LOVE WITH AN
Imperfect
COWBOY

LONE STAR DYNASTY BOOK 1

ANN
MAJOR

To Jerry for the
wishes best!

Copyright 2016 Ann Major
ISBN 10: 1942473141
ISBN 13: 9781942473145

MAJOR PRESS LLC
241 Rosebud Ave.
Corpus Christi, Texas 78404

Cover Design and Interior format by The Killion Group http://thekilliongroupinc.com

DEDICATION

This book is dedicated to Caleb Zane Huett, Willow Vale Huett, Jack Major Huett, Nathan Cleaves, and Nicholas Cleaves, my grandchildren. I'm especially proud of Caleb, who has just sold his first novel to Scholastic.

I owe a special thanks to the following people who helped me with this novel: Genelle Sanders (executive editorial assistant), Colonel Mike Kershaw (research), Graciela Rogerio (research), Carol Major Inouye (research), Kay Major Telle (research), Linda Early (research), Joe Knolle (research), Captain Mike Kershaw (research), Jenna O'Connor (proofreading), Jennifer Jakes (formatting), Kim Killion (cover) and Shannon Godwin (editor)

"She was becoming herself and daily casting aside that fictitious self which we assume like a garment with which to appear before the world."
Kate Chopin, "The Awakening"

"The pieces I am, she gather them and gave them back to me in all the right order."
Toni Morrison, *Beloved*

PROLOGUE

Dead Man's Curve
South Texas

Help! Daddy!
Muddy floodwater poured through the windows as Valentine sank his teeth into Jack's collar and tugged him out the window of the car. Jack took a final gasp from the air pocket before he was in the river. Then he was ripped from the golden retriever's jaws and swept downstream.

Which way was up? Which down? Jack's heavy jeans and boots made his thin body feel leaden. All he could do was surrender to the force of the swift water sucking at his body and fight to hold his breath for one more second.

Just one more breath. One more, please, God!
He was five, still young enough to believe God listened to every single prayer a little boy said.

And answered.
His swimming teacher had taught him to blow bubbles under water only the week before in the pool behind El Castillo where he lived, but he was all out of bubbles.

Just as he was about to gulp in water, his head

burst above the surface. He took a breath, and burning air rushed into his greedy lungs. A piece of mesquite floated by and he grabbed and held on in spite of the thorns.

Daddy? Where was Daddy?

In the sinking car. Running out of bubbles.

Jack wanted to scream or cry, to be picked up and held close in his daddy's strong arms, but Daddy couldn't hear him. When a larger tree limb crashed into him, he ignored the stinging pain in his leg and grabbed it, pulling himself on top of it. He felt other blows to his right arm and leg when debris struck him, but luckily he washed up in a thick tangle of reeds that grew on a muddy shore.

Drinking in a frantic breath, he dug into the mud and rocks with bleeding fingers and clawed his way out of the raging river. For no reason, he remembered oncoming headlights swerving in their direction before Daddy had screamed, and their truck had veered off the bridge.

Get down! Damn bastard's heading straight for us.

His father had rolled down the windows seconds before the crash, causing the rain to soak Jack's new cowboy shirt and jeans even before their truck flew through the guardrails into the creek.

"Unfasten your seatbelt," his father had yelled in a hoarse, strange voice.

Jack had obeyed instantly because he hadn't wanted to anger Daddy, especially when he used that terrifying tone.

Even though it was July, Jack began to shiver with cold and despair as rain slashed him.

Young as he was, he knew his world was changed forever.

Gabe. He wanted his brother, Gabe. Gabe was six and would know what to do. But Gabe was home with their cousin, Liam, and Baby Kate, who'd be fast asleep by now. Both the older boys were probably tucked into their warm beds, watching TV. Gabe had been upset because Daddy had said he couldn't keep up with more than one kid at the rodeo, and he and Liam and Gabe would have to draw straws...or rather matches. Jack had drawn the longest match and had galloped around the room bragging about it. Gabe hadn't thought that was fair. Since he was older and less trouble, he'd thrown his match on the floor, saying he should be the one to go.

"I can only take one of you," his father had said in a tone that told Gabe it was pointless to argue.

Wet and shivering, Jack lost track of time. Hours later a light flashed, and a dog barked

Valentine?

Jack almost called out to the golden retriever, but a prickle of uneasiness made him freeze and hunker lower as a cone of light swept the tops of the reeds.

"Jack? Are you out there? Are you okay? Just call out to me, son, so I can find you."

When the footsteps and thrashing grew nearer, the dog began to bark shrilly.

"Damn dog. Never was no good!"

Jack heard a low growl. Then a shot rang out.

The dog made a whimpering sound. Then the gun exploded a second time.

"Jack? I know you're there. I'm not going to hurt you."

Instead of answering, Jack swallowed at something tight and hard that had lodged in the back of his throat and hunkered lower in the tall, wet grasses.

1

32 Years Later
Early December, New York City

I wonder if I'm the first Park Avenue bride to ever go on her honeymoon alone and with a goal to have revenge sex?

When Hannah Lewis planned her perfect day, she'd never imagined she'd be a bride on the run from her own magnificent, Upper East Side wedding. After all she was a Lewis, who'd been born and bred in a penthouse that crowned one of the truly great buildings on Park Avenue, a building inhabited by titans of industry and their glittering, socialite wives. A building whose smug board had made international celebrities weep when they were denied ownership. But now, instead of sipping champagne in her father's club while her mother basked with pride at having launched her favorite daughter, Hannah's eyes were glued to the minivan's bumper less than a foot in front of the Jag.

Don't think about Mother and how disappointed she is.

Oblivious to the blasts of horns on all sides of her, Hannah pushed her lace veil out of her eyes, hunched over the wheel and gunned James's Jaguar for all it was worth. Tires screeching, she changed lanes, cutting off the trucker to her right who shot her the finger as she raced north along E. River Drive.

Having grown up with a private limo and chauffeur, and later with the use of an elite car service paid for by Daddy, not to mention privately chartered helicopter rides to the family summer home in the Hamptons, Hannah didn't drive much. Unlike her twin who loved cars, she lacked the patience, even when her life was running smoothly.

Today she felt like a joke in her organza wedding gown. And as for patience—she was psycho bride on the warpath.

If only she could have lost the dress before she'd jumped behind the wheel of James's sports car, but she'd been in a panic bordering on the murderous. Her only thought had been to escape James, their extravagant reception, her twin sister, and all the guests who might have witnessed her humiliation. And Mother. No way could she deal with her mother who would consider this *her* tragedy.

This was supposed to be *her* perfect day! *Hers*! Not Nell's! Not Mothers either!

Driven by her mother to excel as a bride as she'd always excelled in everything, from French to physics to classical piano and her career in medicine, Hannah had spent days, hours, weeks…years—well, *fifteen months exactly*, planning her wedding down to the last detail.

Okay, so maybe she'd become obsessed about the wedding being perfect; so maybe juggling the long hours she put in as an anesthesiologist and organizing the wedding had made her edgy; okay, more than edgy. So maybe she'd gotten over-stressed and hadn't paid enough attention to James. Men were high-maintenance, right?

Maybe she'd had a few doubts herself about marrying James these past few weeks. When she'd gone to her mother, her mother had reminded her that she loved James.

When James asked her if anything was wrong, she'd shaken her head and said it was just nerves. He'd seemed to understand that weddings made brides and their mothers crazy, especially Upper East Side, detail-oriented brides and their competitive, helicopter mothers. She'd reminded him that after their wedding he and she were going to have a month all to themselves to honeymoon. A whole month at the dude ranch he'd chosen in the middle of nowhere, where she would have nothing else to do but devote herself to him and indulge his every whim.

He knew doctors were busy; they'd been together for a while, hadn't they? He was an extremely ambitious attorney, who worked all the time himself. Did she ever complain about that when he tried a case and she was on her own for days…and nights? No, she used the time to get more done herself.

He'd admired her family's position and status. He knew she'd wanted everything to be perfect for him. It had all been to please him.

Well...and Mother and Daddy.

And then her very own twin sister, Daddy's *favorite* had had to ruin everything. Had Nell simply been jealous?

Tears leaked from Hannah's narrowed eyes as she remembered what she'd caught Nell doing to James at the reception. Hannah hadn't cried since her first year in medical school, but surely utter betrayal by her sister and brand-new husband deserved a tear or two.

On her eightieth birthday, she'd still remember his goofy smile as he'd stared down at Nell and the glitter of triumph in Nell's lovely, dark eyes.

Her twin! Her own twin!

Hannah's flesh felt clammy. The Queen Anne Venice lace beneath her underarms was soggy. Not that she cared that she might be doing permanent damage to the designer lace gown with its chapel length train as she stomped on the accelerator again and swerved left onto the bridge. She would shred it or maybe burn it as soon as she got to the airport.

The sun was out, and little white diamonds danced on the water's surface. Normally she would have admired the pretty view of Roosevelt Island. Not today. All she wanted was to leave New York as fast as possible. She had a month off and two tickets to Texas.

Texas? Why of all the lovely places to honeymoon had James chosen Texas? She knew the answer to that: his favorite aunt had lived on a ranch in South Texas, and he had fond memories of visiting her there as a boy. In addition the weather was warm there this time of year.

Luck was with her. The traffic thinned. Twenty minutes later she was inside the parking garage at the airport hunting the perfect space for James's precious XK. It took her a while to find a roomy spot where it wouldn't get dinged.

She pulled in carefully, watching the visual indicator on his touch screen to make sure she wasn't too close to the battered truck on her right while listening to all the audible warnings that cautioned she was dangerously near other objects. It was only after she turned off the engine and opened the door and saw how perfectly she'd parked his fantasy car, that she banged her fists in frustration against the steering wheel.

Was she out of her mind? Why was she still trying to please James by taking such good care of his car?

Remembering his grin and Nell's triumphant gaze, she saw red. She couldn't breathe as a scream bubbled to her lips. In a blaze of temper she slammed the door shut, restarted his car, backed it up, hitting the brakes so fast they squealed. Tightening her seatbelt and positioning her seat as far from the steering wheel as she could, she took aim at the big black 5 stenciled on the wall in front of her. Then she rammed her foot down onto the gas pedal. Seconds later glass and metal and his airbag exploded.

Ouch!

Although her nose and cheeks stung from the impact, she almost welcomed the pain. Not bothering to shut off the engine or silence the Jag's audible alarms, she got out and dusted her hands. When she grabbed her purse and took a step, her train snagged on a tiny lever. Yanking at the white lace, she ripped the fabric she'd paid thousands for.

Behind her a gentle voice said, "Are you okay, Miss?"

Braced for a judgmental attack, she whirled to face a worried young mother and a dark-eyed little girl with saucy, brown curls, who were carrying bags stuffed with Christmas presents.

"Are you okay?" the darling little girl repeated. "Your nose! It's all red!"

She was *so* not okay. "I'll live."

Brushing a tendril of gold out of her eyes, which were probably smudged with runny black makeup, she struggled to take a breath.

"Are you a princess?" The child's big, dark eyes, which studied Hannah's designer gown and her tiara, were filled with awe. "Did you just marry the prince?"

"Hardly."

Since she'd been brought up in the rarefied atmosphere of a stylish, moneyed world, and James had been handsome and wealthy, most New Yorkers would probably think so. Real princesses were probably taught to eat sushi instead of pizza, as she'd been. They were probably taken to galleries instead of amusement parks, just as she'd been.

Hannah let out a strangled breath. "I-I...married a frog pretending he was a prince. No! He was more like a giant toad!"

"Is he under a witch's spell?"

She thought of her twin's sultry beauty. "Possibly."

Kneeling beside the child, Hannah pulled her rings off her left hand and handed them to her.

The little girl held the rings up to the light, and the three-karat diamond sparked like fire. "They're pretty," she squealed.

Hannah remembered how her breath had caught when James had joined her on that bench a year ago in the Conservatory Garden in Central Park, her favorite spot outdoors in the city. Looking at the ring brought back the eager warmth in his blue eyes and the memory of how his hands had shaken as he'd slipped the ring onto her finger.

He'd never hidden the fact that he'd been anxious to belong to her set, but had he ever loved her…passionately?

She'd always wanted someone to love, someone who loved her; someone who didn't expect her to constantly compete and win; someone who simply loved her for who she was, as Daddy had always loved Nell. Hannah still wanted it so badly.

She should have paid more attention to James, made more time for him. Maybe then she wouldn't feel so clueless and lost now.

Fighting tears again and hating herself for her weakness, Hannah closed her eyes. She'd cried enough over James and Nell. Medical school had taught her that sentiment made her a sap and clouded her judgment but that anger made her strong…even calm.

Hannah's hand clenched. "They're yours."

"Are you sure about this?" the child's mother asked.

"Pawn them. Do whatever you like with them." Hannah stood up. "I've never been more certain about anything in my whole life."

If only that were true. For years she'd known exactly where she was going—because her ambitious mother had always been right behind her to point the way.

With a grim smile, Hannah remembered her mother standing over her at the kitchen table every afternoon after the nanny had rushed her home from pre-school so a private tutor could prep her for the ERB, the entrance exam that was vital to get into the right kindergarten.

Her whole life had been about planning and achieving, so Mother could bask in her reflected glory. Nothing else had mattered but pleasing her parents—Mother because she needed Hannah to be perfect, and Daddy because she hoped that someday he would love her best.

Where had all her accomplishments gotten *her*? She'd humiliated herself and her family. There was no way she could go to her mother and father and explain, not when status and position were everything to them.

Hannah had the sickening feeling that she'd been on the wrong track for a long time. Maybe her entire family was off course. In a functioning family a twin wouldn't have done what Nell had done. Twins shouldn't be constantly vying for what the other had. They should support each other.

What was wrong with us?

No, she couldn't face her family now when they were a big part of what was wrong.

Hannah felt as if the foundation of her life had shifted, as if she was no longer sure about anything except that she had to get out of New York and be on her own.

The one thing that offered a ray of hope was the fact that she had nearly the whole month of December off before she returned to her killer schedule at the hospital and had to face James, the holidays, her family and her colleagues again.

Even though she couldn't imagine what she'd do for nearly four weeks at the Hideaway Ranch alone other than lick her wounds, she knew that this hadn't happened out of the blue. A lot was wrong about her life.

She was taking December off.

She needed space and time to process. She had to figure out why her life had fallen apart and what she could do about it.

And maybe, just maybe if she got the chance, she'd indulge in some revenge sex. Maybe then she could erase James Colt's silly grin and Nell's awful triumph once and for all.

Lonesome, Texas

2

The country music that whined from the vintage jukebox at the Lonesome Dove Bar was having a hard time competing with the norther blasting the wooden building with gale-force winds and rain.

Liam Stark liked the racket. It sure beat listening to Homer Gonzales, the local sheriff and his best friend, and Gabe Stark, Liam's older cousin, who'd both stopped by to give him their weekly lecture about what he needed to do to turn his life around. Gabe, who was probably worth nearly a billion dollars, was used to people at Stark Energy, his international oil company, doing what he said.

Check out an online dating service. Meet a woman. Go to church. He'd heard it all.

Go to church? Give me a break! Coming from Homer and Gabe, that was a joke. Was that their best?

Liam breathed a sigh of relief when Homer's mobile buzzed. Hopefully someone in the county was up to mischief, which meant his nosy, interfering friend Homer would have to get off his

back and go wrestle handcuffs on some trespasser
or drunk.

Homer sighed wearily as he put his phone to
his ear. "Hell. Why can't people in this damn
county ever behave?"

Liam smiled. "It's a weekend. What the hell do
you expect?"

"You're right. If people started behavin' better,
I'd be out of a job."

Homer slapped a couple of dollars on the bar.
"I'd have to move, and you'd only have Gabe
here riding your sorry ass."

"Did you find out what happened to that
woman who went missing last weekend?"

Homer frowned and shook his head as he
listened to the caller.

A drug detail saleswoman's battered car had
been found on the side of the road about ten miles
to the south of Lonesome. The woman, a Corpus
Christi local, had vanished without a trace.

Homer ended the call. "Sorry, gotta go. See
y'all around."

Homer was tall, handsome, and black. Since
there weren't any other black men in the county,
he stood out.

"You okay?" Gabe leaned in closer, filling the
gap Homer had left.

Okay? Liam fought to suppress a shudder. Not
that he wasn't used to going through the motions
when his older cousin, who was practically like
his big brother since they'd been raised together,
expressed concern.

Hell, when in recent memory had he been
okay?

"Doin' fine," he growled defiantly.

He knew Gabe and Homer had dropped by the Lonesome Dove Bar tonight because they wanted to help. But they couldn't help. Nobody could.

They were worried he was like his mother and would do what she'd done. But he wasn't like her. He'd get through this anniversary... somehow...like he had last year.

Another gust whistled outside in the eaves.

Northers never used to bother him, but that was before Mindy had had the accident at Dead Man's Curve while driving in a winter storm two years ago.

Don't think about Mindy. Or Charlie. Or Dead Man's Curve. Or all the others who died on that nasty stretch of road.

He forced his mind to his ranch and wondered if the old roof on his barn would hold. If he were back at the cabin, he'd probably be drinking himself into oblivion because this was one night he hated to face sober.

"Business sure is off," Gabe said. "Weather..."

"Not my problem. Not my mortgage," Liam replied. "Just filling in for Hector because Ben is home from college and Sam wanted to celebrate.

"You never say no when it comes to Ben."

"Neither the hell do you," Liam replied.

Hector and Sam Montoya had grown up at El Castillo on the North Star Ranch side by side with Liam and Gabe. Even though they'd been his aunt's housekeeper's sons, the four of them had grown up cowboying and had been as close as brothers.

When Kate, Gabe's younger sister, had become pregnant by Sam and had had Ben, Liam's relationship with the Montoyas had thickened. After her accident at Dead Man's Curve, she'd relinquished her parental rights to Ben and had fled Lonesome.

Ben was kin who'd been abandoned by his mom. Maybe since Liam had been orphaned young, he found it easy to identify with the kid. Maybe he was doing' it for Kate.

Draining his whiskey glass—the first and hopefully the last for the night, at least, till after he drove home—Liam directed his steely black gaze past Gabe to a couple of rough looking truckers who were getting too rowdy.

Gabe followed his eye. "I've got an early plane in the morning."

"Always wheeling and dealing," Liam said. "Where are you going this time?"

"The Middle East."

One of the truckers kicked over a chair.

"Hell, looks like we let the sheriff escape too soon. You gonna need backup with that pair before I go?"

"No, but thanks for stopping by…and for offering."

"You'd do the same for me." Gabe pushed away from the bar and Liam followed him to the door where they said a final goodbye.

When one of the truckers kicked a second chair over as Liam was on his way back to the bar, Liam stopped dead in his tracks. A fight would be just the thing to take his mind off the fatal anniversary that had him in the mood for the kind of oblivion only a bottle of whiskey and a willing woman could give him.

Suddenly he was glad Hector had asked him to help out. Alone at the ranch, it was too easy to think. Too easy to remember getting off that plane, expecting Mindy and Charlie to come flying into his arms, only to have Gabe walk toward him instead, his expression so grim, Liam had known instantly his wife and son were gone.

Hell of a thing to come home to after the nightmare of Afghanistan.

Not that he wanted to dwell on what had happened in the desert any more than he wanted to dwell on the accident that had robbed him of his family, but whether he was drunk or sober, alone or in company, those losses ate at him every time he let down his guard.

The first year, he'd stayed drunk; this past year he'd stayed to himself and damn near worked himself to death. A working ranch was good for that, at least. Tonight he'd stared at himself in the mirror of his medicine cabinet in his downstairs bathroom for a longer time than he usually did when he felt this down. Then he'd remembered finding his mother lying white and cold on her bed, and he hadn't opened the cabinet. Instead, intending to pour himself a drink, he'd been on his way to the kitchen when Hector had called.

His eye on his liquor on the counter, Liam had said he was busy, but Hector had countered, "Busy with a bottle, I bet. Hell, tonight's no night for you to be alone. Besides, I need you. Ben's home."

"Get Bobby B." B was a local who hung out at the bar a lot and liked to tend bar.

"I'd rather have you."

Aside from four tables of truckers, only a few of the local regulars, including Bobby B, had shown up to occupy their usual perches. Liam didn't blame Lonesome's citizens for drinking at home tonight, the weather being what it was.

Suddenly the two burly truckers near the door stood up roaring, their fists raised.

Stealthy as a cat Liam eased toward them. "Guys, you need to move it outside."

The bigger man leered. "Just a friendly little discussion." His wide grin was short a front tooth. He had a hooked nose and a dark complexion. A prematurely gray thatch of hair stuck out from under a grubby baseball cap turned backwards.

"Move it outside," Liam repeated.

Fists tightening, Hooked Nose puffed out his barrel chest and meaty shoulders. He had an impressive two inches in height and more than fifty pounds on Liam. But when Liam repositioned himself so that his back was to the wall and leaned in close enough to be hit by the boozy stench of garlic and cigarettes, something the man saw in Liam's eyes made the color drain from his cheeks.

"Sorry." His flabby jaw slackened. Unclenching his beefy hands, he raised them in mock surrender. "Hal and me here, we ain't lookin' for no fight." Keeping his hands in the air, he sank back into his chair.

Hal scowled down at his friend and then at
Liam before he, too, fell back into his chair and
took a grudging pull from his bottle.

Satisfied he'd put out the fire, Liam was on his
way back to the bar when the doors behind him
banged open. As he turned, a rush of icy, wet air
and a slim, stylish woman unlike any he'd seen
around Lonesome for a spell blew inside.

Breathing hard, she was clutching a soggy
Texas roadmap and her cell phone as if her life
depended on them.

Hell.

The last thing he needed was a smoking hot
woman in his bar. No sooner had the dozen or so
truckers in the establishment gotten an eyeful,
than the atmosphere grew super-charged with an
overdose of adrenaline and liquored-up
testosterone.

Despite the fact that her long, light-colored hair
was dripping all over the scarred, oak floor, her
mascara was smudged, and her clingy, aqua
blouse and butt-hugging jeans were soaked
through, the city gal was a stunner.

This was bad. She was dynamite, and his job
was to keep sparks from flying.

Not that she paid the men or him any mind.
Oh, no, she was in her own little world. Sticking
her nose in the air, she marched past the rough
crowd to a table in a corner where she sat down,
hung a black, puffy down jacket on the back of
her chair and turned her back on the lot of them.

Like most civilians, she wasn't paying nearly
enough attention to her surroundings. Too intent
on her phone, she kept punching buttons with a

ferocity that told him she was royally pissed about something.

Hell. She made him feel invisible.

She was probably the kind of woman who never looked twice at anybody she considered beneath her…certainly not a guy she'd see as a hick cowboy bartender in an out-of-the-way bar filled with lonely truckers. Probably nothing mattered to her—except what *she* wanted. She wasn't like his sweet, selfless Mindy, who would have sacrificed anything to make him happy.

Mindy… Loss slammed him so hard he knotted his fists. As he fought the wave of pain that grabbed his heart and squeezed so hard he couldn't breathe, he almost hated the city gal for making him pine for his beloved wife as well as his other losses.

Grief: one second he was okay, that is, if being half dead and needing a long gulp of whiskey to hold himself together for one more hour was 'okay'. Then something would set him off, like this cocky piece of city ass with her haunted eyes and *attitude*, who had no business sashaying into his bar in that look-at-me outfit on a Friday night with four tables of horny truckers. Then suddenly, because of her, he wasn't okay.

Why the hell would a cold fish like this gal make him think, no ache, for his precious Mindy? But she did. She brought it all back. The yearning… the sweetness… the closeness… how good it had felt… living with and loving a good woman after years of feeling all alone after his parents and Uncle Vince had died. This gal made him remember how nice it had been to wake up in the middle of a cold night and feel safe with Mindy's bottom curled warmly against his thighs.

All gone now. He'd learned early, after his parents' deaths, there was nothing he or anybody else could ever do to make it right again. Not that Uncle Vince hadn't tried—but then he'd died too.

An accident, they'd called it. But who knew? Uncle Vince had left a big estate, so there had been odd skid marks and rumors that his truck had been run off the road deliberately into that raging creek. When Liam's aunt had been quick to remarry, the gossips had had a field day.

Suddenly Liam's grief was as fresh and visceral as it had been when he'd gotten off the plane and Gabe had been there instead of Mindy.

Furious at this woman for making him yearn for what he spent every waking moment trying to forget, Liam turned his broad-shoulders on her and strode to the bar where he quickly poured himself a whiskey.

Trying to ignore her, he stared into his drink. The truckers could eat her alive for all he cared.

Still, when the truckers invited her to their table, and she coolly refused them, and they muttered a few lewd insults under their breath, Liam stood up taller.

The guys in his platoon had said he had ears like a cat. A man learned to stay alert, when the price for relaxing might be a bullet between his eyes or a piece of shrapnel severing his windpipe.

Her silky voice with its rapid, Yankee cadence curled inside his gut and made him feel warm and needy, something it had no right to do.

He'd shut that part of himself down in Afghanistan. He'd shut it down even further when he'd erected two more white crosses at Dead Man's Curve after Mindy and Charlie had been buried.

He didn't want to feel, but suddenly his heart was pounding inside his ribcage, and he couldn't think about a damn thing but the woman.

In a barely audible tone Hook Nose called her a bad name. When Liam looked up and found her blushing and staring daggers through *him*, not the trucker, shock lit every nerve in his body.

Excuse me. Why did she see him as the problem?

Frowning, she held up a hand and signaled.

Okay. He got it. She saw him as a servant and wanted him to come over to her table and take her order and was annoyed because he hadn't.

Fusing her eyes to his, she beckoned him again, this time with a single fingertip.

He looked down at his whiskey glass. *When hell freezes over, lady.*

3

No sooner had Hannah put the toe of her shiny, new, red boot—a boot that pinched her instep like all get-out—into the scruffy bar, she'd almost fled back out into the driving rain. If the all-male crowd that sat hunched over their beers looked rough, the lean bartender with the broken turkey feather in his Stetson, whose hard gaze had stripped her before he'd turned and stomped back to the bar as if *she'd* pissed *him* off, terrified her even more.

Although the bar with its rough clientele and bartender frightened her, the wild weather and narrow two-lane road scared her more.

She couldn't drive another mile in this blinding rain. Not until she knew exactly where she was going. Her nerves were badly frayed from the three-hour drive from San Antonio and from having been lost on strange roads in the storm for the last hour. The signal had failed on her phone, so she hadn't been able to call the Hideaway Ranch for fresh directions or use her GPS app.

She'd had to stop somewhere—and other than an unmanned, self-service gas station, this poorly-lit, lousy excuse for civilization was the first sign of human life she'd seen in an hour. Shaking but glad to be off the road, she'd pulled into the lot and parked just as the county sheriff drove away.

She needed to calm down and figure out where she was going before she got back into her rental again. Surely, she couldn't be that far from the Hideaway.

Hideaway. If ever a place was aptly named...

When the big guy with a hooked nose and the baseball cap called her another bad name, her heart began to knock. Keeping her eyes on her useless phone, she held up her hand to signal the bartender.

When he refused to so much as look at her and focused on his whiskey, her fear and frustration found a new target—*him.*

Why did he just stand there, his bronzed hand grasping that empty whiskey glass so hard she was afraid he'd shatter it? Couldn't he hear his customer insulting her? Why was he the only man in the bar deliberately ignoring her?

What was *his* problem?

When he finally did look up, his eyes were so diamond hard and soullessly black, the sheer force of his fierce presence slammed her.

Only when he banked his emotions and turned away, did she let out the breath she hadn't realized she'd been holding and gasp in another. Why did he unnerve her so? It was as if he'd sucked all the oxygen out of the room.

He was tall, muscular, and lethally handsome, if you went for the primitive, earthy type, which she didn't. He had prominent cheekbones, black hair, and harsh, sun-darkened features. He wore a faded blue shirt and stained jeans that fit him like a glove.

When he'd made his way back to the bar, he'd moved with the sure solid purpose she associated with athletes.

In no way was he like James or any of the intelligent, refined men she knew—men who could hold their own in boardrooms or in the salons of the very rich on the Upper East Side. Men who drank wine instead of beer and could debate the merit of one bottle over another with a sommelier endlessly.

Dangerous. Untamed. Those were the words that came to mind. When he read, if he read, he probably mouthed each word out loud.

But, oh God, what a beautiful mouth he had.

She was *so* not interested in his mouth—she wanted nothing to do with men at the moment.

Then the burly guy with the hooked nose and the baseball cap got up and swaggered unsteadily toward her table.

Oh, my God.

With a little shriek she jumped out of her chair and ran toward the bar and the formidable stranger with the gorgeous mouth as if he were her savior.

Not that he looked up from his empty glass. No, the only way she knew he'd noticed her was because the frown lines between his dark brows deepened, and his hand tightened around his whiskey glass.

"Mister, what…what does a girl have to do to get service around here?"

When his gaze seared her again, she went motionless, too stunned by the impact he had on her senses up close to breathe.

"Exactly what kind of service do you want from me—*honey*?"

Wow—she kicked herself for not having seen that one coming. No, he was the one she should kick. Not only was he deliberately rude, he talked slow and deep and made one-syllable words sound like they had two.

"I'd like some...er...coffee," she said in a rush, looking down in an attempt to ignore both his hostility and the sexual innuendo.

"Coffee?" It took him so long to get the word out she wondered if he was dull-witted.

"Yes...please," she snapped, looking up at him again.

"First time I ever got that request...in here...on a Friday night." He pointed to a row of liquor and beer bottles. "This is a bar, lady. That's our selection. Take your pick."

She wanted to scream that the word *night* did not have two syllables. "Couldn't you make a pot?"

"No."

"Do you have club soda?"

A dark brow lifted disdainfully.

"I can't drink...and drive out in that weather again," she explained. "I never drive...where I live."

Why was she explaining herself to this rude, over-sexed Neanderthal?

His eyes bored holes into her. When she didn't back down, he grabbed a glass and splashed soda water into it.

"Could I have some ice...and a lemon...please?"

When he dropped a single cube in her glass and handed her a lime, and then began to scowl into his empty whiskey glass again, she decided that maybe she'd better not point out his mistake. What if he didn't know a lemon from a lime?

After a while, she said, "Could...could you be...so kind...as to tell me how...to find the Hideaway Ranch?"

"Honey, around here, everbody calls it the Honeymoon Ranch."

Everbody? She cringed. His butchery of the English language was too much.

He misunderstood the reason for her grimace. "Sorry. Inside joke," he muttered.

"It's the way you said everybody. It should be *every*. *Every* has a y in it."

He looked up, his hard gaze drilling her as he leaned in closer.

"Okay," he drawled. "Ever-Y-body."

His fierce gaze burned her. "Happy now—honey?"

Honey. The way he said it had her blushing to the roots of her blond hair and biting her bottom lip, a habit she'd quit years ago.

"Sorry," she said testily. "I shouldn't have corrected you. Bad habit of mine."

"So how come a pretty city gal like you is out looking for the Hideaway all by herself on a bad night like this? You get stood up at the altar or something? 'Cause maybe you corrected *him* one time too many, and he got interested in a gal who knows how to please a man?"

Again she saw Nell kneeling before James, her dark head moving back and forth.

"I did not correct him…or at least…"

"Bingo," he whispered.

Suddenly Hannah's eyes felt so hot the handsome bartender's face blurred.

"I'll have you know my life is none of your business," she blurted in a broken voice that probably revealed too much.

When his dangerous gaze fixed on her face again, he tensed, as if he felt the rawness of her humiliation and distress.

"You're right. It isn't. I shouldn't have said that."

He sounded genuinely sorry. Almost human. She was stunned by how touched she felt when his hard features softened.

Why should he care? Why should she care if he cared? She didn't want his pity or his kindness or for him to be a real person. Didn't want anything from him but directions.

"I'm dead on my feet and really anxious to get to bed," she said.

At the word *bed*, his dark, male gaze swept her again, lingering on damp aqua silk that now clung her nipples.

"Don't look at me like that!"

His face tensed. His eyes grew cold. "If you don't want me lookin', maybe you shouldn't have walked up to the bar dressed like that, flaunting yourself."

Flaunting? His crude manners were *so* not her fault. "If you'd please just give me directions to the Hideaway, I won't bother you further."

"Directions won't do you any good. You're not sleeping at the Hideaway. Not tonight."

"Excuse me? Will you leave off the advice and please just tell me how to get there?"

"My cousin Mary Sue, well, she runs the place. She closes the gate at 10 p.m. sharp. It's 9:30 right now, and you're looking at a forty-minute drive."

"Forty minutes?" She gaped at him. She was *that* lost?

"That's if you know where you're goin'."

She groaned. "Are there any motels near the Hideaway?"

"No, ma'am." His polite phrase slapped her like a careful insult.

He grabbed a piece of paper and a pencil and drew a map to a motel that he claimed was the closest to the Hideaway. "Here, you can use Hector's phone to ring them and make your reservation."

"Hector?"

"Hector Montoya. He owns The Dove. The bar."

She stared at him so long when he tried to hand her the phone, he gave up and dialed the number himself.

"You're mighty anxious to get rid of me," she said.

Nobody answered, so he hung up. When he leaned across the bar, she caught his clean, lemony scent and felt his warm breath stir her hair. "Not really, honey. Instead of the motel, you could come home with me."

Instead of leaning even closer, he jumped back, looking stunned, like his words had surprised him as much as they'd surprised her. But he recovered faster than she did. Men usually did, didn't they?

Heat and annoyance flooded her. "What did you just say?"

He didn't flinch. His gaze zeroed in on her mouth. "You heard me."

She was glad he was on the other side of the bar. "What do you take me for?"

"You dress like a woman who wants to forget the sorry bastard who stood her up so she can move on. I could help you with that."

"I don't need any help. And certainly not from you!"

But he'd opened a secret vault of hurt inside her as well as the thought that sexual revenge might be just what she needed.

As her pulse thrummed, he dialed the number again. Damn him for tempting her with his lewd suggestion that a night of passion might soothe some of the pain and misery she felt.

This was crazy. She couldn't actually be considering his proposition. This wasn't happening.

I am not considering it.

"Hello," he said to whoever answered on the other end.

Hannah's heart had begun to thump so madly she could barely sputter a coherent hello when he shoved the phone toward her. The whole time Hannah talked to the receptionist on the other end, the cowboy stared at her so hard, Hannah couldn't think for wanting him to reach out with those strong, dark hands and touch her.

Revenge sex so wasn't her.

"You don't know anything about me," she said to him when she was through making her reservation.

"I know what it's like to feel pain and want to forget. To want it so bad you can taste it."

"You could be a serial killer," she whispered, clutching the receiver she'd forgotten to hang up.

"But I'm not." His eyes were hard, but his tone was as soft as velvet, and it lured her.

"I could get a disease," she said.

He took the receiver from her and hung it up. "Not from me. I'd protect you."

Why was she having this conversation?

She thought about James's betrayal. Were all men dogs?

"You'd probably go to bed with any woman who walked in here tonight."

Much to her surprise, he smiled, and his smile lit his dark eyes and softened his hard features in a way that utterly charmed her.

"Not tonight. If you change your mind, you know where I am. And I'll make you a promise. Tonight...no matter who else walks in that door...I won't ask another gal to share my bed." He placed his hand on his heart.

"As if I care who you sleep with in the next few hours? I'm not that desperate," she lashed.

"Lucky you," he whispered, unmistakable pain washing his carved features.

She heard the dark anguish in his voice, saw it carved in the harsh lines of face and wondered what had happened to him.

With grammar like his and that hick accent, he was probably a high school dropout.

But he got to her. He made her forget what she was running away from way better than her exhausting flight, her hellish road trip or her shopping spree for a sexy revenge wardrobe, floral shampoo and soaps in San Antonio had.

How could she have thought even for one second she could indulge in revenge sex? She was much too logical and inhibited.

"Why you? Tonight, of all nights?" he muttered.

Stunning them both, he reached across the bar, cupped her face, and drew her closer. "You know something? I wish to hell you'd never walked through those doors tonight."

She could have freed herself. Instead, she stood, transfixed, as he slowly leaned into her and kissed her lips with a tenderness that shocked her.

Warmth and an incredible, radiating lightness spread through her until she felt as if every cell in her being was aglow. Never had she felt such a hot rush of pleasure. It was Nell who demanded passion from her relationships, not her; Nell who reached for what she wanted and took it.

Inhibited Hannah closed her eyes and half-opened her mouth, inviting the bartender's tongue, wanting to taste him, wanting to throw her arms around his neck and pull him closer. Wanting. Wanting.

Wanting to know what making love to him would be like if a mere kiss was this good.

Where had that come from? She did not want anything so frighteningly intimate from this ignorant bartender in this God-forsaken bar. Especially not after the heartbreak she felt over James.

Just as she felt herself melting, the man ended the kiss as quickly as he'd begun it, leaving her a trembling, needy mess.

"Come home with me," he repeated.

Out of the corner of her eye she saw the man with the hooked nose glaring at them.

"Can't!" she whispered desperately, defiantly.

"Won't," the bartender corrected gently, allowing her to glimpse the pain smoldering within him once more.

"I'm sorry," she whispered, pressing two fingers against his warm mouth. "For what it's worth, I wish you well and hope you feel better someday with someone else."

"Not likely. This isn't a fairytale world, princess."

"No, it isn't."

She saw that every day she worked at the hospital. Patients were lucky, till they weren't. She saw it in her own family, too. Her parents' palatial home, which seemed so perfect to outsiders was a place of sorrows and secrets. Her parents rejected each other on every level, sleeping on different floors and in opposite wings, never speaking to each other unless they had to. They'd even divided their daughters, their father preferring Nell while Hannah was her mother's favorite. Why? There was never any shouting, but their home was a cold war zone. Each twin had fought for the love of the parent who rejected her.

Hannah stared at the bartender's empty whiskey glass and wished she could think of something comforting to say.

"Thanks for the directions…and for the soda. What do I owe you?"

"It's on the house," he murmured.

She pulled out a ten and laid it on the bar.

When his mouth curled derisively, and he neither reached for the bill nor thanked her, she wondered if she'd insulted him.

Quit thinking about his feelings! He propositioned you!

Fighting to ignore him, which wasn't easy since her lips still burned from his kiss, she rifled noisily through her purse for her car keys.

"Be careful out there," he growled. "There's a nasty curve."

Without looking at him or the other men, she turned her back on him and headed for the door, not that she didn't deliberately swing her hips a little, just to taunt him.

The man with the hooked nose jumped in front of her, blocking her way. "How come you were so nice to him?"

"Leave me alone," she said, trying to sidestep him.

But he was faster. "What's he got?"

"Let her pass," the bartender drawled with lazy menace.

For a breath or two, she felt a spark in the air. Then the man with the hooked nose gave her a sly look. "Later," he whispered as he backed to one side.

She didn't turn to thank the bartender or acknowledge his help in any way. It was his job, right?

Pulling on her down jacket, she stepped out into the wet wildness and ran through the downpour to her car.

When she was inside her rental, dripping all over the seat and floorboards, she started the engine. Leaning back against the upholstery, she let out a long sigh.

How strange. Who would have thought she could have shared such a moment with a stranger in a bar in the middle of nowhere?

Things like that happened to Nell. Not to her.

Still, it had been a moment. She'd felt totally connected to him, as she'd never felt connected to another. He'd made her feel special, which she'd needed after James.

If he'd been a banker or a lawyer or someone with a prestigious education who'd been born in a lavish Park Avenue apartment, someone her mother and her father would approve of, would she have taken him up on his proposition?

It didn't matter.

It had been a moment. That was all.

He'd probably kiss the next woman who walked into the bar, and they'd have their moment. Maybe he'd proposition her and she'd go home with him and they'd have more than a moment.

Nell would have gone home with him in a heartbeat, but not Hannah.

So I'm a snob. Big surprise. What else would a little girl who had a French nanny and a German one as well, since she'd been three be? Especially when confronted with a man who could barely speak his native language?

I have one brief month to figure out where I went wrong and decide where to go from here. I don't have time to waste on another loser.

She ran her fingertip across her burning lips and trembled.

When the doors of the bar swung open, and the barrel-chested trucker and his shorter pal slammed outside, panic welled inside her.

For a fleeting second she considered running back into the bar to the bartender.

When she shifted into reverse and hit the gas instead, the truckers rushed to their large truck and did the same.

4

Rain peppered the metal roof like bullets as the country singer on the ancient jukebox whined about lost love. Liam went still as he and every other man in the bar watched the woman he had just kissed, the woman whose name he didn't even know, swing her ass like a pro as she walked toward the doors and out into the storm.

God, what he wouldn't give for a piece...

When the hooked nosed trucker stepped in front of her to block her exit, Liam fought the urge to hurl himself over the bar and pulverize the bastard. Instead he whispered, "Let her pass."

The trucker's eyes narrowed. He took his time before slowly stepping aside.

Liam felt ridiculous for feeling so protective. Especially when she never looked back, making it clear that he was nothing to her.

Why the hell had he kissed her?

It had been a mistake because now he couldn't forget how her floral scent clung to her skin. Nor could he forget the way she'd tasted sweet but tart because of that damn lime, or how she'd melted into him, her heart racing as he'd snugged her against his chest.

She was taller than he'd thought. He liked the way she moved with an easy sureness, her body carving its way across the room.

Poetry in motion.

Just because he was struggling to forget his wife, whom he'd loved most of his life and had needed more than air itself, didn't mean he wanted to feel such an inexplicable attachment to another.

He was glad the blond was gone, glad she'd said no, glad he'd never see her again.

He was grabbing a bottle, intending to pour himself a drink, when the trucker with the hooked nose exchanged a grin with his pal before they bolted after the blond. Liam set the whiskey bottle back down.

It was bad enough that she was heading toward Dead Man's Curve where he'd lost Mindy and Charlie and Uncle Vince and his cousin Jack in different accidents, where his cousin, Kate, had had that wreck and Lizzy had died. But what if those badasses chased her? He thought about the missing drug detail saleswoman.

Grabbing his jacket off a peg, Liam exploded from behind the bar and strode over to Bobby B's table.

"B, will you cover the bar for me? You might have to close. I gotta check on somethin'."

B grinned too knowingly and then nodded. "Hector won't like it if I have to close."

"I'll deal with Hector."

By the time Liam started his truck, the girl and the truckers had vanished.

Good thing he knew which road she had to take to get to the Hideaway.

He opened his glove compartment, pulled out a flashlight and a box of shotgun shells and dumped them into his pocket. Then he hit the gas. His heart was hammering as he sped down the slick pavement, faster than he liked, given the blinding rain and wind.

Adrenaline had him gripping the wheel. Damn it. He'd known she was heading for Dead Man's Curve. He'd known the truckers were a problem. Why the hell had he just let her walk out?

Liam's windshield wipers slashed back and forth, but they could barely keep up with the rain. Leaning forward, straining to see, he wiped at the foggy windshield with the back of his hand.

Normally rain was a good thing, something all ranchers in South Texas prayed for. Just not tonight when a woman who didn't know these roads was being chased by a pair of truckers.

When he didn't see another car for the first few miles, Liam began to worry he'd lost them. At one point he hit deep water on a low water crossing and skidded off the road before he regained control.

Two miles later as he rounded the first loop of Dead Man's Curve, he caught up with two vehicles, racing at high speeds as they approached the bridge. Highway signs warned him to slow down for the figure eight curve. Instead Liam stepped on the gas. As he squealed around the second loop, he made out a small dark car struggling to stay in its lane as a larger truck rammed it.

Hell. Were they trying to kill her?

Liam slammed his foot on the accelerator.

The sedan rocked violently. Veering off the road, it plowed over the five white crosses before hitting a fence post.

When the truckers braked a few feet ahead of the wrecked car, Liam pulled off behind the sedan.

Turning his lights on high, he grabbed his shotgun out of the gun rack behind him. He kept it loaded with the safety on in case someone surprised him on the ranch when he was working a pasture alone. He got out of the cab.

Taking cover behind his truck, he pumped the gun and made sure the safety was off. He would have preferred a different gun, but his bird-hunting gun would have to do.

When he pushed his Stetson back, cold water dripped all over his shoulders. Not that he noticed. He could hear the swollen creek, but he wouldn't let himself think about his uncle, who'd drowned here, his cousin, Jack, who'd vanished or Mindy and Charlie. Nor did he think of Lizzy, Kate's best friend who'd died here when she'd been a teenager, or Kate, whose life had been destroyed as a result. No, his entire attention was riveted to the shadowy figures that were moving toward her car.

Crouching in the high wet grass, Liam low-crawled through mud and slime and bits of splintered white wood to the wrecked car.

While Hooked Nose pounded on the driver's window, Liam snuck up behind Hal. Looping his forearm around the man's neck, he mashed the man's carotid artery. Within seconds, the trucker went limp and slumped to the ground.

At the heavy sound, Hooked Nose whirled. Aiming to the left of the big bastard, Liam fired. Birdshot bounced off the hood of her car and tore up the ground around Hook, who yelped and sprang backwards, hopping on one leg. The girl began to scream.

Liam had four more shots before he had to reload.

"You crazy? You tryin' to kill me?" the trucker yelled.

Liam's trigger finger tightened as he aimed at the man's belly. "Put your hands up and back away from her car."

The man on the ground began to stir.

"What did you do to Hal?" Hook Nose yelled.

"Move! Nice and slow."

"You better not have done nothin' to Hal. We wuz just tryin' to help her."

"Get your friend here and get into your truck! *Now!*"

When Hal sat up and groaned, Liam blasted the mud to the right of him. Not even when they shouted they were going and loped toward their truck with their hands in the air, did Liam lower his gun.

No, he stood where he was, the butt of his gun digging into his shoulder as the icy rain pelted him until long after their taillights had vanished.

Only then, did Liam lower his weapon and walk over to the driver's window and pound on the glass. "Can you open the door for me please?"

When she cringed lower in her seat, he went to the right hand side of her car and asked her to open it. When she shook her head, he rammed the butt of the shotgun through the rear window.

At the sound of glass shattering she sprang up out of her seat. "Are you crazy? What did you do to that man out there?"

"He got in his truck and drove off, didn't he?" Liam opened the door and slid inside, dripping mud and icy water all over her upholstery. Shrinking away from him, she hunkered lower against her ruined airbag and steering wheel.

She was shaking and rubbing her arms from the cold. Her lip was cut. Her cheeks were white and bruised.

"Are you hurt?" he demanded in a low, steady tone that was meant to reassure her.

"Just go away and leave me alone."

"Right. And if your trucker buddies come back, what then?"

"Go."

"I asked you if you were hurt."

"No."

"An air-bag can pull quite a punch. I see a trickle of blood on your lip and forehead."

"Scratches."

"You're coming home with me."

"We had that conversation already."

"I'm damn sure not leaving you here on the road, especially not *here*." He couldn't help remembering the night Uncle Vince had died. He thought of Jack, whose body had never been found, and all the trauma that had surrounded his disappearance. He thought of Kate who couldn't be a mother to her own son because she still blamed herself for Lizzy's death.

Hell, he'd lost enough people here. He didn't want anyone else on his conscience.

"A saleswoman's car from a nearby city was found not far from here last weekend. The authorities are still looking for her."

"You are not responsible for me," she said. "I can call a road service."

"With what? There's no cell service here. This discussion is over. You've got a head injury. You could be hurt, bleeding on the inside and not know it."

"If I was hurt I *would* definitely know it."

"You could be in shock," he countered. "Or so stubborn you won't admit you need my help. You've been through a lot. Somebody needs to keep an eye on you for a couple of hours to make sure you're okay. "

"Did it ever occur to you that maybe you don't know everything?"

"And you do?" He pursed his mouth. "Who got herself lost, came into my bar, lost a drag race with two crazy truckers, and wrecked her car on Dead Man's Curve?"

She swallowed a breath.

"Did you see those five crosses? Four people have already died here... And another, a little boy, my cousin, who went missing is probably dead too. If I hadn't come along, what kind of party do you think those truckers and you would be having right now?"

Her eyes widened, and her teeth began to chatter. When he saw that she was afraid, he decided to ask a couple of practical questions, to distract her.

"Did you get any numbers off their license plate? I had my shotgun on them, so I couldn't use my flashlight."

"I think the last number was a 9," she said. "And maybe the next to the last one was a 2. Texas plates."

"That's good," he said, impressed.

In the darkness all he could make out was the contour of her skin and the reflection of his truck's headlights in her eyes as she stared back at him.

"We need to get you out of here, before they come back...maybe with friends," he said. "If you can walk, I won't touch you. If you're hurt, I can carry you. One way or the other, you're coming with me. If there's anything in the car you need, tell me, and I'll get it."

She didn't say anything for a long moment. "I saw what you did   to...to that trucker."

"Will you forget that bastard? He's lucky I didn't do worse."

"You're not going away, are you?"

"I'm not leaving you here in the middle of nowhere in a damaged car all by yourself, hurt—no."

"So, now you're the good Samaritan."

"Not exactly. When I saw you leave the bar, I saw the same jerks I'd had trouble with earlier get up and follow. I was afraid they'd pull some crazy stunt like this. So, I came after you. I can handle myself; you obviously can't."

"Usually…I can."

"Probably at cotillions and tea parties."

"I'm surprised you know about such things."

"Look, I'm wet and muddy and cold as hell. I shot my weapon. I choked a man out. You're hurt. I gotta get home, woman. We're through talking here."

He slid across the back seat, leaned forward and opened her door. Then he got out into the rain, came over to where she was, knelt and began to examine her.

She cowered, pushing at his hands. But he was determined. Running his palms over her limbs, he shone his flashlight into her eyes to make sure she didn't have a concussion.

"You're blinding me!"

"Other than being stubborn and shaken up and about as ungrateful as a bad-tempered polecat, I think you're okay." He lowered his light.

"I could have told you that."

Putting the safety on, he pointed the shotgun at the ground. Then he helped her out of the car and let her lean on him as they walked to his truck. Getting into the cab was a bit of a climb since she was shakier than she would admit. He secured his gun in the gun rack.

"You're going to need to talk to your insurance company," he said.

"The car's a rental."

"Do you have the papers?"

"They're in my suitcase."

"I'd better get it then." He went to her car and got her suitcase, which was silver and new and shiny, and threw it into his back seat.

"I'll call the sheriff later. We'll see about your car in the morning." He slid in beside her and started the engine. When he turned on the heater, frigid air blasted them.

She began to tremble and her teeth to chatter. "W-would you t-take me to my motel please?"

"Too far. You're spending the night at my place."

"N-no, I want…"

He stared straight ahead. "This isn't just about what you want anymore. I'm not your servant or some cabbie for hire, so I'm damn sure not driving forty miles to your damn motel and then forty miles back in a storm just because you were fool enough to get yourself lost and into trouble on Dead Man's Curve."

The heater warmed up and began to feel good, and she shut up.

"A reasonable woman might take a notion to…say thank you, you know," he said a few minutes later.

She stiffened and looked away.

"They'd say, 'thank you, Liam, for saving me and getting yourself and your truck all muddy. Oh, and for risking your damn neck on my account.' Yes, ma'am, a thank you at this point would be mighty nice. Not that I expect one from the likes of you."

She let out a long, quivery sigh. "Are you calling me a snob?"

She lifted that slim, aquiline nose of hers and sat up straighter, staring out at the road with her soft bottom lip stuck out in stubborn silence.

His jaw clenched. His fists tightened on the wheel.

Why the hell did he care if a snob like her said thank you?

To distract himself, he turned on his favorite radio station, which was country, of course. Unfortunately, the song being played was about love gone wrong.

Hopefully she hated it even more than he did.

"Liam, is that your name?" she whispered, turning her head toward him.

The sound of his name on her lips made the air in the cab feel too close; made every male cell in his body too aware of her slim, feminine form in the dark. He caught her scent and suddenly it was hard to breathe.

"Thank you—Liam. I am...very grateful to you."

Nodding, he grunted an acknowledgement, not liking that her saying it made the tension between them build instead of lessen.

"What's your name?" he said a long time later as his tires hummed on the wet, slick road and the singer on the radio whined about broken hearts.

"It's Hannah."

"Hannah," he repeated, saying it aloud so he'd be sure to memorize it. "Hannah."

She bit her bottom lip as if his saying it grated on her nerves the way everything she did grated on his.

The tension was so thick neither of them dared another word until he parked outside his cabin.

She got to him, like no one else had been able to since he'd lost Mindy.

How the hell would he ever make it through a whole night alone with her and stay sane?

5

The fragility of life stunned her.

Hannah felt strange, almost disconnected from her real self. Was it only two days ago when she'd been planning a life with James? She'd been so sure of herself and her future. Then suddenly, irrevocably the foundation of her Upper East Side existence had crashed around her and cut her off from everyone and everything that was familiar.

When she'd entered the bar, she'd felt adrift, scared of driving in the storm. Then a pair of crazed truckers had chased her and had run her off the road.

She'd been too charged, too determined to survive, to feel terror then. Even now she couldn't feel it. It was as if she were numb.

Her memories darkened. Again she remembered how she'd steeled herself for the worst when the truckers had rammed her and she'd sped up, causing her to lose control and careen into that fence piling. When she'd managed to get her bearings after the airbag had slammed her, she'd seen the truckers grinning as they'd stalked toward her. Maybe that's when she'd gone numb.

The rain had let up by the time Liam braked sharply in front of a mean looking log house that squatted at the end of a lonely, rutted road. She had no idea where he'd taken her. They'd driven at least thirty minutes. He'd had to get out into the rain a couple of times to open and shut gates, which he'd done uncomplainingly. Other gates had opened and shut automatically. Besides the gates, they'd rumbled over several cattle guards.

Because of his battered truck and grubby attire she couldn't imagine him being the owner of a large, private ranch. No, he was probably some absentee rancher's hired hand, a minimum-wage cowboy who had to moonlight as a bartender to make ends meet.

She slanted her eyes in his direction. He was so broad-shouldered and strong looking. Again, she remembered how he'd barely touched the larger man, who'd dropped like a rock.

If he wanted, Liam could easily overpower her, kill her even and then bury her somewhere on this God-forsaken place. If he turned bad on her, nobody was coming to her rescue.

She was too numb to feel fear. Still, it was probably better not to dwell on how helpless she was or how powerful he was, or all the things he could do to her if he took it in his mind to do them.

Yanking his key out of the ignition, Liam jumped out on his side and then came around to hers. When he opened her door, a blast of cold, damp air hit her. Even though she was anxious

about what he intended once he got her alone
inside his cabin, she didn't resist when he put his
big hands around her and lifted her down. She
was too tired. And maybe—not that she was
emotionally coherent enough to know—too
shaken by thoughts of what might have befallen
her if he hadn't rescued her.

He wasn't her type. So why had his nearness in
the dark cab, despite her numbness, produced a
strangling tension inside her—even before he'd
put his hands around her waist and she'd slid the
length of his hard, mud-splashed body.

He'd made his intentions clear when he'd
propositioned her in the bar. She could tell by the
way he was looking at her lips and pressing her
against the truck after her feet were solidly
planted on the ground that he hadn't forgotten
their kiss any more than she had.

She hated how she swayed a little and clung.

He waited until she steadied before he released
her.

"You're going to be okay, Hannah," he
whispered against her brow. "You're safe now.
The bad guys are gone. For the record, I'm not a
serial killer."

Strangely, his deep voice and the way he said
her name reassured her a little. "I never really
thought you were," she admitted.

"You could have fooled me." He got her
suitcase, climbed the stairs to his porch and
unlocked the front door.

"Hold on a minute," he said. "I'm not much of
a housekeeper, and I don't want you stumbling
over something in the dark after what you've been

through. I downsized a while back. Haven't had company in a spell, so there's a lot of stuff on the floor."

So he didn't bring women here all that often. Or not the kind of women he bothered to clean his house for.

Dodging various items on his scuffed floor, he switched on a lamp on a low table beside a gray sofa and two beige plastic lawn chairs that had seen better days. She saw a stack of unopened mail by the door as well as several boxes that looked like they contained items he'd ordered off the Internet.

His cabin was small and ice-cold. It smelled of dust, dirty dishes, unclean laundry and old newspapers. He did have a small desk in a corner with a modern-looking laptop on it, but someone had propped a motorcycle against one wall. Oil cans, parts, and greasy tools circled it. A telephone sat in a tangle of disconnected wires in the middle of his kitchen table.

Men.

At least James, who wasn't all that neat himself, had a cleaning lady once a week. How could anyone—even a man of cruder tastes—live in such squalor?

For a second she imagined the grandiose, antique-filled rooms of her mother's palatial penthouse, the gleaming perfection of every carefully-selected item.

"Sorry that I can't offer you the Waldorf. You're probably used to fine things."

Growing up on the Upper East Side with Audrey Lewis for a mother, how could she not

be? All things material had been important to her
mother, so naturally she'd taught those values to
her child.

A person's name or job title had mattered far
more than his character. The right address, the
right career, a name in the social registry—those
things were what counted.

Practically from the day Hannah had been
conceived, her elitist mother had battled to make
sure she got her favorite daughter into the correct
kindergarten, elementary school, and the most
prestigious private high school.

Only the best for *Hannah*. Not that Audrey had
fought those battles for Nell.

Hannah hadn't questioned the rightness or the
wrongness of how she'd been raised until the
disaster of her wedding. But her sister's betrayal
had thrown her off balance. When they'd been
younger, her twin had tried to please their mother.
It was only later that she'd given up and had
become jealous of Hannah and had rebelled.

For no reason at all, *his* saying she would be
happier at the Waldorf than in his cabin made her
aware, that, no, she didn't prefer the Waldorf
tonight.

The dark flush that stole across his cheekbones
as he grabbed a pile of clothes slung across the
arm of his sofa and tossed them toward a door
made her wonder if the state of his cabin
embarrassed him.

She was surprised he'd even heard of the
Waldorf, but, hey, even badass, whiskey-drinking
cowboys who lived in the middle of nowhere
watched television, didn't they?

She sucked in a breath and let it out. So much had happened in such a short time, she was waiting for the next bad thing.

He hadn't tried to touch her, hadn't made even one untoward move. Just when she told herself maybe she should take another deep breath and try to relax, she saw the rifle and large pistol beside the front door—and froze.

When he took off his Stetson and placed it beside a stack of cowboy hats on the end table by his couch, a heavy lock of black hair fell across his brow. He was tall, and he seemed made of solid muscle. He looked so sexy with his thick disheveled hair that she longed to smooth it back for him.

Biting her lip, she tried to focus on the lopsided stack of hats instead of his hair or the two guns by his door. Why did one cowboy need so many hats?

When he strode over to the front door and locked it, she forgot the hats and refocused on his guns.

"Are those things loaded?"

He took a measured breath. "An unloaded gun wouldn't be of much use, now would it?"

She stiffened. The cold air was getting to her, but she tried not to shake. "I-I wouldn't know. I-I've never been around guns. They make me nervous."

"Where the hell are you from anyway?"

"New York. Manhattan."

"Figures. The accent…the know-it-all attitude…and the way you talk so fast… I was afraid you were a Yankee."

A Yankee. The way he said it was a careful insult.

Her? An accent? He was the one whose lazy drawl and abuse of vowels made her wonder if he'd ever get to the end of a word, much less a sentence.

Scowling at her, he leaned down and picked up the guns.

"What are you doing?" she squealed, jumping backward and flattening herself against a wall when he approached with the firearms.

Her numbness vanished. Fear gripped her.

"Moving them. They make you nervous, don't they?"

You make me nervous.

"You're trailing mud everywhere," she pointed out, so he wouldn't see how scared she was.

"It's my house. I can do what I want."

Oh, my God. If her Mother was profoundly upset with Hannah for running off from her wedding reception without a word, and then for not bothering to call to explain, she would be even more horrified to find out she'd stayed with this man, here, alone, even for one night, despite the circumstances.

"Before I go put these away—your face is scratched. If you want adhesive bandages, they're in the bathroom. Over there." He pointed toward a door.

Without waiting for her to reply, he turned his broad back on her. Leaving a trail of mud behind him as he stomped quickly up a narrow staircase, he disappeared.

Not that she didn't know where he was. The ceiling shook every time he took a step. His filthy boots were probably kicking off little flicks of mud up there too. Was he throwing things?

He was so rough and uncouth, she half expected one of the guns to go off and blast a hole through the ceiling.

Eyeing the mud-streaked floor and the depressing living room, she began to shiver. When her teeth began to chatter in earnest again, she rubbed her arms in an attempt to warm herself. Closing her eyes, she wished she could magically beam herself out of this awful place to the motel room she'd rented, which was probably safe and warm and dry… and clean. She imagined herself showering and sinking into a warm, soft bed.

But he wouldn't be there. She'd be alone. He'd saved her. He'd said he wasn't going to hurt her, and she was beginning to believe him and feel more secure around him.

Still shaking from the cold, she opened her eyes and took in his lumpy couch and filthy windowpanes. Upstairs, he was still storming about in his muddy boots as if he were as upset by her presence in his home as she was.

Suddenly he stopped moving. After a while, she heard something hit the floor with a clunk. Another clunk followed, and then silence.

What on earth was he doing up there?

Why was it that as much as he annoyed her, now that he was gone, she wanted him back?

Her cell buzzed in her bag.

Well, what do you know? Will miracles never cease? He has cellular service.

When she pulled out her phone and saw James's name lit up, her heart thudded so violently with fresh hurt and fury she declined the call.

When she saw that he, Nell, her mother and various friends had called repeatedly, her skin grew clammy, and a fist squeezed her heart so hard it cut off her breath.

She'd turned her phone off as she'd boarded the plane. She hadn't turned it on again until she'd landed. When she'd discovered texts and voice mail messages from nearly everybody she knew, she'd deleted them all. She hadn't felt like explaining herself to anybody, even her family. They knew all they needed to know for now— she'd left James. The only family member she intended to call in the near future was Uncle Tommy, James's boss—because she wanted Uncle Tommy to start working on obtaining an annulment.

James had no right to call her. She considered texting him and telling him to stay out of her life forever.

No, he didn't even deserve that much of a response. Not yet anyway. She *so* couldn't deal with some stupid apology or explanation. She was through. Finished.

But what if he used the phone to somehow find her and then he turned up here? Or what if her parents were panicking that she was hurt?

Deciding maybe she had to let her family at least know she was alive before she put her phone in airplane mode or turned it off again, she texted her mother.

I'm ok. Sorry. Can't talk. Need time alone. Love you.

Sinking down onto one of Liam's plastic chairs, she blocked James's number and her mother's and Nell's.

Turning her phone off, she plunged it into the sodden pocket of her jeans.

"Are you all right?" Liam's deep, male voice demanded from behind her.

She couldn't have exploded out of his chair faster if he'd fired one of his guns.

"How dare you sneak up on me!"

"Sorry."

"How did you come down here without me hearing you when you were stomping around like an elephant before?"

"Hey...easy...I took my boots off."

Noting his socks as he set a pile of sheets, blankets, and pillows on the end of the sofa, she nodded. Strangely, she felt slightly reassured that his socks weren't *that* dirty.

"Sorry. I really didn't mean to scare you," he said.

"I-I'm just a little jumpy, that's all."

"No wonder—after what you've been through."

She heaved in a breath. She didn't want to think about that, couldn't let herself—or she might break down.

"You can sleep here. Or in my bed. Your choice," he said.

He made the offer casually, as if he didn't care, but his hot black eyes that devoured her gave his preference away.

"Where will you be?" she whispered, alarm trilling through her.

"I'm damn sure not sleeping on that lumpy couch."

"Th-then I-I'll be just fine down here…alone…lumps and all. Thank you very much."

"Indeed." His tone was neutral, but again, his eyes weren't. Still, he let it go. "You're cold, aren't you?"

"M-maybe just a little."

He went into the kitchen and turned on the oven. Then he lit the burners of his stove, actions which horrified her so much her teeth stopped chattering.

"Isn't that unsafe…heating the place with your kitchen stove?"

"Did anyone ever tell you you've got a bossy streak?"

James. All the time. Every surgeon she worked with. Nurses in the OR. Nell too. Practically everybody she knew, even Mother, who adored her and thought she was perfect. But Hannah didn't want to think about New York, James, her career, her mother and her former life there—the life and career she'd built achievement by achievement for the last fourteen years before she'd screwed it all up by marrying James. She'd known he'd been born poor in his youth and was ambitious, but she hadn't faulted him because she'd been ambitious in her career as well. She'd understood his desire to climb and to be important. She'd wanted him to seek status because those things had mattered to her. But she'd believed he'd cared about her...until...

Liam left the kitchen and strode to his fireplace. Kneeling, he poked at a pile of twigs and logs before he lit a match. Five minutes later, he had flames dancing in the stone hearth.

He was good at everything he took a mind to do, she noted with cool approval.

Drawn by the warmth and fiery glow, and maybe by the broad expanse of his back and his devastating male appeal, if she were truthful, she joined him there.

"Why do you keep guns everywhere? In your truck? By your door? Are you paranoid?"

His eyes narrowed. "This is South Texas."

"And? Don't you feel safe...even in your own home?"

"Safe?" His tone was flat. "Do you?"

"Usually."

"Must be nice."

His tone chilled her.

"Tonight didn't shake you?" he asked.

She didn't want to think about what had nearly happened to her. Even so when she hugged herself, her fingers dug into the flesh of her upper arms.

When she didn't reply, he said, "Let's just say I don't mind having a gun or two around."

"All the time?"

"Is that a problem?"

"I don't like it."

A muscle jumped in his jaw. "Well, you don't have to, do you? You're just passing through, right?"

"Have you ever shot anybody?"

He sucked in a breath. His jaw flexed, but he didn't answer. Instead, he deflected. "You ask a lot of questions."

"Aren't you afraid maybe you'll shoot someone someday?"

His expression hardened. "Honey, I never pick up a gun without knowing I'll use it if I have to."

Her heart skittered. "Like tonight when you shot at those truckers?"

"I didn't shoot *at* them. They walked away, didn't they? We may be a hundred miles north of Mexico, but this is still border country. Folks who can't travel by car, because they don't enjoy chatting with the Border Patrol at the checkpoints, hike north through private ranches like this one. Used to be, the folks we saw out here didn't bother us ranchers much. They were nice and polite and looking for a better life, so we understood.

"Now we get all sorts. Mostly they're still okay. But we get smugglers and traffickers, and terrorists too probably. The closest inhabited house is thirty miles away. I'm on my own out here."

You didn't answer my question. Have you ever shot anybody?"

His mouth thinned; his gaze seemed haunted. "What gives you the right to ask me so many damn questions?"

"You *have* shot somebody?"

Again, he deflected, which made her feel even warier.

"What I've done or haven't done is my own damn business, not yours."

"I just want to know who I'm spending the night with."

"Do you now? Ever think that maybe knowin' would be a whole lot scarier than not knowin'?"

When he shot her a look that was probably meant to quell her, she met his unflinching gaze.

"Ever think maybe you'd be happier if you stopped poking your pretty nose in my business— where, by the way, it doesn't belong?"

"You're right." Her heart rate skipped and her palms got sweaty. Why was she goading him? Maybe he'd saved her, but she didn't know him, didn't have a clue what he might be capable of or what might set him off.

"I can see I make you nervous. Why don't we forget about me being a scary guy with guns and focus on practical matters? I need to call the sheriff, and you need to call your rental car agency. We need to figure out what we have to do about your car, too. If you need to get on the Internet, you can use my computer. My password's on a scrap of paper underneath my laptop over there on the desk."

"I can't believe I'm here with you."

"You won't be for long." Tension rippled through his massive frame. "Honey, the less we get involved with one another on a personal level tonight, the happier we'll both be come morning."

The unexpected endearment made her tummy flip again, which scared her as much as his talent for violence.

They sat down together with their phones. While he called the sheriff, who sounded like a friend, she turned her cell on and called her rental car agency.

When he hung up, he told her the sheriff would want to talk to her tomorrow about what had happened, that he would need written statements from both of them.

Strangely, after making those calls, she felt better.

They had a plan. In New York she'd been a planner.

It no longer mattered quite so much that Liam had snuck up beside that big trucker and had so easily vanquished him with his bare hands.

Where would she be if he hadn't?

6

"Can I get you anything? A drink, before I turn in?" Liam asked after he'd shown her where everything on the lower floor was.

When she met his eyes, she resented how his classically handsome face with its sharp cheekbones and hard jawline had her hitching in a breath.

Liam leaned against the wall at the foot of the stairs, his bronzed fingers gripping the long neck of his whiskey bottle. He looked so disturbingly virile, a ripple of unwanted heat flooded her.

His dark gaze sharpened. "What? Have you got a problem?"

"Could you please cut off the kitchen burners?"

"Sure." He went to the kitchen and did as she asked. "Anything else, princess?"

"You showed me where the bathroom down here is, so I'm good."

Like the rest of the cabin, his bathroom was in need of a good scrubbing. He'd pointed out his adhesive bandages and his abysmal selection of toiletries.

When he'd shown her the kitchen, he'd opened his poorly-stocked fridge and had offered her a ham sandwich or a slice of cold pizza.

Somehow she'd managed to resist commenting on his terrible food choices. She'd refused a snack because the thought of him slicing bread and slathering it with fatty mayonnaise for her in his tiny kitchen had seemed much too intimate.

When she frowned at the whiskey, he'd lifted a dark brow.

Having seen the empty soldiers in his trash, she didn't like the thought of him going upstairs with that bottle either.

"What?" he asked.

"It's a bad habit—drinking alone," she said.

"Right."

"You should read a book or take up a hobby. Or get a dog. Or maybe a cat."

Why had she bothered saying anything? She knew better than to get involved with him or worry about his bad choices.

Involved? Where had that crazy thought come from? Was it because so much had happened to her and she wasn't reacting normally?

"You can drink yourself to death for all I care," she snapped.

"Good. Not that I needed your permission." He paused. "For your information, I do have a pet. A horse. A very bad horse, by the way. I don't need another cantankerous animal. Or a bossy woman trying to run me."

He turned and strode up the stairs, but long after he was gone, her thoughts were consumed by him. Why did she care so much whether he drank or not? Why did she strain to hear every sound that came from the room above her as he padded back and forth on squeaky floorboards. When he stopped and she heard the sound of water, she imagined him stripping out of his torn jeans and faded shirt, and fought not to imagine his ripped, bronzed torso and thighs naked. When he slammed the bathroom door and then the shower door, the walls were so thin, she could still hear him sing, "When the Saints Come Marching In."

All he sang was the first verse, but he sang it over and over again. He probably didn't know the whole song and he definitely couldn't carry a tune. But as he sang, slowly her fear of him ebbed, and she even laughed.

After a while the fire died down and the cabin grew quiet. Imagining him upstairs in his warm bed, she made up the couch and went into the downstairs bathroom, intending to shower and see to the scratches on her face. But his tub was gray, his shower curtain black, and the mirror of his medicine chest so smeared with tiny white droplets and fingerprints, she could barely see herself. Did the man ever clean anything?

Curious, she opened his medicine chest where she found a row of bottles crammed into the shelves above bandages, condoms, floss and toothpaste.

Condoms? Amazed that he had so many packages, she flipped through the small boxes before tossing them back in the cabinet in disgust. He worked in a bar. What did she expect? He probably carried a few in his wallet all the time.

Ignoring the adhesive bandages, she lifted a bottle, and then another, only to wince in shock when she understood their significance.

He was hoarding psych meds.

To what dark purpose? And what was his diagnosis?

Her frown deepened after she counted his bottles and then looked inside them. Why had he filled two years' worth of prescriptions and never taken a single pill? He'd saved up enough to kill that cantankerous horse of his.

She remembered the pain she'd seen in his eyes after they'd kissed, remembered wondering what had happened to him that was so awful.

Suddenly it was all too easy to imagine him gathering up the bottles and walking upstairs with a bottle of whiskey one night. If he took the pills along with the whiskey all the way out here, who'd find him in time?

Well, that wasn't going to happen. Not if she had anything to do with it.

Her frown deepening, she deliberately uncapped a bottle and tossed the pills into the toilet. With the same determination she emptied the rest of them, bottle by bottle. Flushing the toilet, she replaced the empties on the medicine shelf so he wouldn't notice till she was gone. If he needed refills, no doubt his doctor could see to that, but she wasn't turning a blind eye to a pill-hoarding situation.

After that she found some Clorox and got to work rinsing his tub and shower and scrubbing his mildewed shower curtain. Only when she had the bathroom sparkling did she take a quick shower

with the scented soap she'd bought in San
Antonio and tend to her face, which wasn't too
bad, considering.

Wrapping herself in a towel, which—
surprise—was clean and soft, she stepped out of
the tub and opened her suitcase, tensing when she
saw nothing but the sexy new garments she'd
purchased.

Suddenly her revenge-shopping spree at the
River Center Mall this morning didn't seem so
clever. She'd still felt so crazed and insecure
about Nell being the sexier twin, Hannah had
decided she needed a wardrobe makeover.

Selecting clothes that would make people
notice her for her looks instead of her brains for a
change, she'd chosen tight-fitting jeans and
sparkly sweaters, revealing blouses made of
shimmery fabrics and short leather skirts like the
ones Nell wore, instead of the more tailored
clothes she preferred. To top it off, she'd bought
shampoo, soap, and that toe-pinching pair of
outrageously-embroidered, look-at-me red boots.
For the first time in her life she wished she owned
and had packed jeans a size or two too big or
some bulky sweats.

When her eyes fell on the neatly-folded scarlet
silk gown and robe, she studied them critically,
remembering how the soft fabric had clung to her
body. Not the smartest thing to wear when sharing
a cabin in the middle of nowhere with a rugged
cowboy who'd gone to bed with a bottle.

She pulled the gown and robe out of her
suitcase and slipped into them. When she looked
in the mirror and saw her nipples and belly button

with a clarity that made her gasp, she quickly fastened her bra. Then tying the robe, she went to the couch and buried herself under the covers.

Not that she could fall asleep. Or forget him. Oh no. The wind whistled in the eaves much too noisily. The rain pattered on his roof, and a shutter hammered against an outside wall. Once or twice she imagined hooves on the porch. When she heard a large animal snorting outside her window, she froze. Then the coyotes began to yelp.

Above her, Liam was silent—even when some small creature, no doubt chased by the coyotes, screamed in mortal terror.

How could *he* sleep through all this carnage? Was he sleeping? Or was he thinking about her, too? What if he came down?

Go to sleep! Don't think about him.

For a while she felt both exhausted and crazed because, no matter how many imaginary sheep she counted, she couldn't fall asleep. Then shortly after midnight, after she finally drifted off, a man's wild scream tore through the cabin.

Breathless, she sat up and listened to the shutter bang. If Liam had only screamed once, she might never have found the courage to go check on him. But when he continued to cry out, sounding as if he were terrified, her heart filled with compassion.

Getting up, she stole across the icy room to the stairs where she hesitated until he screamed again. Then she climbed stealthily, so as not to further alarm him.

When she pushed his door open, her gaze went to the bed and the mound of covers that was illuminated by the gray light sifting in from a single window.

"Liam?"

One minute, he lay in his bed thrashing wildly. In the next he leapt out of it like a wild man, charging her so fast, she had no time to react. His right hand clamping around her mouth, he dragged her back to the bed. Falling on top of her, his legs imprisoned her lower body against the mattress.

His other hand wrapped her throat in a stranglehold. He was strong, powerful, muscular. He felt like he was made of iron as he held her down.

Terrified, sputtering for each breath, she kicked and scratched him on the shoulders, causing him to curse.

"Stop," he growled.

A silk spaghetti strap ripped, and the red gown slid beneath her breast, exposing her black lacy bra. When his leg moved between hers, forcing hers apart, she felt his aroused manhood.

He was as naked as the day he'd been born.

She was a doctor; she was used to bodies, used to male bodies. Just not under these circumstances.

She had to imagine him as a patient in need of her care, not as an aroused man who had her underneath him in his bed. Not as a possible sexual predator.

Stay calm. Reassure him.

"Liam? Liam, wake up!" She spoke in her firmest, most professional voice. "Snap out of it! It's me, Hannah."

"Hannah?" He froze. He opened his eyes, which were glazed and wild as he shifted and stared down at her body in the silky red gown.

"Hannah. Oh, my God." He groaned. Easing his grip, he lifted the edge of her gown to cover her bra. "I ripped your gown. Nearly tore it off you."

Her fear abating, she was both amazed and pleased at his remorseful, respectful tone.

Slowly, carefully, he rolled off of her. Breathing hard, he sat up and then gently pulled her to a sitting position. Grabbing his sheet, he covered his bare legs and thighs.

"Are you okay? Did I hurt you? Tell me I didn't hurt you."

"I'm fine," she said, even though her heart was still thundering. "You screamed. I was concerned and came up here to check on you."

"Don't ever sneak up on me like that again, okay? The guys used to say I had ears like a cat."

"What guys?"

His eyes narrowing, he pressed his lips together. "It doesn't matter. All that matters is that I could have hurt you. Seriously hurt you. Do you understand me? Next time, if I'm asleep, touch my ankle or say my last name. Stark. Say, 'Stark, wake up.' Whatever you do, be sure and say my last name. If I don't wake up, scream it. Do you understand? I have to know you're a friend. Not the enemy."

"The enemy?"

"Just a turn of phrase," he muttered, looking away. "Do you understand?" he repeated.

"Okay." She didn't understand, but she didn't know him and never would, so she didn't suppose she really needed to.

He swept that thick, unruly lock of dark hair that had a tendency   to tumble across his brow out of his eyes and then turned back to her. "I couldn't have stood it if I'd hurt you. You know that, don't you? I'm not...some serial killer, like you said." His expression was grave, his low voice tender and sincere.

Instead of slowing, her heart sped up. She didn't want to find him so attractive. Not now, when she felt so exposed and afraid of him. "Like I told you before, I know. I just said that...because..."

Her hand closed over his where it rested in his lap. Her touch was meant to reassure, but when he threaded his fingers through hers and drew her nearer, sweet forbidden fire shuddered through her. No longer was it remotely possible for her to imagine they were in a professional setting where he was her patient and she his caring doctor.

"Hannah?"

She heard the question in his rough voice, felt his fierce, hot need because it matched her own. She knew she should release his hand, get up and go; knew she should fly down those stairs; knew she should bury herself under her covers again on his awful, lumpy couch.

"If you're not going to stay, you'd better go," he said huskily.

"I know."

So why couldn't she move? Why was she so drawn to him?

Because the sight of his bare chest and the outline of his powerful legs beneath the sheet excited her too much. He was made of bronzed, sinewy muscle, and the hard ripple of male flesh over his rib cage sent feverish darts of awareness racing along every feminine nerve ending.

He was the polar opposite of James.

Considering how everything with James and Nell had worked out, that was an almost welcome alternative.

But Hannah wasn't thinking about James or Nell as she feasted on Liam's incredible cheekbones and memorized his black brows and the nose that was slightly crooked. His gaze was as hungry as hers as he stared at her with urgency.

James had crushed her. This man had risked his own life to save hers, and the fierce need that blazed in his eyes was having a profoundly different effect. He made her feel feminine and infinitely desirable.

Her gaze devoured his beautiful sculpted lips. She didn't care if he was a lowborn cowboy with no aspirations who would probably drink himself to death before he was forty. She wanted to kiss him again, wanted to taste him. Her gaze wandered lower, down his strong arms and further, down the solid length of his ripped, muscular torso.

He was gorgeous. Perfect... And she, who loved beauty in all its forms, was sorely tempted.

"Oh my God," she whispered, her voice quivering, when she saw the jagged scars with rivets in the skin where flesh had been held together with wire clamps on his right arm. "Oh my God." Next she saw the melted curl of flesh on his shoulder and the letters tattooed in bold blue capital letters across his magnificent chest.

INFIDEL.

As a rule she didn't like tattoos, but his tattoo and scars merely enhanced his aura of primitive, all-powerful masculinity.

Her heart knocked. "What happened to you?" she asked as she brushed her fingers down the length of the puckered red scars on his arm and then the tangled flesh on his shoulder.

At her touch he clenched his jaw and stiffened. "I got shot. And burned. What of it?"

"But, why?"

"Afghanistan. Combat. The first time I got hit, I was on my bunk eating a ham and cheddar cheese sandwich with a buddy. Then I heard a sound like rubber whizzing past my right ear, and my buddy was dead and I was deaf. I'll spare you the grisly details."

"No, tell me."

He was silent until she squeezed his hand.

"Bullets began slicing up the floor. We'd been hit before I heard the gunfire."

"You were a soldier?"

"Army. *Were* being the operative word."

"And the second bullet wound?"

"It doesn't matter."

"And the tattoo?"

"You ask a lot of questions, lady."

Without checking the impulse, she lifted her hand and traced each hideous letter with trembling fingertips.

Although her touch was light, he heaved in a breath, his eyes narrowing to slits as he watched her face and fought not to react. When she continued to stroke him, his muscles bunched, and he knotted his hands.

"Why?" she whispered. "Why this particular word?"

When his gaze lingered on her lips, she began to tremble.

"Tattoos are always a mistake." Seizing her hand, he removed it from his chest.

His palm was callused, but his tight grip was pleasantly warm and unimaginably gentle.

"The mood of a moment," he continued. "Then the moment passes."

She liked the way her hand felt wrapped in his. As he studied her mouth, she remembered their kiss. The mere thought of his lips on hers made every part of her tingle.

"Like tonight? Like us?" she murmured in the dark.

"I'm going to have it removed. I just haven't gotten around to it. I'm a rancher, so I work. All the time."

"What does it mean?" she asked.

He loosened his grip on her hand, but kept his palm flat and warm, oh so pleasantly warm, against hers—a gesture that was somehow both deeply reassuring and wildly erotic.

"Nothing…now…here."

He lowered his head, letting his mouth brush hers in subtle warning. "Nothing for you to worry about, honey. That part of my life is over."

Not if it haunts you. Not if it has you screaming in your sleep and hoarding psych meds.

Mesmerized by his lips hovering so close to hers, she forgot she wanted to ask more about his scars. Her hands fell to her sides. His hard, warm body, his clean male scent, his deep, husky drawl, and most of all the thought of his mouth on hers or his mouth touching other places—everything about him stirred her. She'd never been with a man who was so irrevocably and unapologetically masculine, or a tenth as sexy. *One time. Only once,* she promised herself. *Then I'll return to my own world, safe and sound, and settle down again where I belong.*

"You'd better go," he said, even as he leaned closer and took her mouth in a hot, sensual kiss that destroyed the last of her will to fight him.

Hannah opened her mouth and yielded, letting his hot, expert tongue slide inside and mate with hers. "Yes…I'd better," she breathed between kisses. "That would be the smart thing for a smart woman to do."

But she wasn't feeling smart. Forgetting every rational argument against sleeping with a stranger, especially him, she slid her arms around his neck and surrendered to the burning tide of desire that was sweeping her past reason. Drawing him closer, she kissed him back, the tip of her tongue grazing his and then tangling with his.

He barely knew her, yet he made her feel so desirable. More desirable than she'd even imagined she could feel. Was this what Nell felt all the time? Was this what her twin was looking for when she hopped in and out of all those strangers' beds, including James's?

Hannah, who had always been deeply passionate about her work, was amazed she could feel so aroused sexually. She'd studied so obsessively, missed so much.

"How can you taste so good?" Hannah whispered.

"Careful, maybe you have a secret weakness for whiskey," he murmured dryly.

"I don't think it's whiskey I have a weakness for. I'm thinking it's cowboys."

When she touched her tongue to his lips, he sucked in a long breath. Then his restraint broke and his arms tightened around her.

Gripping her fiercely, he kissed her with raw, savage hunger. Sensing the wildness in him, her own heart began to race, and she kissed him back with a greediness that matched his.

Never had she felt so hot or so shockingly aroused. Or so wet. His hands moved over her, exploring her hair, her breasts, her pelvis and the incriminating dampness there.

Barely able to catch her breath, she clung to his hard body, trying to pull him down on top of her as she stretched full length underneath him on his bed.

Suddenly she knew that in his arms, she could erase the memory of Nell with James, which was the most devastating hurt and humiliation of her life. With Liam she could forget her twin's superior sensual appeal and betrayal and find peace.

"No," Liam said abruptly, pulling back and pushing her away with both hands.

"What?"

"Not tonight, honey."

"Not tonight?" she cried in anguished disbelief. "You're rejecting me? You don't want me?" she pleaded, feeling even more lost than when she'd discovered James with Nell.

"When you were in your right mind, you told me no in the bar. And then again downstairs. You chose the couch over me, remember?"

"What? Now you're being noble?"

"You've got to admit, it's a whole lot better than me being a serial killer."

"Not funny," she snapped. After feeling rejected and humiliated by James and Nell, and now by him just when she'd realized he could make her forget what she badly needed to forget, she was in no mood to joke.

"It's ego-deflating and infuriating," she finished.

"And you're playing with fire. Go back downstairs before you get burned."

"But we started...and now I want you," she pleaded hoarsely.

"Maybe right now you do, but you won't be happy in the morning."

"What?"

"You heard me. Believe me, you'll thank me tomorrow."

"If I don't kill you tonight."

He laughed. Then he pulled her close and tousled her hair, and the gentle touch of his blunt fingertips against her sensitive scalp coupled with his warm, masculine laughter soothed her, lessening some of the hurt and sense of rejection.

"I do want you," he said, touching his brow to hers. "Too much I think. It isn't a question of my not wanting you. I went to bed nursing a whiskey bottle. You didn't approve. You were so cute when you scowled with your face all scratched up and told me to read a book or get a pet. I couldn't sleep for thinking about how cute you were...and that you were downstairs."

"Don't tease me now," she said sulkily.

"But when you heard me scream, you rushed up here to help me." Gently he traced the adhesive bandage on her chin with the rough pad of his thumb. "You didn't come up here to be seduced into my bed when I'm half liquored up and you're still so shaken by whatever made you run from New York and then those truckers. You barely know what you're doing."

"I can't believe I'm having this discussion with you, *you* of all people."

He smiled again. "What do you mean?"

"I thought you were just another whiskey-drinking, horn-dog cowboy in a bar who wanted to get laid. You said you would have slept with anyone who walked through that door."

"I probably would have earlier tonight. That's the problem."

"Meaning?"

"You're not like that."

"You know me so well?"

"You've been hurt...pretty badly by people you loved...and trusted."

She swallowed.

He ran a fingertip along her jawline, letting it hover again on top of the bandage she'd applied. "I get you're pure city and kind of a princess-and-the-pea type, and, therefore, complicated...while I'm rough around the edges and pretty low maintenance."

"*Princess and the Pea*? Complicated? I don't think I'm like that."

"Good. It would definitely be better for both of us if you go downstairs and sulk about it for a spell."

"Now I know you're trying to get rid of me."

"I am. So scram." When she hesitated, she felt his warm breath against her ear. "Honey, don't you know I'm not strong enough to fight this much longer?"

"But you don't have to. I-I don't want you to."

"I've got a lot of regrets. I don't need any more. This is the anniversary of a very bad night for me. You and our adventure with those thugs helped me get through it this year. I owe you for that."

She thought about the pills she'd flushed down his toilet and slowly stood up. He might not be so grateful when he discovered the bottles in his medicine cabinet were empty. Not that she felt guilty about that.

A bad anniversary? She didn't know him, didn't know what he was going through or why and had no right to ask.

What she did know from what he said and from the dates on his meds was that he'd been fighting unbearable pain for two years. He hadn't surrendered to it, and he'd put himself out for her tonight...risked his life even. Now, in addition, he was fighting to protect her from his own base desires as well as hers.

He had more to him than she'd originally thought. It would be wrong to use him to assuage her own feelings of inadequacy because of James and Nell. Hannah didn't know much about Liam Stark, but she knew he deserved better than a one-night stand with a woman who was only out to use him for revenge sex.

7

Liam woke up to the sound of floorboards creaking downstairs. It was pitch dark and still hours before dawn.

His heart beat faster. If she came upstairs again, he damn sure wouldn't turn her down a second time.

The bathroom door downstairs opened and closed. He held his breath when she came out of it and listened for her light tread on the stairs. But she didn't climb them. No, she began moving about in the kitchen. Cabinet doors banged. Water splashed. Next he heard the washing machine.

What the hell? Washing in the middle of the night? What was wrong with the woman? Okay. Maybe nothing was wrong with her. Maybe she was simply so shaken by all that had happened she couldn't sleep, so she was doing practical things to take her mind off what had happened.

Strangely, as he listened to the racket she was making, his annoyance faded. A peace that he hadn't felt for two years settled in upon him. For no reason he remembered how good it used to feel to hear Mindy running the vacuum cleaner or mowing the yard or doing anything in the house or on the property, even if they weren't interacting.

Hannah wasn't Mindy. She could never take her place. No woman could. Still, it was just nice having a woman—no, having *her*—down there.

He lay back down, savoring her presence. This was way better than getting drunk and screwing his brains out and waking up to a headache and remorse.

When he put his head on the pillow, he fell into a deep, dreamless sleep, the first since he'd lost Mindy. Who knows how late he would have slept if a violent thud hadn't walloped the roof directly over his head just as a new blood-red sun shot scarlet rays over the horizon.

He burst to a sitting position, squinting in the rosy light. What the hell? Remembering the truckers that had been after her, he threw off his covers despite the arctic chill, grabbed the pistol out of a top drawer and strode to his window naked.

The norther had settled down. The air that could be so dense and humid in the summer that it sat on a man like a warm blanket, was cool and crisp and light. Slanting sunlight sparkled rosily on the bare branches of the mesquite and lit up the trunks of the two leafy live oaks out front.

Pharaoh, Mindy's prized Arabian gelding, stood directly beneath him staring up at the house. When the mischievous rascal spotted him, he lifted his black head and snorted.

Liam's trigger finger relaxed.

You devil! If I didn't know better, I'd think you were taunting me.

No way did he need a dog. Not with this big baby demanding constant attention. Mindy had delivered him in the dead of winter. Then she'd raised him from a foal and spoiled him rotten.

Guilt swamped him as he realized how little time he spent with the horse she'd loved nearly as much as she'd loved little Charlie and him. But he couldn't spend time with the animal—not when just looking at Pharaoh brought back memories of the way she used to stroke him and tease him by stuffing carrots and apples in different pockets of her garments.

Suddenly, he was remembering how pretty she'd looked riding him, her long dark hair flying behind her in the wind. The memory made his heart constrict. A lump big enough to choke a full-grown horse solidified in his throat.

Damn horse. I should have sold you to somebody with kids. Somebody who has time to deal with an ornery, demanding cuss like you. But I can't sell you... 'cause you're all I have left of her.

So what the hell have you chunked onto my roof this time? Last I checked the barn doors were rolled down and the porch was free of clutter.

As if to answer his question, Pharaoh sprinted out of sight and quickly returned with something black dangling out of his mouth that he jauntily began whipping from side to side.

Damnation! Is that my favorite snake boot?

It was.

You rascal! How the hell did you get it?

When Pharaoh looked up at the roof and began to toss his head as if he meant business, Liam opened the window, waved his gun and shouted down at him.

"Don't you dare throw it or I'll shoot you. Or I'll sell you for glue! I will! I swear I will!"

Taking aim in a way that would have made a talented sniper proud, the Arabian tossed his head and smacked a second boot onto the roof, easy as you please.

There was a resounding clunk above Liam's head as it landed beside the first one.

Liam swore. "Now you've done it!" When he aimed his gun at the animal, the horse lifted his head and snorted triumphantly.

"Calling my bluff, are you? Well, we'll see about that! You're glue!"

Liam slammed the window shut and jammed his pistol back into the drawer. Dragging his briefs and a pair of clean jeans on, he grabbed a shirt off a hanger and shoved his arms through the sleeves. Buttoning it with one hand, his other skimming the banister, his mind on how to deal with Pharaoh, he bounded down the stairs two at a time.

He was halfway across his living room when a soft feminine sigh and a shiny gleam of flaxen hair spread across a pillow on his couch brought him to an abrupt standstill.

Hannah. Even from this distance, he caught the scent of flowers.

Knowing she'd been up most of the night, working herself to death when she'd been hurt, he took pains to soften his tread on the creaky floorboards when he resumed walking to the door.

Shiny floorboards.

Hell, he didn't see a speck of mud anywhere. Not a single speck.

She'd waxed the damn floor. The kitchen sparkled like a surgeon's operating theater. Mindy had always been so proud when her floors had sparkled like that. Not that they had all that often. As a rancher's wife and a mother of young son, she'd been way too busy.

Do not think of Mindy.

Still, a rebel thought teased. *Mindy would approve of her.*

Stacks of neatly folded laundry graced his table that had been cleared of its usual piles.

Where was all his stuff that he'd carefully stored on his living room floor?

And where the hell were his hats that he always kept on the end table where he could find them?

His snake boots?

So, that's how...

Not knowing about Pharaoh's penchant for throwing things, she must have unwittingly set them outside on the porch. He began to notice other prized possessions that weren't where they belonged—or were downright missing. Like his bailing wire.

What kind of crazy woman cleaned up a stranger's house and hid a man's bailing wire in the middle of the night?

Just as he was about to shake her awake and demand answers, the clatter of hooves on his porch sent him stomping to the front door before Pharaoh could grab another treasure and get up to more mischief.

Liam opened the door. "Get!" He waved his arms as Pharaoh grabbed a plastic sack, no doubt filled with more of his valuables, stuff she'd deemed trash.

Pharaoh began to swing the sack.

Liam lunged for the sack, but Pharaoh was having too much fun to let go.

"What's going on?" Hannah asked in a sleepy voice that was sexier than all get-out.

Just as he was turning to answer her, the sack broke, and he fell backward, trash exploding all over him as he crashed onto wooden planking.

Pain knifed through his elbow, causing him to curse and say things no lady should hear.

She burst out laughing.

"Now get," he said from the floor of his porch in his sternest tone. The horse, who was smart enough to know Liam wasn't kidding, hoofed it.

When Hannah couldn't stop giggling, he twisted his neck so he could see her. "This is your fault. You can't set all my valuable things out on the porch 'cause Pharaoh here is a mighty curious, not to mention a mischievous animal."

"Valuable?" Her expression dubious, she rushed out into the cold, half-naked in that sexy red silk gown he'd torn last night. "Are you hurt?"

All he saw was irresistible tawny skin and voluptuous, soft curves as she knelt over him.

"Get back inside," he growled.

Hell, she was so cute and smelled so good he almost forgot how mad he was at her. Suddenly all he wanted was to take her in his arms and kiss her and let nature take its course.

"It's not only valuable, it's dangerous," he forced himself to say. "If he gets into the bailing wire, he might cut himself."

"I didn't know. I'm so sorry. I was trying to do something for you...to say thank you."

At her heartfelt apology and thank you, he softened, despite his best intentions not to. But the sunlight looked so pretty in her hair, and her concerned blue eyes as she hovered over him were as bright as sapphires. Even without her makeup, she was a damn fine looking woman. All of a sudden he was remembering how long it had been since he'd had a woman underneath him.

In combat he'd had to do without for months. When he'd return home, he and Mindy would go at it like rabbits till he left again. Only the last time he'd come home to an empty house and an emptier life. And no sex.

He'd let Hannah think he hit on women all the time. The truth was, there'd only been one since Mindy, a woman he'd picked up at the Lonesome Dove on the first anniversary of Mindy's death. It had been a mistake. He'd felt even emptier and needier afterward than before, not to mention guilty.

God, Hannah was beautiful with the morning light on her face and in her hair. Suddenly he was so hard, all he wanted was to pull her closer and carry her upstairs and get this thing that was between them settled. Maybe then he'd feel sane again. Maybe afterwards they'd have breakfast

and a conversation over coffee...like normal
people, like friends, before saying their goodbyes.

He was feeling almost sociable. Which meant
she was super dangerous.

Which meant he had to get rid of her before
this *thing*, whatever the hell it was that was
building between them, really took hold and got
out of hand.

"Put somethin' on. Your teeth are chattering
and your gown is torn."

"W-w-hat?"

"You heard me, woman," he said, staring at her
breast covered by her lacy black bra as if it
offended him, which caused her to blush and yank
the gown up. "I warned you off last night, didn't
I? What does it take?"

Her bottom lip quivered.

"I'll deal with this mess," he said gruffly. "And
the horse. Then we'll have breakfast and get you
on your way."

"R-r-ight." She turned white, and her blue eyes
filled with fresh hurt.

All of which made him feel guilty. *Him.* Not
that he said he was sorry. Better to be a little
rough on her and break it off before things got any
hotter.

Holding her gown above her breasts she fled.

Ten minutes later she emerged from the
bathroom in a pair of tight jeans and a tighter
sweater with her hair done up in a golden topknot,
like the hairdo of that pesky fairy that flitted about
in green, torturing Peter Pan. By that time, Liam
had hauled everything she'd dragged onto his

porch back inside and had dumped it square in the middle of the floor.

Her brows knitted when she saw the mess he'd made. "What do you think you're doing?"

"Putting my things back where they belong. So I can find them and Pharaoh can't." Only he said 'cain't' and added a second syllable, which he drug out, just to rile her.

"In the middle of the floor?"

"I can see them there." He gave "there" two syllables.

Instead of fussing at him like he'd expected— hell, like he'd *wanted* her to—or acting hurt, or giving him a lesson in diction, she smiled, which made him madder for some reason.

She was too damn pretty when she smiled, and her smile softened something in him that left him aching for all that he could never have again.

"Men. You're all impossible," she chided sweetly.

"I could say the same thing about your sex. Who washes clothes in the middle of the night?"

"You were right about the lumpy couch, and right about me being the princess-and-the-pea type." She held up her hands. "After everything that happened, I couldn't sleep." Her voice was much too cheery, not nearly argumentative enough.

"Hell," he grumbled.

"Makes you wonder how the planet ever got so over-populated," she said, eyeing him from beneath her lashes in a way that made him hot.

Sex again. Before he thought, his gaze ran the length of her body.

Not wanting to go there, he averted his eyes. But with that black sweater clinging to her nipples and those jeans hugging her thighs, and the room suddenly so small and warm, he couldn't think of anything else but sex.

Specifically, sex with her. It was too easy to imagine her naked in his bed, lying underneath him like she'd lain beneath him last night, only this time with their sexes connected as he moved rhythmically above her.

No sooner had he shoved that image from his mind than she leaned over the couch to fold up her bedding and tilted her butt at him in a provocative angle.

Heat flooded him again. Was she doing that on purpose? Was it an invitation? Or was he like some dirty old man who'd been living alone out in this damn cabin so long?

He took a deep breath in an effort to calm himself.

"It's nice now that the rain has stopped," she said, turning back to him after she'd made a neat pile of the covers at one end of his couch.

He couldn't take his eyes off the lush curves of her breasts and rounded bottom, couldn't forget how small and light and warm that bottom had felt when it had been planted on his bare thighs and he'd held her in his arms last night.

"Yeah. Real nice," he muttered.

"Amazing day...after yesterday."

He nodded like one struck dumb. He was mesmerized. It didn't take much for a clever woman like her to bring a man who'd done without for as long as he had to his knees.

She probably knew exactly what she was doing.

All he could think about was sex. Sex. A steady drumbeat of urgency pounded viciously in his temple and throbbed along every nerve in his body. He was as hard as a brick.

Was he the only one who felt the air between them was as charged as a fuse about to blow? His body felt swollen. His need was becoming more explosive by the second.

Determined to fight it, he swallowed. Then he took a deep breath, and looked away from her, out the window. Not that he could focus on Pharaoh. Hell, who could focus on a horse munching on grass in a distant pasture with her there?

"Do you mind if I take a walk?" she asked.

"What?" His goal was to feed her and get her on her way and out of his life as fast as possible. "This is a working ranch. I've got chores," he said grumpily. "I need to check in with the foreman and his crew."

"Then do that. Like I said, it's kind of pretty out there now that the rain has cleared and the sun is shining. I mean, in a stark sort of way. It's so empty…and… quiet…and…peaceful."

"Peaceful?" There'd be no peace for him—not in this cabin, which had been his sanctuary these past two years—till she was gone.

"Yes. Peaceful. Here there's nothing but cacti and open pasture. It's so different from what I'm used to. In New York there are so many people and cars and busses everywhere. Constant fumes and chaos, sometimes I can't hear myself think…"

He couldn't think either because one slender woman with corn silk hair had him so wired to jump her, his circuits were jammed.

Good thing he wasn't on the frontline with other men depending on him.

Remembering what had gone down on his last tour of duty, his mood darkened.

"Yeah. Go ahead. Take your walk. Do whatever the hell you want. Stick to the road though. Can't have you getting lost again. It's easy to get turned around in brush country if you wander off in a pasture 'cause the country all looks the same. I don't want a bull chasin' you either."

She laughed, and that made him want her even more. Which made him madder.

"Sorry I've been such a bother," she said.

"How about takin' a gun? Maybe a pistol."

"No!"

"There's no tellin' who or what might be in the brush."

"Whatever's out there, I'm sure I don't want to shoot it."

"Then don't go too far from the cabin."

"Look, I'd probably shoot myself if I took a gun. Or you."

"Then I'd better teach you how to shoot…" He stopped himself. "Never mind. It's not like you'll be here more than a few more hours, at the most."

"Right." She swallowed, her expression a little sad, before she looked away.

The moment grew awkward as they stood there. He tried not to feel regret that he'd never know her better but found it impossible. Suddenly he realized he was going to pay for last night. Because if he didn't bed her, he'd never quit fantasizing about her, and he didn't want that.

If he was going to pine for a woman—it should be Mindy. Not some snooty young woman from Manhattan.

Frowning, she grabbed her down jacket off the back of a chair at his kitchen table and walked past him with her nose tilted upwards, that scent of flowers that stirred him trailing in her wake. He inhaled it deeply, drawing it in, savoring it as if he were seeking her essence.

Damn.

He stomped to the kitchen and began to open and slam cabinet doors. He had to stop thinking about how sweet she smelled and how soft she'd felt last night…and how much he wanted to have the lost opportunity back to make love to her.

"Where'd you put the damn coffee?" he shouted. "And the filters? Not to mention my coffee pot?"

She laughed merrily as she opened the door.

"Never mind," he growled. "Just get out of here and enjoy your damn walk."

"Oh, I will," she said, her tone relentlessly cheerful. "Top cabinet to the right beside the fridge. No! Not there! To the right like I said! You should listen."

"You should have left them out on the counter where I could see them."

"Cabinets were invented for a reason."

"Right. So were flat surfaces and floors. Cabinets were invented by some woman who wanted to drive men crazy hiding his things."

When he grabbed the coffee pot and filters, she slipped outside, shutting the door softly behind her before he could ask where she'd hidden his damn hats.

While the coffee brewed, he went upstairs and took a long, icy shower. He was blue and shivery when he stepped out of the stall, but he didn't towel off or hurry to dress.

Better to suffer from the cold than to suffer from wanting her. The compulsion to have her was growing faster than the speed of a bullet whizzing across the desert and catching a man unawares.

Suddenly, he remembered he hadn't warned her to stay away from the big house. Nosy as she was, she'd probably go inside and snoop.

Don't borrow trouble. He'd told her not to get out of sight of the cabin, hadn't he? If she did what he asked, she'd never see the house. If she did see it, he'd deal with it and with her.

What did it matter if she *knew*, since he was getting rid of her first thing?

8

The air was cool and light. Hannah lifted her eyes and watched buzzards a thousand feet above her lazily riding thermals.

After being cooped up in her car yesterday, she loved being able to walk in the sunshine, especially since she didn't have to dodge other pedestrians, stop for traffic lights, or look out for cars.

Being from Manhattan where real estate was calculated by the foot and people were stacked on top of each other in tiny apartments, what struck her most was the vastness and the silence. No planes roared. She couldn't even hear the sound of a car, and she could see forever.

She was hugging herself and savoring the hush when she heard hooves approaching from behind the cabin. She turned, smiling, as Liam's black horse approached.

"Pharaoh? Is that your name?"

The magnificent beast stopped. Snorting, he refused to come closer until she turned and headed toward a tall metal barn. Then he trailed her.

The barn doors were rolled halfway down, so she had to hunch over to get inside. The barn, which was ice cold, was a bit of a mess. Two barn cats jumped down from boxes of wood shavings and scurried out of sight.

Someone had ripped a feed sack open and had shaken feed all over the concrete floor. Two small ranch vehicles were parked against the wall. Tack hung from the walls. Blankets as well as several saddles sat on sawhorses.

Moving further into the barn, she opened a door and was surprised when she found a modern office that was both orderly and functional. Desks, computers, scanners, faxes, printers, and dozens of filing cabinets all appeared in working order. *His* office—at least, she suspected it was his, since a cartoon drawing of him in combat gear and a cowboy hat labeled L.S. was taped to the glass window of the door and a stack of hats littered the filing cabinet behind that glass— looked functional. When she moved closer she saw two framed college degrees on the wall behind a massive desk with his name on them.

A framed photograph of a younger Liam in a maroon football jersey stood on his desk. Several guys his age in boots and Stetsons flanked him.

She took a breath. Maybe he couldn't speak English, but somehow he'd managed to obtain a graduate degree from one of the state's top universities.

Everbody? Could she help it if she had a doubt or two about the quality of that university?

Whatever. Liam was college-educated and had a staff.

She had no right to be here. No right to
investigate further, but as she turned to leave, the
top file folder on a desk caught her eye. Someone
had scribbled in a bold hand on a sticky note
attached to the file. "Louise—please type and get
these in the mail and file my copies where I can
find them. L.S."

Curious, Hannah opened the file. In it she
found copies of a hunting lease signed by Liam.
He'd written a letter to the CEO of a Fortune 500
company detailing the amenities of his ranch's
hunting camps and its private airstrip. He offered
to send the Stark jet for the man's hunting guests.
Although Liam didn't waste words, his letter was
articulate and welcoming. Clearly he was on a
first name basis with the CEO and had no trouble
holding his own with such a sophisticated
businessman.

The Stark jet?

She flipped through more files, some crammed
with hunting leases. Others had to do with records
on cows or invoices from feedlots or oil and gas
leases. Liam's letterhead read 'White Tail Ranch,
Liam Stark, Owner.'

She sank down on the edge of a smaller,
desk—maybe Louise's. Was she his secretary?
Did he own and manage an empire far bigger than
Hannah had imagined? An empire big enough to
impress her mother—even if it was in Texas?

But if he owned all this, why did he live in a
dirty cabin that lacked central heat and air, tend
bar, and exhibit zero pretensions? Weren't rich
Texan guys supposed to be arrogant braggarts?

Again, she remembered the pain meds he'd hoarded and she'd thrown away.

What was going on?

Before she'd specialized, she'd always been interested in her patients' lives as well as their illnesses. Sometimes she wondered why she'd gone into anesthesiology. Even though she loved the drama of surgery and loved knowing she was helping surgeons save lives, she missed getting to know her patients in depth. She put people to sleep and woke them up again. That was her job.

Liam was more than some loser, gun-crazy cowboy who moonlighted tending bar in a local dive. Why had he deliberately misled her?

Intrigued as she left the barn, she forgot what Liam had said about staying close to the cabin. With Pharaoh following her, she set a brisk pace and didn't stop walking until she came to a lovely cluster of live oaks beside the road.

As she studied the sunlight sparkling in their tangled branches, a sculpted trunk caught her imagination. Pulling her phone out of her pocket, she turned it on and snapped a picture.

On either side of the trees, fat red cows stood knee-deep in high brown grasses that undulated in waves toward the horizon. His ranch felt huge. Its vast spaces made her feel freer than she ever had in her whole life.

An owl hooted from the top of a twisted oak before taking flight. Then coyotes began to yelp. When they stopped, the world grew so amazingly quiet she could almost hear the silence. She'd never felt so at peace.

Navigating the crowded sidewalks from her townhouse in Sutton Place to the hospital sometimes had her frazzled long before she got to work or made it back home after a stressful day.

What would it be like to live in such a remote part of the world?

A roadrunner dashed eagerly down the middle of the road with a thin lizard dangling from his mouth. When Pharaoh nickered, she turned and took a picture of him too. Loving the attention, he hammed it up, throwing his head back and snorting. Then he struck a thoughtful pose. After she got a few shots, he came closer, inviting her to talk to him and stroke him while he sniffed each of her pockets for treats.

"I don't care what Liam says about you, you're a good boy," she whispered.

His nostrils flared. Then he snorted as if in agreement.

"That's right. You are. You're just bored and don't like being ignored. Who would? I'm sorry I don't have a carrot or an apple in my pockets, but I will next time. Promise."

Pharaoh nickered and then tried to stick his nose in the pocket of her jeans again.

"Nope. No carrot," she said in a sympathetic tone. "Next time. Come on. Let's walk a little further."

A hundred yards down the road past the trees, she came to a large, white, rambling house that crowned a slight rise. Shaded by live oak trees, the house had lovely lines and sat at the end of a lane. She knew a little about architecture and imagined it must have been built in the late

1800's. Whoever had built it must have been wealthy enough to erect a mansion like that in the middle of nowhere.

When she headed down the lane and got closer, she saw that it needed paint.

"It would be very impressive if it were tended to," she said to Pharaoh, who listened thoughtfully.

The vast, fenced lawn with its shade trees surrounding the house was overgrown and brown. Leaves and branches lay in the lane and littered the high grasses.

"I'll bet you know who lives in this house, and why he's not keeping it up."

White metal lawn furniture in need of paint graced long, wrap-around porches. Large white urns filled with leafless, brown ferns stood against the house's outer walls. Cobwebs swung from the eaves where wasps and hornets had built nests.

As she climbed the porch stairs, oak leaves crunched beneath her feet. No longer interested, Pharaoh lowered his head and nibbled grass.

Rapping briskly with the back of her knuckles on the front door, she called out and waited. When no one answered, she walked the length of the porch and peered through the dirty windowpanes.

From what she could see, the front room was charming. The furnishings, a clever blend of modern and antique styles, were bright and cheerful. Bookshelves lined two walls. But even from the windows she could see that a layer of dust coated everything.

She went back to the door and twisted the knob. To her surprise, the door opened invitingly.

"Anybody home?" she called as she pushed it a little wider, her voice echoing in the high-ceilinged room.

Liam had asked her not to venture far. He was probably impatiently waiting for her to return so he could rid himself of her. Even though she knew she should shut the door and go, she was too curious about the beautiful, neglected house to do so. Was he connected to this house in some way?

Across the room, she saw an intimate grouping of photographs on the mantel. She had no right to look at them. No right to step inside the room.

Still…she was here, wasn't she? If she were fast, who would know?

Feeling like Goldilocks, she tiptoed inside. All was dark. When she was sure nobody was home she crossed the room and lifted the first silver frame.

Oh, my God.

Liam.

Her breath caught. In the picture a much happier Liam smiled down at a dark-haired woman, who vaguely resembled Nell.

Hannah set the picture back down. In the next picture, he was holding the same woman, who wore a wedding gown, in his arms.

Hannah took another breath. He looked so happy. Clearly, he'd adored his wife on *their* wedding day.

In the next shot, a proudly smiling Liam held a newborn against his wide shoulder. In the last photograph, Liam, in military dress now, was throwing a red ball to the woman and a dark-haired little boy while Pharaoh chewed grass beside them.

They all looked so happy. Where were his wife and child? Was he divorced? Or...

Hannah's heart began to knock as she shakily replaced the photograph. Had his wife and child died? Was that why he'd hoarded all those pills? Why he'd said he knew what it was like to want to forget, to want it so bad he could taste it, after he'd kissed her in the bar? Why he lived in that awful cabin instead of this lovely home he'd once shared with them?

Death, which could be so sudden and shocking, was so irrevocably permanent.

You don't know they're dead.

Her gut said they were. Had they died two years ago?

If they were dead, compared to his pain, hers didn't seem so bad.

The last object on the mantel was a small bottle that contained a tiny metal object. Lifting the bottle she shook the piece of metal into her palm.

It was a bullet. A single bullet. Her fingers clenched around it. Why had he saved it?

Frowning, she dropped the bullet into the bottle and replaced the bottle on the mantel. Had Liam put the bullet in the bottle and kept it there for a reason?

Of one thing she was sure—she had no right to be here, no right to invade his privacy, when his loss was still so painful he hoarded meds, drank at night, couldn't face his own home or talk about any of it.

Stumbling blindly across the living room, she ran outside,

Shutting the door, she fisted her hand and brought her clenched knuckles to her lips. She wished she'd never come here, wished she'd never had seen this, never seen the pills in his cabinet, never thrown them away.

Hating herself as she pulled out her phone, she googled Liam's name and the name of his ranch. It didn't take her long to discover what she'd suspected—that he wasn't poor. Not only that, he was the descendant of a legendary ranching family, and he operated a vast cattle ranch, which also had elite hunting and fishing camps. There were stories about the mystery surrounding his uncle's death, stories about his wife's death, stories about him receiving the Purple Heart.

She liked the fact that he hadn't tried to impress her as every other man she'd ever met had, that instead he'd gone out of his way not to.

When she finally got her thoughts in order and descended the stairs, Pharaoh came up to her, his narrow face solemn, his dark eyes infinitely comforting.

"You miss them too, don't you, fella? You miss her, I bet. She carried treats for you in her pockets, didn't she? You're as lonely and grief-stricken as Liam is, aren't you, my big darling?"

Hannah laid her head against his neck and held onto him until she looked at her watch. Then guilt sent her hurrying down the road toward Liam's cabin even though she dreaded having to face him.

9

Liam knew where she'd gone the minute she stepped across the threshold and then stood there, flushing as she twisted her hands.

Tension made his muscles tighten as he stepped out of the kitchen. He didn't want her pity. He was tired of pity.

"Did you have a good walk?" he asked.

She refused to meet his eyes. "Yes. Lovely...walk. Very peaceful. Didn't see anybody I needed to shoot either."

He pressed his lips together and nodded.

"Good." He couldn't look at her either.

He'd seen her head toward the house and watched Pharaoh follow her. Seen them disappear together around the bend. When she'd taken her time about returning, he'd imagined her walking through that tomb of a house that he still couldn't enter, not even to get essentials—because to do so cut off his breath and made him remember that terrible day of the funerals when he'd sat in the living room all alone with a loaded gun in his hand. For hours he'd struggled to make himself take the next breath and then the next.

Whenever he needed something from the house, Gabe or the Montoyas had to go there and retrieve it.

He'd liked Hannah not knowing. It had freed him a little. Hell, he should cancel the insurance on the place and burn it down. He was never going back there. Never.

But he was frugal by nature and hated waste of any kind. Besides, the house wasn't just his. It was historic. His great, great, great, great, great granddaddy had built it after he'd made a fortune on a cattle drive, and the family regarded it as an important part of the Stark legacy. He'd been told that his dad had dreamed of having it moved to the main square of Lonesome and turning it into a museum. But he'd died, and Mindy had wanted to restore it and live in it.

He shut his eyes and tried not to think about the photographs and the bullet he kept on the mantel or Charlie's favorite toys Hannah might have seen inside the house. Had she picked up Zebo, Charlie's beloved bear, the bear he'd slept with and carried everywhere? Had she tossed it carelessly back on his bed as if it were of no importance?

Grabbing the skillet, he slammed it on top the burner so hard she jumped. "How do you feel about fried eggs and bacon for breakfast?"

When she turned up her nose, he asked her if she was a vegetarian.

"Mostly," she admitted. "I don't really like eating things that used to have eyes."

"Does that include eggs?"

"I think humans should eat a lot of greenery. I'm not perfect though. I allow myself four eggs a week."

"Four," he repeated. "Four exactly?"

"Look, you don't have to go to so much trouble for me."

"I'm having fried eggs and bacon. Four eggs to be exact. That should please you."

"Cereal would be…"

"Do you want eggs or not?"

"One egg, no bacon…would be just great."

He grabbed four pieces of bacon and slapped them onto the skillet that was already so hot they instantly began to sizzle and pop. Lowering the heat on the burner, he shoved four pieces of bread into the toaster.

"Can I help?" she murmured from the doorway, as if she sensed the reason behind his anger and wanted to appease him.

Last thing he needed was her in his kitchen, getting his mind off cooking and onto her.

"Nope. I'm good."

"I'm not used to being waited on, you know," she said, although he was pretty sure that wasn't exactly true.

"What are you used to?" Why had he bothered to ask? It encouraged her to linger and maybe pry into parts of his life that were off limits. The less they knew about each other, the better.

"What exactly do you do in New York City?" he heard himself saying. *Was he crazy?*

"I'm a doctor."

"Impressive." He'd known she had a head on her shoulders and was used to bossin' people.

"Not really. It's just what I always wanted to do."

Orphaned young but knowing he was his father's sole heir to an impressive piece of a huge historical ranch that was part of Texas history, Liam hadn't had much choice about his profession. From birth he'd been told by his aunt and everybody in Lonesome that his dad would be proud of him when he was old enough to run the ranch. Ranching had been expected of him.

"Why did you want to be a doctor?"

"Because my father is a doctor. It was the only profession he had any respect for."

"Ah."

"My mother didn't work, so it was the only profession I was acquainted with. He loves his work."

Liam frowned. Like ranchers, doctors tended to take a narrow view.

"You don't dress like any doctor I ever knew."

"You've heard of revenge sex?"

His eyes fell to her mouth, which was soft and wet, and then to her breasts in that clingy sweater. Damn. The word *sex* had reignited the molten hunger in him to have her—as if that spark needed any fresh heat. Why the hell couldn't she stay on a safe topic?

"Well, I went revenge wardrobe shopping. In San Antonio. You see, I ran away from New York so fast I didn't even bring a suitcase."

She had him now.

"I needed something to wear, but I was so upset...that I bought things...I'd never usually buy. And I'm sure I'll never wear...except for now...because I don't have anything else."

"Sexy things...like that see-through red gown I ripped?"

Her blue eyes narrowed. "It's not see-through."

"Wanna bet? When the light's behind you, it's worse than see-through."

"I usually wear shorts and a t-shirt to bed. Or sweats in the winter."

He pictured her breasts in a tight t-shirt and her long, tawny legs. On her, anything would be sexy as hell. Better to concentrate on cooking breakfast than on her legs and what she wore to bed.

"What kind of doctor are you?" he asked.

"I'm an anesthesiologist. Daddy was a cardiologist. At least, originally. Now he's mostly on television."

"So, he's a celebrity doc?"

"Just in the New York area. He's got his own local show."

"You must have been a good student."

"I was."

"I wasn't. At least, not in school. So chalk that up as another thing we don't have in common."

"Are we making a list?" she whispered, slanting her eyes up at him in that way that made his blood heat. "I've always been a list-maker."

He shook his head. "I got better at studying when I got older and there were things I wanted to learn."

"What sort of things?"

He shook his hand as he thought about the sophisticated weapons he'd been so eager to know

about. He still loved guns. She was a doctor who
didn't like guns, not at all, so she wouldn't
understand. And for some reason, he wanted to
please her this morning.

"Never mind," he growled.

"I studied so hard because I wanted Daddy to
love me."

"Did it work?"

She hesitated and her eyes grew haunted.
"Well, at least, now he can brag about me at
cocktail parties."

"I wouldn't know much about cocktail parties.
That's another thing we can add to *our* list."

"Or at least he could...brag about
me...before...I..."

"Before you what?"

"Ran away... Day before yesterday."

She went chalk white as she remembered
whatever the hell it was that had made her hightail
it to Texas. The sadness in her eyes tore his heart,
so he worked faster, checking on the toast,
flipping the bacon, lowering the fire under the
eggs.

He had to get breakfast over with and her out
of here.

He grabbed a couple of plates and handed them
to her. "You could set the table. Maybe down at
the end not devoted to my laundry."

She laughed. "Sorry about that. Didn't know
where to put them."

"That didn't stop you from hiding all my hats.
Or my coffee stuff."

"Your hats are in the closet. Up high. On the
left."

"Found them already." He filled their plates with food and sat down.

"You've got a lot of hats." She sank into a chair opposite him.

"A man needs one for all occasions. And I grow attached."

"I wouldn't know," she said.

"You probably have a lot of shoes. And belts and scarves."

"Now that's different."

He grinned. "Right. My stuff is junk but yours is necessary?"

"Accessories are necessary." When she grinned, a hot dart of excitement flared in his gut.

"How can a doctor run away? I mean, don't you have obligations? A practice? Patients? Partners who expect you to cover them?" He nearly kicked himself for asking more questions and giving her the impression he cared.

"All of the above. But I have been working extra hard for a while just so I could have the whole month off."

"Because?"

"Okay, if you have to know—because I got married two days ago. I was going to honeymoon with my husband for a month at the Hideaway."

Her husband.

She was married?

The news hit him like a blow.

"You all but guessed the truth in the bar last night…that I'm a runaway bride, and, therefore, a joke," she said.

"Yeah. And I lobbed it at you like a live grenade. Real sensitive, right?"

She toyed with her egg before she lifted it to her beautiful mouth. "Only he didn't...stand me up at the altar."

Her lovely eyes grew shadowed. "But what he did...*after* we were married was way worse."

After. Damn it. She'd married the jerk.

"Like I said, we were supposed to honeymoon at the Hideaway Ranch. James chose it because he used to visit an aunt on her ranch in Texas. He said the Hideaway sounded quiet and remote. We agreed to an entire month because we hadn't been spending enough quality time with each other."

Quality time? What the hell was that? When he hadn't been overseas, Mindy and he had just been together whenever possible...workin', hangin' out, ridin' in to town together so they could confide in each other while doing errands. Just being together in the same house and not talking had felt good.

"He said the Hideaway was the go-to dude ranch this time of year. Because of the warm winter weather in South Texas. Ironic when you think how bad the weather was yesterday, I know."

"At least it almost never snows here. What about *him*? This James guy? *Your husband?* Does he know you're here, on *his* honeymoon without him, in Texas?"

"I don't care about him. It's over."

Right. Liam wished relationships were that simple. He wished feelings could be turned off like a light switch.

She was still married to the bastard. They had a history, so she'd probably stay married to him.

Which gave him another huge reason to leave her alone.

"Does *he* know it's over?"

"He'll figure it out when I call Uncle Tommy, the family lawyer—his boss by the way—first thing Monday morning and tell him I want an annulment."

"Okay. So you're down here honeymooning alone? At least, till your husband shows up and sweet talks you back into his arms and takes you back home for the holidays?"

She shook her head. "Not going to happen!"

"The guy is rich and sophisticated and from your world. You thought you belonged together until you had this little misunderstanding."

"There was no misunderstanding. He'd better not show up. I need to figure out my life…where I go from here now that he and my sister have pulled the rug out from under me."

"Your sister?" *The bastard was involved with her sister? This was bad.*

"My twin. But I don't want to talk about her. After what she did, she's dead to me."

Dead? He could tell her about dead.

If her twin was still on this earth, living and breathing, she wasn't dead. Families could be hell on each other, but it took a lot for them to give up on each other for good. He had a big-ass, badass family that was hung up on land, oil, greed, and power. At the moment Gabe, who'd been thrown out of the family business, was trying to oust his mother from a position of leadership in North Star Oil and Gas, the family oil company, and get himself reinstated.

Liam thought about Aunt Miranda, who'd
raised him after his mother hadn't awakened one
morning not long after his father's accident.

Aunt Miranda had been the farthest thing from
a loving mother figure after his biological uncle,
Uncle Vince, had drowned and her son, Jack, had
vanished at Dead Man's Curve. She wasn't blood
kin, and she wasn't maternal by nature. If his
cousin Gabe hadn't been the next best thing to a
big brother, and Hector and Sam Montoya, the
maid's sons, his best buddies, he probably would
have run away from his aunt's loveless home as
her own daughter, Kate, had when she'd gotten in
trouble. Now that Miranda was estranged from
Kate and warring with Gabe over who should run
North Star Oil and Gas, Liam was trying to stay
neutral. Like his father and his Uncle Vince, Liam
was a rancher first and an oilman only because a
huge gas and oil reservoir had been discovered
under the White Tail Ranch.

As Liam watched Hannah eat, he thought about
her mouth and all the erotic things it might have
done for him last night, if only he'd let her.
Maybe if he had, he wouldn't be fantasizing doing
her on the table.

"How long were you and James together?"

Damn it. Why didn't he just shut the hell up?

"A couple of years. I thought he loved me. He
was so sweet. He was my best friend too, or at
least I thought he was. Maybe he just loved the
idea of being with me."

*Their relationship isn't over. So back off fast,
Stark.*

"He probably likes going to plays and the opera*.*"

"We enjoy the theater, yes. And music and art. *Enjoyed*!" She all but growled the last.

"I bet he likes vegetables. Maybe sushi too?"

She nodded. "He's smart. He takes care of his body, yes. And Daddy loves him."

Had Hannah really loved this artsy-fartsy, pseudo vegetarian? Or had her marriage been another ploy to make Daddy love her?

Liam hoped for her sake she didn't love James and that she was able to get over him quickly. *But her twin sister?* A betrayal between kin of that magnitude would be hard to live down.

Liam had been sunk in his own misery so long, it had been a spell since he'd appreciated all the good things in his life. Maybe he'd lost Mindy, but Gabe and the Montoyas and his other cousins and Homer all had his back.

And Mindy. Maybe she was gone, but she'd been so damned good to him. Always. They'd both been little kids when his father had fallen in the barn and died. She'd always been faithful, kind, sweet and patient, even when he'd been a royal jerk. All his Army buddies and everyone in his family, especially his cousins and the Montoya brothers, had loved her and had envied their relationship.

He'd had to be there for his men on more than one occasion when their wives had cheated on them or had given them real grief for being on a tour so long. Mindy had rarely complained. She'd run the ranch and had raised their son. Liam had been loved and supported, utterly and completely

by a good woman. He'd made it back from
Afghanistan alive and whole, at least physically,
when too many of his buddies, including Charlie
Clark, had been shot to pieces.

*Made it back with a head full of grief and guilt
to nothing,* he'd told himself after he'd lost her.

But that wasn't true. He could stand. He could
walk. That was huge. His friends and family,
especially Gabe, big executive that he was, and
Homer, worried about him, checked on him,
invited him out—even when he told them to mind
their own business. Like Hector—making some
excuse to ask him to tend bar so he wouldn't be
alone last night. People here cared about him and
let him know it all the time.

Hell. Maybe it was time he quit grieving about
what had gone wrong and started thinking about
being there for his family and buddies. It wasn't
like their lives were perfect.

He thought of Charlie, who was in rehab
because he'd lost a leg. Hell, he'd named his kid
after Charlie, but so far he'd only gone to see him
once.

Liam hadn't stayed long or gone back because
he hadn't been able to see his big powerful friend
in a wheel chair with a stump for a leg, knowing it
was his fault Charlie wasn't whole.

Not that Charlie blamed him. No. His
postcards and emails begged him to come again.
But seeing Charlie made him face stuff he
couldn't face.

Hannah got up and bussed their plates,
bringing his thoughts back to the present. "Thanks

for the breakfast," she said. "I'll clean up. I should do something to earn my bed and board."

He wouldn't let himself look at her because then he'd think of all the ways he'd prefer her to earn it...like lying back on his kitchen table and letting him take her on that pile of fresh laundry.

He nodded grimly and stood. "While you do that, I need to call my cousin at the Hideaway and let her know I'll be bringing you. Then I'll call the wrecker your car rental company's sending so we can meet him at the scene, as well as Homer, the sheriff.

She tensed. "Sounds like you're anxious to get rid of me."

His gut knotted. He wanted to reach out and pull her close. But on top of everything else that made him know sex with her was a bad idea, she was married.

"What's your full name?" His voice was crisp, all business.

When she gave him a blank look, he said, "Homer, I mean the sheriff, will need it."

"Hannah Lewis Colton. No! Just Hannah Lewis. I...I haven't changed my name on my insurance yet. And I won't now!"

"Right."

She scowled at the sarcasm in his low tone. "I won't."

"When do you want to talk to the sheriff?"

"The sooner the better, I guess."

He pulled his phone out of his pocket. "Mind if I step outside to make the necessary calls?"

Shaking her head, she went to the kitchen and turned on the faucet and began rinsing their plates.

He liked the sight of her in his cabin, doing simple domestic chores. It seemed so natural and so right; it was too easy to imagine her here indefinitely.

He shook his head to dispel that fantasy. She was a fancy, New York doctor *married* to a fancy, New York attorney who worked for *her* uncle's law firm. A woman like her would get buggy out here in a week. Then she'd pine for the bright lights, the bars, shops, and restaurants where fancy chefs sculpted food and made it look like art. She'd miss the plays, the cultural diversity and everything else New York had to offer. Like o-per-a. She'd long for the kind of man who fit into her world.

That man could never be him.

Besides—she was married.

10

"Mary Sue?"

"L.S.? Sweetie Pie. So good to hear from you. It's been a coon's age."

He groaned and brushed a lock of black hair back from his brow. "Sorry."

"We've all been so worried about you being on your own out there and then actin' so out of sorts with any family who dares to drop by."

"Not that that stopped y'all from pesterin' the hell out of me."

She laughed. "Especially not Gabe, I bet."

"Definitely not Gabe."

"Bless his heart. Because of you, he's spent more time in Lonesome these past two years than he has in the past decade. I thought he was too high and mighty to ever come back."

"Look here, I've got a client of yours over at the White Tail. She got herself lost last night on her way to the Hideaway and blew into the Lonesome Dove Bar."

"I heard you followed some woman and a couple of truckers out of the bar and left B in charge. And that there was wreck at Dead Man's Curve."

He didn't like the speculative lilt in Mary Sue's tone. He wished B had kept his mouth shut.

"A couple of the Dove's patrons ran a customer off the road at Dead Man's Curve. She mowed down the crosses and wrapped her rental car around a fence post."

"Don't tell me you played hero and took her home, for which she was properly grateful!" Mary Sue giggled

"Damn it, M Sue, don't you go around town sayin' I did that, you hear?"

Mary Sue laughed harder.

Why had he given her so much ammunition?

"Are those...er...patrons dead...or alive—if you don't mind me askin'?"

"What if I do mind?"

"They're dead?" She sounded thrilled.

"Alive," he thundered. "Her name's Hannah Lewis Colton."

"Oh, my God! Not James's Hannah."

James's?

The mere thought of her going back to the husband who'd run her off and damn near gotten her killed, or worse, stuck in his craw.

"Is she okay?"

"She's fine. I'll drop her off as soon as we see about getting her car towed."

"Tell her that her husband's been callin' and callin'. Bless his heart, he's just frantic."

"She had good reasons for leaving him, M Sue. So, don't tell him where she is. Let her tell him in her own good time, okay?"

"Got it." He heard the questions in her voice, but he hung up before she could ask for more details.

Liam had enjoyed his morning with Hannah much more than he'd expected to. She'd held the ladder for him when he'd climbed onto the roof to retrieve his snake boots. She'd caught them, easy as you please, when he'd tossed them down, one by one.

Everything they'd done together—talking to Homer, filling out the necessary reports, talking to the wrecker, and then stopping by the grocery where she'd made him buy apples and carrots for Pharaoh and had made him promise to give them to the four-legged pest after she was gone—had been made more pleasurable because she'd been with him. Not that he'd liked being seen with her in Lonesome, because he knew the gossips would make too much of it.

The Montoya brothers, the wealthier Sam, Ben's father, and the more easy-goin' Hector, who owned The Dove, had tipped their hats and had made a special point to say hi to him and come over in order to get a good look at her up close.

In no mood to introduce her to the two handsome bachelors he'd grown up with or to discuss why he'd left the Dove in B's hands last night, he'd rushed her along even though they'd done everything they could to provoke an introduction.

Rita Callahan Kirby, a local hairdresser and fortune-teller and his Uncle Wes's younger sister, had pulled her truck snub up to his. Then she'd rolled her window down, refusing to move even though they were in the middle of the street till he introduced her to Hannah.

"What's this I hear about you bein' run off the road and stayin' out at his place last night?" Rita said, fluffing her bright red hair as she leaned out of her window after the initial pleasantries had been exchanged.

Liam's jaw hardened and his hands tightened on the wheel.

"Mary Sue told me how you saved her and all. How Homer dropped by this morning. I hope he catches them and locks 'em up. Bad as that was for you two, now that the danger's past, we're all ever so thrilled. You know how we've all been praying for somethin' or someone to come along and get you out of your funk. So, the good Lord sent her."

"Last night was an emergency, so don't go readin' anything into it that isn't there, the way you do in those tea leaves of yours, okay?"

Rita's quick smile was all teeth, and her gray eyes were sly. "Whatever you say." She eyed Hannah. "Dear, whether this stubborn cuss knows it or not, you're the best piece of luck that's happened to him in quite a spell. And he was yours. He's the man I'd want in my corner if ever I was in trouble like that."

Liam growled low in his throat. "You're blockin' the road."

"So?"

"We're on our way to the Hideaway where she has a reservation."

"I hear she's staying for a whole month," Rita teased. "A lot can happen in a month."

"Damn it, Rita, for once in your life, mind your own damn business."

Rita was about to say something when a car came up behind her and tooted. Frowning, she waved a sulky goodbye.

"Gossips, all of them!" Liam said when they were on their way again. "Small-town folks love nothing better than sticking their noses into their neighbors' pots and stirring till they work up a froth."

Hannah had laughed. "So I see."

When the two of them hadn't talked much for a while, he'd found their silences easy.

Why had he ever thought Hannah would be difficult to be around just because she was a fancy doctor from New York? Or that they wouldn't be able to find common ground to enjoy each other?

Usually he wasn't a talker, especially not of late, but once she got him talking, he'd chatted about everything. She told him how shocked she'd been by her first cadaver in medical school, even though she'd been thrilled and honored that she'd been accepted to her daddy's alma mater.

"It was the remains of a real human being, but it reeked so badly of formaldehyde, I gagged. When the other students laughed, our professor told me to leave class and not to come back until I could show some respect."

He told her about attending A&M College Station, his father's alma mater.

"I was three years old when I found my daddy on the barn floor. I thought he was asleep, and I tried to wake him. But he had a broken neck."

She didn't say anything, but he felt her compassion.

"I wish I could have known him. Everybody loved him. He was strong and able and tough. All my life I've wanted him to be proud of me. So, of course, I had to go to his university and take over his ranch. Sometimes I think that my whole life has been about finishing his life and making him proud."

"All I ever wanted was to make my father as proud of me as he was of Nell," she said.

Hannah seemed amazed to learn that in his family, attending UT Austin instead of A&M would have been a worse betrayal in the eyes of his family than changing his religion.

"So you see, we're all Aggies through and through. Have to be!"

She was as curious as his son, Charlie, had been, asking him questions, demanding to know the name of every damn tree and bush and flower in the pastures as well as the name of every bird and animal they saw. Hell, she even made a list.

Huisache, mesquite, scissor-tailed flycatcher, white-tailed deer.

She repeated each name to make sure she was pronouncing it correctly. She was smart too; she didn't have to ask him twice. The next time she saw the same bird or plant or cow, she said its name.

She seemed to hang on his every word, which he liked more than he should have. Because she was with him, the morning flew by. They were both laughing when she spotted the sign that marked the turn-off to the Hideaway.

Then it hit him. Nine miles of private road and she'd be gone. Forever. James would come for her at some point during the month. They'd have a ruckus probably. They might even throw things. Maybe she wouldn't go back to him, but she'd definitely return to New York and marry another man who was just like him.

A cloud passed in front of the sun, and Liam's smile died. He took his foot off the gas. As the truck slowed, she fell silent too. Putting a fingertip to her mouth, she tore off a cuticle. When she started biting at a second cuticle, he wanted to grab her hand. But that would have meant touching her.

The silence stretched. Only this time, a fresh thread of tension hummed between them as they drove through Mary Sue's carefully landscaped brush country and groomed pasture.

Funny, Hannah didn't ask about the Hideaway or its history, even though she'd been so interested in everything else. No, her face went chalky and her fingers, which she pulled out of her mouth, knotted as she stared out the window, studying his cousin's overly manicured acreage.

Like his own ranch, the White Tail, the Hideaway had once been part of the vast legendary North Star Ranch, originally founded by Abraham Stark, Liam's great, great, great, great, great grandfather way back in the 1800's, not too long before the Civil War.

Not that Liam was sure how many greats there really were, but Mary Sue had it down pat. According to legend, old Abraham had won the first 50,000 acres in a poker game, Abe's four aces beating Jimmy Callahan's four queens.

The Callahans, who'd held onto a few prime acres, some of which had the best oil and gas production in the county, held a grudge to this day because Tommy had been drunk on the fine whiskey Abe had supplied during the game. There had been more than one lawsuit and more than one settlement made to the Callahans through the years, but no exchange of acreage. And no softening of feelings.

As soon as Liam drove through Mary Sue's main gate, shiny hearts and stars sprouted up on all the gates and fences. Mary Sue, who was sentimental about love, liked to fussy things up almost as much as she liked to gossip.

Liam parked in front of the big house with its perfectly manicured lawns and freshly painted shutters. Without a word or a glance toward his passenger, Liam opened his door and got Hannah's suitcase out of the back. Then he went around the front of his truck to let her out.

"This place should be fancy enough, even for you," he whispered as he put a hand on her elbow and nudged her up the stairs. "I bet the pillows match and that you won't find a spot of mildew on Mary Sue's shower curtain. You can probably eat salads and green stuff here till you gag."

"Sounds wonderful." Her voice was low and dead.

Damn it, was she wishing James was here with her instead of him? Did she miss him already, despite all she'd said to the contrary? How long would it be before she called the bastard and begged him to join her here?

A young couple waved at them. Honeymooners for sure, he decided, since their bodies were tied up in a knot at one end of a wide porch swing.

"You two here to honeymoon, too?" the girl, whose lips were bruised from too much kissing, asked in a husky tone.

Letting out a little cry, Hannah turned to Liam in a panic, her pretty face leached of color.

Her eyes huge, she made a strangled sound that damn near broke him. He knew what it was to ache for what you couldn't have. Did she long for that bastard?

One minute Liam was a man on a mission, determined to deposit her safely with his gossipy cousin and be shed of her. Then her forlorn wail tore his heart like a blade, triggering a response that left him reeling.

Quicker than a flash fire can lick across a dry pasture in August, his arms wrapped around her, and he snapped her close. Her soft body nestled into the hard planes of his massive frame in a way that made him feel like they were one.

He was crazy. She was married to another man. And even if she wasn't, she was city born and bred and no good for him. But she felt so deliciously hot, she had him on fire.

"What are you doing?" she whispered.

Damned if he knew. "Are you missing him?"

"No—I just feel...out of place...here...all alone."

He felt her heart pounding and his own blood searing his veins.

"You're not alone, honey. Not yet."

"What?"

"You're with me."

She opened her mouth, whether to protest or to agree he'd never know, because he said, "You came to Texas to honeymoon, didn't you?"

"What are you saying?"

As she stared up at him, the heat between them grew intolerable. Did she feel it too? Or was this insane wanting all in his head?

He kissed her long and hard. When her knees went limp and she sighed, when he felt the rhythm of her heart knocking like thunder against his chest, when her arms wound around his neck, tight and sure, and she kissed him back for all she was worth, desire punched through his gut like a fist.

This wasn't happening.

It sure as hell was. Two years of living with ghosts, without a real woman's softness, without tenderness, without *this*, and aching for it deep in his iced-over soul had created a void. A night sharing a cabin with *her* sleeping downstairs after she'd begged him for it had him over the brink.

It didn't matter that she was a fancy, big city doctor, who was on the run from her crappy, lawyer husband. It didn't matter that she liked opera and art and he preferred shooting guns, hunting wild hogs, and his job included castrating calves. It didn't matter that she probably paid

more for her French, designer purses than he did
for his truck.

Details.

Nothing mattered but her taste and the
wildness in his blood as he pressed her against his
body.

He'd never wanted any woman, not even his
precious Mindy, more than he wanted her.

Maybe his feelings were a normal reaction to
the stark, wretched emptiness that had filled him
so long. Maybe guilt and a reassessment of his
true feelings would wash him later. But not now
when he was in a fever to have her. Not when he
was starved for warmth and a real woman's flesh,
and she was willing to give him everything he
wanted.

From the first moment he'd laid eyes on her,
he'd known she was all-wrong for him and had
craved her anyway.

He wound one hand in her silky hair and
cupped her breast with the other, not caring as he
usually would have that the rapt couple on the
porch had become untangled and were now
leaning so far forward on their swing to get an
eyeful, they were in danger of falling out of it.

"My God," the girl whispered. "Did you
see…"

Normally, Liam would never have made
himself a spectacle. But he was past sanity. He
couldn't stop kissing her.

His feelings were a crazy, mixed-up blur of
lust and protectiveness as he pressed her into the
wall and against his hardness, liking it when she
melted into him. When she gave a sigh of pleasure

and squirmed against his pelvis, his heart pumped at rocket speed.

He couldn't leave her here, pining for some jerk in New York, her only companions baby-faced, honeymooners whose happiness tempted her to cry.

"You have no business staying here all by yourself," he whispered.

"I don't?"

"A busy, energetic, not to mention bossy person like yourself? Alone? Broken hearted? With these honeymooning lovebirds? You'd have nothing to do except pine for James while they smooch."

"You're so wrong. I'd be thinking about my life and planning for my future. I'm a planner. Besides, where else would I go? I don't know anyone."

"You know me."

"So?"

"This is the first place James will think of looking for you."

She whitened. "If he shows up here, I'll blast him to hell and back."

Imagining their fiery lovers' squabble followed by torrid make-up sex pushed him over the edge. He was damned if he'd let that happen.

Tightening his arms around her waist, he snugged her closer. "You could come home with me."

"What?"

"You've got a month. We could indulge in a helluva lot of old-fashioned revenge sex in thirty days. During the days when I'm working, you

could think and plan. You can clean all you want,
even at midnight. I'll even consider your insane
idea about hiding some of my stuff in cabinets."

"That's the craziest idea I ever heard," she
whispered, but she hugged him closer.

"You could give me English lessons. Teach me
how to say everbody like all y'all good Yankees
do."

She laughed. "It was bad of me to correct you.
It's a very sweet offer, really it is, but I'm sure
it…"

"Wouldn't work a day, me and you," he said,
filling in for her. "No way could it work for thirty
days. And nights. I was crazy to ask."

"You'd be sick of me as soon as we had sex.
As soon as I bossed you about one tiny thing or
hid something, you'd be driving me back here as
fast as you can say 'ca-in't'."

He chuckled. "You don't know my cousin
Gabe's mother."

"What does she have to do with anything?"

"Aunt Miranda raised me. She was bossy as
hell. Worse than bossy. Cruel. She drove my
cousin Kate, her own daughter, into running
away. Honey, I'm used to bossy, and I don't think
you're cruel."

"Being used to it might make you less tolerant
of it."

She had a point about his liking her being
mostly about sex. He'd been on his own so long,
three days together in his tiny cabin would
probably break him.

Still, what he wanted was for Hannah to say
that she'd get stir-crazy here, being pampered by

Mary Sue. When she didn't, he didn't blame her for preferring a well-groomed resort with all the amenities to his crude cabin where she'd have to put up with the likes of him as well.

"I know my place is a mess and I'm a mess. But you're an organizer. My wife was an organizer."

He couldn't believe he was talking about Mindy. To her.

"Since her death two years ago, I've let a lot of things go. Not just the cabin or the ranch, but the home we once shared and all the people who matter to me. I've been a real bastard to my friends and family, especially to my cousin, Gabe and my best friend, Homer, who both refused to give up on me. Gabe has an international business, but he's come back to Lonesome at least once a month to check on me since I lost Mindy."

"Grief," Hannah murmured in a low, compassionate tone. "It wreaks havoc. You probably felt half-dead and were unable to do more than you did. It's not like you wanted to hurt them."

How did she know that if they had nothing in common?

"Maybe I could hire you to help out. You could be like those people on T.V. who show people how to get their lives and houses back in order."

"Hire me?" she said, surprise in her voice. "You mean put myself in a position where technically you're my boss and can boss *me* around?"

"A boss who would listen and take your organizational advice very seriously."

"No more dumping stuff I've organized into the middle of the floor again?"

"I'll even move my motorcycle to the barn."

"You are serious."

When she studied him thoughtfully, as if she were actually considering his offer, he was surprised how sorrow loosened its chokehold on his heart.

Then she shook her head and sighed, he felt like he was tumbling back into the black hole again.

"A month with me annoying you might get you over James," he said.

She rocked back on her heels, still saying nothing.

"Okay then," he said. He smoothed a strand of flaxen hair from her eyes. "I knew I was asking the impossible. At least you'll be safe here with Mary Sue, and I won't worry about you being chased by truckers."

"You'd worry?"

"I'm not going to repeat it just to stroke your ego. Here you'll have a gourmet cook, salads galore, a masseuse, a heated in-door pool, hot tubs, kayaking, biking, horses to ride, a posh suite with lavish furnishings and no telling how many of those matching pillows. Plus, there's bound to be more amenities."

"Like a spa?" she murmured, her sparkling eyes teasing. "It sounds like heaven."

"So this is goodbye?" Backing away from her, he fought to hide his disappointment.

She shook her head and smiled, causing that dark place at his center to light up. "Now don't you go putting words in my mouth, cowboy."

When she slid closer and kissed him full on the lips, tasting him with her tongue, his heart sped up. "If I stayed here, sure I'd be in heaven, of a sorts, but I wouldn't have you."

Hope spiked through him. She looked so pretty with her blue eyes peering up at him from beneath her dense lashes, with her golden hair falling over her shoulders.

"No, ma'am, you wouldn't."

"So, I was thinking maybe…maybe you're right about me being a doer. Maybe I could think and plan better if I made you and your place into one of my projects and spent the month helping you while I figure my own life out. But this place really is heaven, so I'm thinking… You know James and I bought the pre-paid honeymoon package, and I'm dying for a salad. It'd be a shame to waste all that money we spent. So maybe before you and I drive back to your cabin, we should check out my posh suite with its lavish furnishings and all those matching pillows and wonderful amenities you've been telling me about."

His dark eyes dropped to her mouth and lingered there. He knew he shouldn't be doing this, knew he'd fuel the gossips if he didn't leave her the hell alone. "Did you just say yes?"

She kissed him full on the lips. "With an exclamation mark."

Forgetting about the gossips, he yanked off his hat and sent it sailing across Mary Sue's emerald green lawn. Then he cupped her chin and grinned down at her.

"I might have to order this special coffee off the Internet that I'm addicted to…"

"No problem," he said. "If we order it today, you'll have it in two days."

"Really? And I'd need work clothes as well."

"There's a second-hand shop in town."

"And I was thinking that once we check in, maybe we could have room service deliver us a gourmet lunch," she suggested.

Thoughts of Mary Sue's cooking made his mouth water. Hell, maybe he'd even try a salad.

"Maybe we could enjoy a private lunch out on my balcony together. And then afterwards…you could indulge me in my first-ever round of revenge sex."

Hannah was saying yes!

He swooped her into his arms. Spinning her around, he kissed her lips harder. When she opened her mouth and let his tongue inside, he pushed her against the wall again. They weren't anywhere near a bed and he was brick hard and burning to have her. He sank his hands into her hair, his grip tightening as he kissed her again and again.

Damn. Would a month be enough for him to get his fill of her?

It had better be—because there was no way in hell two people like them could make it long term.

No way.

11

Throughout lunch Hannah's heart raced faster than the ever-present voice in the back of her mind.

Revenge sex? Really Hannah? I mean really? So what if you made a silly vow in Manhattan! This isn't you. You're not Nell. You've known the guy, what, less than twenty-four hours. You have nothing in common with him.

I like him, and I don't want him to kill himself.

That's no reason to go to bed with him.

For once in my life I want to be as uninhibited as Nell!

She remembered the violent storm and her terror when the truckers had run her off the road.

Your mother will die if she finds out you slept with a tattooed cowboy who eats spaghetti sauce and chili out of cans and lives in a shack—even if he's a decorated war hero and owns a big ranch.

Who's going to tell her?

He saved me. I like him. He makes me feel safe and protected. And Sexy. Was her wanting to be with him as simple as that?

Maybe I can help him.

Beneath the warmth of an outside gas heater, they dined in the shade on Hannah's private balcony while longhorn cattle, wild turkeys, and white-tailed deer grazed nearby.

Lunch was Quiche Lorraine, grilled tuna, arugula, the bitterest greens in the universe, at least, according to Liam, even when served with goat cheese, a fresh baguette and homemade butter. For dessert they had a superb *crepe et fruit* that melted in her mouth while she sipped her freshly brewed coffee, which reminded her of her favorite coffee in New York and made her anxious to order it.

"Are we in the Garden of Eden or what?" Not wanting to spook the animals, she was careful to keep her voice down.

"Frankly, my fantasy of the Garden of Eden is whole lot greener. But then I'm a rancher. If the grass ain't green, it ain't eatable."

"Ain't?"

"Just teasing you." He paused, concern in his dark eyes. "You've barely touched your tuna."

"I ate all my arugula," she said.

"Rabbit food."

"You really should try a second leaf," she said.

When he leaned closer and shook his head, her stomach curled in tingling awareness as he gazed at her lips.

"Why, when I'm sure it's as bitter as the first?"

"It's an acquired taste," she said smoothly.

"I'll have to take your word for that."

"Do you want the rest of my tuna?" She pushed her plate toward him. "You've got to be starving."

"I'd rather watch you eat it."

His intense gaze had her nerves quivering as she fantasized about what he would soon be doing to her in bed. Mental images of their naked bodies in a tangle had her much too excited to eat. "I'm satisfied."

"You sure about that?"

When she smiled, he exchanged their plates.

"Who would have expected we could enjoy a light French lunch as good as any I've ever had in Manhattan—or Paris—here?" she said, trying to keep her voice light as she changed the subject.

"Certainly not a woman forced to endure last night in my cabin after getting herself run off the road by a pair of lust-crazed truckers. By the way, thanks for lunch."

"I owe you for last night. You could have left me to those guys. After the way I treated you in the bar…"

His expression hardened. "You still think I'm capable of that?"

The tension in his jaw brought back the terror she'd felt when he'd bashed in her back window after he'd finished off the truckers. Caked with mud, he'd looked fiercer than they had.

She remembered the loving photographs she'd seen of him in his former home. "No. I don't think you're capable of that."

He settled back in his chair even before she reached across the table and touched his clenched fingers.

"I don't," she whispered.

"Who knows why things happen the way they do?" He lifted a final forkful of tuna. "You and me? It's crazy—me sharing your tuna while watching you eat arugula."

With his black hair and eyes and tanned skin and powerful shoulders, he really was gorgeous, but a big part of what made him so beautiful was the lethal aura of male power he exuded.

Other women found him attractive, too. When she'd been doing errands with him in Lonesome this morning, she'd seen them watching him covertly with sly, envious eyes.

Men respected him. The townsmen, from the driver of the wrecker to the mayor, had sought his advice on all sorts of problems, both agrarian and mechanical—advice he'd given freely. When he'd spoken to the sheriff again, she'd sensed an easy camaraderie between the two of them.

"Come with me," he murmured, interrupting her thoughts as he pushed his chair back.

Interlacing his blunt, bronzed fingers through hers, he led her inside. He shut the doors and drew the curtains. Releasing her, he tore the covers back from the bed.

Her heart was thumping madly as she watched him toss the pillows on the floor. When he turned back to her, a tremor went through her.

"What?" he whispered. "Is it against the rules to throw all the matching pillows on the floor?"

She laughed and then caught her bottom lip with her teeth. "No. Of course not."

Tension throbbed between them like an electric charge. She couldn't believe she was about to go to bed with a man she barely knew, but being with him was so thrilling. Maybe he was just what she needed to blast her out of the safe, disciplined life she'd been leading when she'd chosen James.

It occurred to her suddenly that one could change ones life in the course of a heartbeat. Had she been in a rut?

"Shut your eyes," Liam commanded. "You're making me feel like a bug on a slide under one of your microscopes."

"Okay," she murmured.

When he stole up from behind her, she gasped when his warm breath warmed her nape. "Easy," he whispered as he buried his lips in her hair.

Savoring his nearness, hoping her nerves would settle, she let him nuzzle her.

"Hannah?"

Excitement arced through her. "Yes?"

His rough hands slid the length of her neck, downward over her shoulders, and then lower, tracing the shape of her waist and the curve of her hips. Pulling her back against his pelvis, his hands slid beneath her sweater and cupped her breasts.

When she let out a sigh, he molded her bottom against his impressive erection. For several seconds neither spoke.

"I've wanted you from the minute I saw you. Wanted you every bit as much as those truckers did. I would have killed them if they'd touched you. Just a little more pressure, and Hal wouldn't be here."

She'd sensed that. "But you didn't," she said in a rush, more to reassure herself than him.

"Killin's easy," he whispered. "It's livin' that's hard."

She shuddered even before his hands skimmed the length of her body. Expertly, he pulled her sweater over her head and unhooked her bra.

She held her breath, waiting for him to strip her, but instead he went still.

"It's a good thing, you having your life in New York, and me having mine here. A good thing us knowing that now...knowing how things stand before we..."

"Meaning?"

"Meaning that our worlds being what they are, and you and me being who we are, our being so different and all... It means that no matter how good this is, we can never truly belong to each other. Thirty days max—that's all we have. Sex. Some good times. But we can't mean anything to each other."

She forced herself to swallow. He was just being honest. His spelling it out shouldn't cause a painful lump to form in her throat, shouldn't make her eyes burn and her heart ache.

"You know that, right? You won't go and do something stupid like fall in love with me, will you?"

"Of course not! Been there! Done that! Learned my lesson!"

"Promise me."

"I promise." Her raw tone was too harsh to sound convincing.

"You won't let sex change your perception of those realities?"

"I said I wouldn't. How many times do we have to go over the same ground?"

"Good. Because I'm done with love and any sort of normal life with a woman. I can't face that sort of responsibility again. Or risk another loss. But I don't want you hurt again either. Not by me, anyhow. And I know women attach more meaning sometimes than men do to sex."

"I'm not like that. I'm from Manhattan, remember?" No need to worry him by telling him that the elite tribe of women who inhabited the Upper East Side were way more dependent on their men than most other modern women.

He took a breath. "The war messed me up. I don't want to talk about it, but I was burned out when I came home. Then my son and wife died on the same cursed stretch of road I'd lost an uncle and a cousin and a friend and another cousin in different accidents years ago. If I could have, I'd have put in for another tour of duty. Only I couldn't go back there either because I would have been responsible for more lives."

"Oh, Liam…" She turned and stroked his cheek with the back of her hand. "I'm sorry. Nothing that happened was your fault."

"You don't know that. Whatever mistakes I made that hurt others, I'm sorry for them." He stared past her. "But sorry doesn't help much, does it? I hurt people. Caused people to die.

"I'm sure you're taking on way too much blame."

"I'm not, but I'm telling you, so you'll understand. I'm nobody to get mixed up with, okay? You don't have to do this, not even though you said you would. You can still say no."

"You're wrong about that."

"Well, I just wanted you to know the truth going in. I'm nobody to count on. I'm just going through the motions. Sure, I get up every morning. Make myself work. Make myself operate the ranch...because the ranch is my birthright, and I'm in business with my extended family, and other people as well. People depend on me, good folks I don't want to hurt. But my heart isn't in it. So, I can't take on anything else... especially not a woman, who needs and deserves more than I can give. I don't want a second chance."

She shut out that last, not wanting to hear it or believe it. He'd put himself out for her, saved her life, taken her home with him. She didn't believe those were the actions of a man whose soul was dead.

At the thought of all the pills he'd hoarded and the beautiful house he'd once shared with his wife and precious little boy, hot tears welled up before she could stop them. She'd been there for patients facing all kinds of heartache. Life could be so unbearably hard sometimes. No words could adequately comfort the wounded. Only time and love eased such pain.

But he wasn't thinking of his pain; he was trying to protect her. Knowing he didn't want her sympathy, she blinked back her tears.

What other man had ever cared about her feelings as much as he did? Only this stranger with the ravaged heart who barely knew her, this man who was telling her he could never love her, but didn't want to hurt her.

Who? Not her father, whose love she'd craved from birth. Not James. Maybe James had been her friend. Or maybe he'd thought he'd be proud to have her as his wife because he'd be married to an exalted Lewis. But he hadn't craved her with his entire being.

Never had James's eyes adored her as Liam's had adored his wife in that snapshot on their wedding day. Someday she wanted her husband to look at her like that and to keep on looking at her like that for the rest of their lives.

And she wanted to look at her husband with the same expression she'd seen on Liam's wife's face. Hannah didn't think she'd felt that passionate about James.

Maybe James had been a suitable husband for a woman in her position, but not the right man for her. Maybe she'd been too caught up in the trappings, the big diamond, their fancy wedding, their glamorous reception, the month-long honeymoon, the fashionable apartment Daddy had bought her in Sutton Place, and her parents' approval. Maybe she'd never loved James as deeply as she'd thought. Maybe he'd sensed it and had turned to Nell.

She felt humbled before the truths Liam was willing to face. He'd known what mattered—true love. He'd given his all to it, but he'd lost it.

Maybe he was to blame for some of the things that had gone wrong in his life. Maybe not. Survivor's guilt was very real.

What he needed right now was to heal. The last thing she wanted to do was burden him with her needs.

"I know we can't be together," she whispered in a choked tone. "Not permanently. I don't expect that. Trust me, I'm not ready for a relationship either."

"You're sure?"

She reached up and cautiously placed her palms on either side of his carved face. Reaching onto her tiptoes, she pressed a soft kiss upon his lips. "My only hope is that I don't do anything to make your life worse."

"Thanks," he said. "I feel the same way about you. It's hell being stuck, isn't it? Maybe I can help you get over whatever happened to you. Nobody's dead. Not even your twin—even though right now you sort of wish she was. But you don't really. You'll forgive her."

"Maybe on my deathbed…in about sixty years…if she's lucky."

He smiled. "Remind me not to piss you off."

She squeezed her eyes shut and tried not to think about Nell—beautiful, sexy Nell, Daddy's favorite.

"You've got your whole life ahead of you," he said. "You've got to forget James and move on. He's not worth it."

"You don't even know what he did."

"I know he betrayed you and that he hurt you. What else do I need to know?" He paused. "Bottom line of this interminable warning—I'm good at hurting people, too. And I don't want to hurt you."

"Then don't. Just make love to me."

12

She lay beneath him, naked, exquisite, trembling. Although he hadn't stripped out of his jeans, he felt equally exposed as her huge eyes devoured him.

Awed by the powerful force that drew him to her, he ran his knuckles across her petal-soft cheek. Then he leaned into her and inhaled her floral scent.

James had crushed her, had made her lose confidence in herself. Just the thought of the bastard ever hurting her again made him clench his fists. But this wasn't combat where he could annihilate the enemy.

With an effort, Liam forced himself to relax. Gently he ran his hands through the length of her silky hair. Next his fingertips traced over her face and then her lips. He touched each freckle, each scratch and each raw place. Then his lips followed the path of his fingers, gently kissing every bruise until the tension went out of her and she sighed.

Reaching for him, she began to stroke his arms and torso, running her fingertips over his hateful tattoo and scars as if in an effort to comfort him.

As if she could. As if any woman could. Not that her hands on his flesh weren't warm and pleasant. They were. Sinfully so, but nothing more. This was hunger, sex, a purely physical need. Nothing more.

"You are beautiful," he said huskily as he arose and quickly tore off his clothes.

Liking the way her eyes burned like blue flames as she watched him, he slowly eased himself down on top of her again, his hands too eager as they cupped her breasts.

"Kiss me," she commanded.

He grinned. "You gonna be bossy in bed, too?"

"Don't you want to kiss me?"

"What do you think?" He gave the tip of her nose a feather-soft peck.

"Not like that!"

"There you go again…bossin' me." He kissed her nose a second time.

"Not there! On my lips!"

"Hush. Close your eyes."

Her mouth quivering, she obeyed, her lips pursed expectantly.

His hand cupped her chin. Then fusing his mouth to hers, he kissed her slowly and deliberately. He'd meant to take his time, to make her wait, to assert dominance, to show her he was the boss—at least, in the bedroom—but the moment his mouth claimed hers, flaming need swept through him, and he was lost to an urgency that was too raw and elemental for him to resist.

It had been too long since he'd had a woman. He'd meant to indulge in lengthy foreplay, to kiss her everywhere, to make her feel beautiful, special even. But he was too hungry, and she was too desirable.

Fierce sexual tension throbbed in every male cell of his body. His heart pounded so violently he could barely breathe. Suddenly nothing mattered but having her, claiming her as his—immediately.

Sensing his need, reveling in it, her answering kiss was shockingly explicit. Opening her legs wider, her body melted into his. She was on fire, and so wet and ready that as soon as his manhood touched the entrance to her sex, he felt on the verge of exploding.

"I want you," she gasped.

He kissed her brow, groaned his fierce pleasure. "Sorry. I-I can't wait..." Barely coherent, he was hanging on by a thread.

Lifting her, positioning himself, he entered her with a single thrust. Joined to her, he felt huge, and shockingly complete.

For two years he'd been dead. She made him feel alive again, and the pain and the pleasure was so raw, it pushed him over the edge.

After a brief moment of savoring her, he began to move again. His rhythm that was fast and hard, carried her with him. Then suddenly she froze and pushed him away.

"What's wrong?" he groaned.

"Condom," she whispered breathlessly.

"What?"

"Condom. You forgot to use one."

"Bossy," he growled. *Damn. Did he even have a condom?*

"Sorry. *We* forgot."

Breathing deeply, he pulled out. "Hell."

Months ago Gabe had told him he'd feel better if he got laid more often. He'd bought him bunch of condoms and had stuffed a few in his wallet. Maybe they were still there.

Kneeling on the floor, he fumbled in the back pocket of his jeans for his wallet.

"I'm a planner," she whispered.

"Right. I get that about you."

His body on fire, his mind crazed from hot, unfulfilled sexual needs, his hands shook badly as he dug through his wallet. When he found the item in question, he was so eager, he could barely tear the package open and roll the condom on.

Sliding into bed, he pulled her underneath him again. "Hannah. Hannah..." Feeling huge and hard, he surged deeply inside her.

"Liam," she whispered, trembling.

He liked how her knees tightened around his waist the moment he was inside her again. Then wildness took him over, his desperate passion driving him.

Not that she objected. Her short nails digging into his back, she met each thrust with an abandoned eagerness that soon had them shuddering as he cried out her name and they climaxed.

Bliss, he thought as he lay beside her afterward. She was sweet and indescribably lovely. For a brief dazzling moment, she'd banished his loneliness and grief. For the first time since Mindy's death, he was glad he hadn't been shipped home in a coffin.

Lowering his lips to hers, he kissed her tenderly. "Thank you."

"My pleasure," she replied. "Can we do it again? Only slower?"

"Bossy…bossy."

"Can we? See, I'm not bossing…I'm asking."

He laughed. "Give me a minute."

Revenge shopping didn't compare to revenge sex. No way.

Her breathing ragged, her mind in post-coital daze, Hannah lay beside him feeling aglow with satisfaction. She hadn't felt this proud of herself since she'd graduated and walked across the stage to receive her medical degree while her father watched.

The dark feelings of inadequacy and humiliation she'd experienced after the reception were gone. Nell and James no longer mattered. Only Liam was important. She felt connected to him as she never had to another, not even James. It was as if in that final blaze of passion, all their differences had melted away.

Stupid, idiotic thought. He was a tattooed gun-lover who was talented at violence, a rancher with issues, who was completely wrong for her.

Maybe. But he saved me, and he's divine in bed. He makes me feel divine too.

Having been awkward and unsure with other men, even James, she quite liked feeling like a sexual goddess. In fact, she reveled in it. Her head and body felt deliciously heavy on the pillow, and she ached and felt raw in secret, feminine places.

Rolling over, he cradled her face with his thick, callused fingertips. "Next time's for you."

He was so handsome with that wayward, inky lock tumbling across his dark brow. How could merely looking at his carved cheekbones and slightly crooked nose and his powerful, bronzed shoulders make her stomach flip? His male body was laced with thick muscle, and he exuded a lethal force. Still, with her he was tender, and he made her feel safe.

He didn't just look sexy and hard, he was those things. In the worst moment of her life, he'd put himself on the line for her.

"Next time?" she teased. Sliding her hand down his body, she circled the thickness of his engorged shaft. "Oh, my, so you really do like me."

"I do. And I have a whole month to prove it."

"Tick tock," she said, her fingers circling and then tightening around him in eager delight even as she grew anxious that the month would not be long enough.

Laughing, he pulled her underneath him. "Then we'd better make the most of it."

13

"Now? You're calling him now?" Liam demanded. "I thought you didn't want to talk to James."

"I didn't, but that was before…" Heat washed her as she recalled the intimacies they'd shared.

"Sex?" he supplied.

Before you. "Please," she begged as she grabbed her phone out of her purse. "Try to understand. I know it's crazy, but I have to make sure James knows it's over. I-I can't start this with you…without…"

Liam started to argue and then frowned and turned away. "Do what you have to do."

Because he was angry, or if not angry, annoyed as hell, she wanted to go to him, to wrap her arms around him and explain, but she couldn't because she didn't understand herself. She knew modern men and women slept together, and it meant nothing. But she couldn't just marry a man and then hop in bed with another, as if both relationships were insignificant to her—when neither was. She had to settle things with man number one, so she'd feel more settled with man number two.

Okay. For her, revenge sex was complicated.

Punching in James's number, she arose and walked out onto the balcony.

When James answered on the first ring, she sucked in a breath.

"I've been trying and trying to get you," he blurted.

"I know." She didn't apologize. "I couldn't talk until now."

"I know what you must be thinking."

"I doubt it. I barely know myself."

"I can explain," he said.

"Don't. I'll do the talking—thank you very much. I'm calling Uncle Tommy first thing Monday and telling him I want an annulment. I wanted to let you know first."

"But..."

"I've made up my mind. I can't marry a man who'd do what you did. With my own sister. My twin."

When he started to say something in Nell's defense or his own, she slammed the phone down and turned around.

Liam, who was standing right behind her, looked grim. "How'd it go."

"It's over," she said, wishing he hadn't followed her outside.

"Right," he muttered as if he didn't believe her. Saying nothing more, he went back inside.

She knew she'd spoiled the mood by making the call, but she'd had no choice. She couldn't kiss Liam again or hold him without some sense of closure with James.

Mindless of the familiar South Texas ranch land with its pastures and sand dunes covered in tall grasses and dotted by occasional oak motts and clumps of tangled mesquite trees, Liam stared straight ahead as he drove them back to his cabin.

Why didn't she say something? Did she regret making love to him?

They'd been getting along fine at the Hideaway until Hannah had said she had to call James.

Liam hated the way he'd immediately started feeling possessive and uptight and locked-down when she'd said she had to call her husband. He couldn't stand her being married, even though she said she hadn't considered herself married since the reception.

Liam had listened to the call, heard every word. He wanted to feel as easy around her as he had before. He wanted to talk to her, but he couldn't. She was married, damn it. The phone call had made James too real.

When Liam finally glanced at her, he was almost relieved that her face was turned away. Despite what she'd said to James, he wondered if talking to him had made her regret the day and the night she'd spent at the Hideaway in his arms? Was she rethinking her decision to remain in Texas with him?

Well, at least, he'd had her. At least the hunger that had pulsed inside him from the first moment he'd laid eyes on her was gone. The trouble was, instead of the hunger, he had new, powerful needs that made him uncomfortable.

Maybe she'd bedded him, but she wasn't really his, and despite what he'd told her, he felt the fierce illogical need to possess her—completely. He didn't want her having any connection to another man, especially her husband.

God how he hated feeling so craven.

When she'd talked to James, he'd stood on the porch with clenched hands, his gaze never leaving her as she'd paced back and forth, her brow furrowed. He should have given them privacy, but he hadn't been able to. He'd felt as if something vital had hung in the balance.

Short and sweet as their conversation had been, the damn call had seemed endless.

He didn't like thinking about her ever having been with that rich New York jerk, didn't like knowing that the man had enjoyed her and had more in common with her than he did.

All these draining emotions he felt, because she'd been his. Because he'd possessed her long legs, her sweet lips, her breasts, her belly— because he'd kissed her and tasted her and had been inside her.

For her part, Hannah hated how her call to James had Liam so tense and cold. Why couldn't he understand that she'd had to settle things with James if she were to stay here with him?

She'd ended the call as fast as she could, but Liam's mood had worsened anyway. Even now he was frowning and refusing to look at her as he gripped the wheel.

"Liam, I can't stand this! Pull over. Stop the truck."

He exhaled. Then, much to her surprise, he did as she asked.

"Okay, what?" he said once he'd stopped.

Despite his tense expression, he was so handsome, her breath caught.

"I know you didn't want me to make that call, okay? But I had to do it, and it's done. He's out of my life forever, and I'm glad I'm coming home with you, okay? I want to be with you, not him."

A muscle on his jawline ticked

"Okay?" she whispered.

"I don't know what's wrong with me." He took her hand and pressed it against his cheek.

Leaning toward her, he gently kissed her lips. "But I'm hellishly glad you're coming home with me. Even though I don't have a clue about where we go from here."

"Why don't we take it one day at a time?"

Hannah had wondered what she, who'd always been so driven, would do day after day on his ranch, which was in the middle of nowhere. After all, she'd never had very much unstructured time to herself before.

Much to her surprise she found she quite liked waking up after a night of vigorous lovemaking to a day where she could do whatever she wanted.

During the first couple of days she took long, aimless walks on silent ranch roads and enjoyed the immense quiet and the natural wonders. She liked watching flocks of wild turkeys search for bugs in the grass. She stood in awe as javelinas

disciplined their odd-looking young. She was
fascinated by the abundant coveys of quail and
odd-looking anteaters. She watched birds, looked
up their names and photographed them. Because
she'd sworn she'd use this precious free time to
rethink her future, she made herself journal every
afternoon.

Homer, the sheriff, called to inform Liam the
truckers had fled across the border and had been
in a hit-and-run accident in Mexico.

"They're gonna be stuck down there in jail...
awaiting trial for a spell," Liam told her.

She let out a long breath.

"If I know the Mexican authorities, it'll be a
cold day in hell before they extradite them to the
U.S.," he said. "They'll probably serve hard
time."

"So, they won't be running any more women
off South Texas roads in the near future?"

He nodded.

The news made her feel more at ease in her
new surroundings. Soon her new life began to
take on its own rhythm. Pharaoh followed her on
her walks, so she always carried treats.

"You shouldn't spoil him," Liam warned.
"Because if you do, he'll really get up to mischief
after you leave."

Sometimes Liam invited her on his errands or
asked her to help in his office, which she enjoyed
because she liked spending time with him. One
morning he drove her to a cattle auction, where
she watched him bid on prize livestock. When a
landman showed up the next afternoon to talk
about leasing acreage for a well, Liam flattered

her by asking her to sit in on their meeting. She was thrilled when he bounced his environmental concerns off her.

"I didn't know Texans had environmental concerns," she'd teased later.

"I'm finding out Yankees aren't nearly as bad as I've been told either."

When a group of wealthy hunters flew in to check out their leases, he took her to meet their plane. They were wealthy businessmen from Chicago. She was impressed at how easily Liam conversed with them and how in awe of him they seemed to be.

Instead of sleeping on his lumpy couch, she now slept upstairs in his bed curled tightly against him. Every night they would climb the stairs hand in hand. Then he would take her in his arms and lead her to his bed. Rarely did they speak as they undressed. When she was naked, he would wordlessly run his hands over her, and she would do the same to him. His eyes would worship her and make her feel like the sexiest, most beautiful woman in the world. And that was before he touched her.

He always got up before she did to get his crews started on various projects and to do early morning chores of his own. Usually when she awoke, she'd find him fully dressed, sitting beside her, watching her as he sipped coffee from a steaming mug. He'd lean over and kiss her, his mouth tasting deliciously of coffee. All too often, one kiss would lead to more.

She watched him, too, and listened for him—constantly. If she was in the kitchen and she heard him on the stairs, she would move closer to the doorway and smile. Then when he saw her, she would turn away, coyly tempting him to steal up behind her and put his hand on her waist as he rummaged for a cup or a spoon. Often all it took was a simple touch to tempt them into bed. Once he pulled her jeans down and took her against the kitchen counter. Afterwards he'd touched her cheek and run his knuckles along her jawline. Then he'd apologized and had been tender. Not that he'd needed to. Even though their sex was sometimes primal and animalistic, she always found it was wildly wonderful and even spiritual.

She was eager not to waste a minute with him because they had so little time.

On the first of January she had to report to work. She'd have to face James and Nell, Mother and Daddy and her boss, and deal with the consequences of breaking it off with James.

To ease the transition back to her real life, she'd emailed her parents and had called Uncle Tommy, her lawyer, asking him to seek an annulment.

Although James hadn't actually lived in *their* apartment, *her* apartment technically, he'd moved most of his things in. She texted him and asked him to remove them and leave his keys inside as well.

She wasn't ready to talk to her mother, so she emailed her parents to reassure them and her boss to tell him she was taking some personal time and would not return before she'd originally planned.

After that her mother emailed and texted her hourly, demanding that she come home at once, demanding that she call, arguing that Christmas was a time for family togetherness and now that the wedding was off, she had no excuse for not spending the holidays in New York.

"I have every excuse! After what Nell did, New York is the last place I want to be this Christmas," she'd e-mailed in response.

Her mother had loudly objected to Hannah's wedding date occurring during the holidays *before* the wedding, saying it messed up their Christmas family traditions, that their friends had Christmas parties to go to. Despite her objections, Hannah and James had set the wedding date and honeymoon during the Christmas holidays because his firm closed and many of his major clients took two-week holidays, which meant that was the best time for the two of them to take time off together.

"But I can't face my friends at parties after the wedding debacle without the comfort of my precious daughter."

"I can't face Nell, New York, or my life there, Mother."

"You won't have to. Because of what she did, Nell is no longer welcome in our home."

"That's nice to know, but I'm not coming home until the date I originally set, and that's final."

"Why are you being so stubborn?"

Hannah closed her eyes.

As always her wealthy, domineering mother refused to take no for an answer, so it wasn't long before the mere sight of another persuasive email from her mother in her inbox or a text was enough to make Hannah tense. As with everything else in the Lewis household, celebrating Christmas was about keeping up appearances and impressing others.

Her mother's next email had been so desperate that Hannah had relented and called her.

"Tell me where you are and I'll come to you," her mother pleaded.

At the thought of her mother showing up at the cabin, Hannah's heart had begun to pound so hard it was difficult to breathe. "I'm a grown woman! I will be home January 1st."

"You always help your father make the mulled wine."

"Let Nell help him. He'd probably prefer that."

"I told you—she's no longer welcome in our home."

"I'm sure Daddy wouldn't mind her being welcomed into your home."

Her mother gasped.

"Why did each one of you choose a daughter to favor?"

Hannah wasn't surprised when her mother refused to answer and changed the subject. She hung up almost immediately and for once didn't call back.

Holding the receiver against her cheek, Hannah imagined the deathlike hush and stillness of her mother's palatial, Upper East Side co-op. Although everything was perfect, something intangible had always been missing. As a result she'd felt sorry for her mother and had probably given in to her demands far too often in an attempt to try to make her feel a little better.

What was it that was so wrong? Sensing some
secret tragedy lay behind her parents' misery, she
had always sought to please her mother and father
while Nell had given up and had chosen to rebel.

The strident tone of her mother's emails made
her decide she needed to quit giving in to her
mother. No longer was Hannah all that sure she
wanted to stay in New York City where Nell and
their influential parents were. Her mother needed
to face whatever was wrong and stop living
vicariously through Hannah.

And Hannah needed to live her own life. But
what did she want? Liam for the next few weeks.
But after that…what?

Even though they'd promised not to become
serious, her feelings for him seemed to be
building rather than lessening, which was bad.

Not that she let on. Each morning when they
began their day, she locked the closeness and
passion she'd felt for him the night before in some
secret chamber of her heart.

Only at night when he shut the bedroom door
and stripped her did she express her need to claim
him and belong to him. All her resistance melted,
and in the white heat of passion, she felt reborn.
In spite of her promises, she was starting to care
so much she wondered how she'd ever be able to
make herself leave him.

On their seventh night together Liam had
another nightmare. When he began to writhe and
scream as he had that first night, she slipped out
of bed before she called him by his last name as
he'd instructed. When he finally awakened on a

dreadful shudder and met her gaze, she rushed back to the bed. Cradling his head against her breasts, she kissed him until the color came back into his cheeks.

"What was your dream about?" she asked.

"Don't ask." His voice was rough, his eyes dark and cold.

"Maybe it would help to talk."

Shaking his head, his arms tightened around her. When he tried to kiss her, she pushed him away. "You just want me to shut up."

He grinned.

"All right. For now," she said. "But if it happens again, I can't just ignore that you're in pain."

He arose and began to dress.

"What are you doing? Where are you going?"

"Out." He stalked out of the room and stomped down the stairs.

She managed to lie in his bed alone for all of five minutes. When her tension built to an unbearable level, she sat up and threw off her covers. Without bothering to dress or put on any slippers, she stole down the stairs after him.

As she entered the living room, he picked up a gun and shoved it in the back of his waistband. She gasped. Without a word or even a glance in her direction, he grabbed a whiskey bottle and slammed out the door.

When she ran to the front door and threw it open, he was already gone.

Not knowing what to do, she went back to bed. Not that she slept much. But in the morning, when she opened her eyes, he was sitting on the bed sipping coffee as if nothing had happened,

When he handed her a cup of coffee, she sighed. "Liam…about last night…"

"Hey, forget about it. I want you to dress. And hurry. My pilot's downstairs…"

"But…"

"It's a beautiful morning, and I'm pretty caught up. I want to fly you over the ranch, so you can see all my pastures, the beaches, and my hunting and fishing camps. If you like, we'll fly out over the bay. We'll fly over Mary Sue's and the North Star Ranch, so you can see how vast the North Star used to be."

"Liam, I'm trying to help you."

He pulled her close. "I know. You're sweet. And bossy. And super determined. I appreciate your concern. But there's nothing you or anybody else can do or say that will help. So just forget about it."

"You're in pain. I care about you."

"There's nothing you can do."

14

"They're up on the fucking ridge!"

At 120 degrees the desert was so hot, Liam, who was weighted down by eighty pounds of gear, felt like he was being boiled alive. Everybody was yelling and cursing, but Liam, whose head was spinning as crazily as a robot's as he searched wildly for enemy fire, could only catch a few words in between the bullets spurting around him.

"How many rounds?" Charlie screamed as Liam and his men low-crawled across rock that ripped their uniforms and gouged holes into their flesh as bullets stitched across sand and ricocheted off boulders.

Not that Liam was sweating from the oven-like heat. Hell no. Pumped on adrenaline, his heart was racing way too fast, at least 170 beats a minute. As a result, he had tunnel vision, and his hands were shaking so badly he was afraid to fire.

He had to get a grip. Suddenly an explosion in front of him that sent dirt pinging against his helmet had him back-peddling fast. A bullet snapped past his helmet so fast it broke the sound barrier, deafening him.

His men were dying; the platoon was losing ground. Damn it, basic military strategy was all about lugging heavy machinery uphill so you could fire down on the enemy. Today the enemy had gotten the jump on them.

His men were exposed, while enemy up on the ridge were having the time of their lives blasting down at them with all the firepower they had.

Behind him Gunter yelled, "I'm hit!" Dropping his gun, he crashed to the ground with the full weight of his body plus his protective gear.

Liam was wondering how he could get to Gunter when to his right, Marcello yelped and grabbed his belly.

Things were getting crazy fast. Or was he crazy from hunger and lack of sleep? In the five days the platoon had been away from base camp, he'd gotten maybe two hours of sleep and four meals. None of them had showered or shaved. Like his men, Liam stank and had fleas and was utterly exhausted. But that didn't matter.

The trees along the ridge took on monstrous shapes. He could hear animals yapping in the crags all around them. Monkeys? Or was it wolves?

Fighting to steady his hands, Liam raised his gun. Just as he got a target in his crosshairs, a flash of red blinded him, and everything went quiet and still.

Suddenly his men were gone. When the noise returned, and the firing started again, he was surrounded by the enemy.

Trapped, he stood up and began pulling the trigger. Not bothering to take aim, he mowed down everyone and everything within range. The enemy was so close, his victims' blood splattered all over his face and body as they fell.

Once warriors had believed in duty and honor and country. With the invention of the assault rifle, war was more like murder, pillage and chaos. It was all about winning, no matter what the cost.

When a dying man grabbed him, Liam struck out, punching hard. When the bastard wouldn't quit, Liam grabbed him by the throat.

A familiar voice screamed his last name. Startled, Liam loosened his grip and looked up.

He was standing in a sea of bodies, but they weren't the enemy.

They were *his* men.

Had he killed everybody in his own platoon?

Charlie groaned.

Not everybody. Charlie was still alive, but he'd been hit in the leg and would bleed out in minutes if Liam didn't do something.

Liam sank to his knees, and fought not to look at Charlie's gray face or the brown circles beneath his eyes that marked him as a doomed man. Grinding a knee into the injured leg between the wound and his heart, Liam pinched off the artery and staunched the flow of blood.

"You killed them, Liam. Did you have to fucking kill *all* of them?"

Sorrow welled in Liam's chest, pooled in his eyes, spilled down the grime on his cheeks.

"Damn it, Charlie, don't you go dyin' on me too. You're my kid's namesake!"

"Why'd you kill 'em all?"

"Shut up! And don't you fucking die on me!" Liam screamed, holding onto him.

Then Charlie's face twisted, and Hannah was there. Lovely, naked, and whole—Hannah, whose hair shone like spun silver in the moonlight.

"Stark! Wake up!" She was digging her nails into his arms in an attempt to make him wake up and let go of her neck.

Tears in her eyes, she was lying beneath him while she fought to remove his hands, which were fisted around her throat.

"Hannah?" he screamed, struggling for air because his heart was still racing. "What the hell?"

"It's okay," she said gently. "You're safe. You're with me. Remove... your...hands...please...so I can...breathe."

Reality hit him like a sucker punch and he let her go.

He blinked. Then he bit his lip hard, not caring when he tasted something slick and coppery.

The blood and the gore—it had all been another horrible dream.

He was in his bedroom straddling Hannah, who was pale as ashes, whose blue eyes were huge and teary with fear because he'd been on top of her with his hands wrapped around her throat.

"What did I do to you?" he growled fiercely, accusing *her* even as he sprang free of her and stared at his bare hands.

Shame and regret filled him.

"Nothing. I'm fine," she whispered, but she trembled and looked shaken as she rubbed her wrist and then her throat. He couldn't help noticing how she winced when she sat up.

"Did I hit you?"

"I'm fine."

"What's that mark on your cheek?"

"Nothing. I swear. Really."

She was lying. Her eyes were enormous.

"Jesus." For a long time he sat in the dark, his broad shoulders hunched. Unable to look at her, he knotted his hands tighter and stared down at the floor.

"Are you scared of me now?" he whispered.

"Don't be silly," she said, but her voice caught as if on a sob.

He swallowed. It didn't take a genius to figure out that when he'd been holding onto Charlie with all his might, she'd been trying to wake him. What if he'd seriously hurt her?

"I told you...the war, Afghanistan, did things to me...made me so angry sometimes...that I'm no good any more, not for civilian life anyway, not for someone gentle and sweet and...normal...like you. I'm a killing machine, a man designed to roll hand grenades into houches and take down an entire platoon with a single assault rifle. You asked me if I've killed... Well, I have. Some of the people I killed were young, really young. Kids."

She bit her lip and swallowed. "You were a soldier."

"Nothing justifies what I did." *And what I didn't do.*

"You know what I wish right now?"

He shook his head.

"I wish I was Mindy. Maybe then I'd know what to say to get through to you."

Hush," he murmured. "It's probably all been said." Cupping her chin, he traced the delicate line of her jaw. "Or there's nothing to say... Crap happens. Sometimes you do stuff that nothing can fix. Not words. Not religion. Nothing. You're just finished."

"I love how you paint such a rosy picture."

Her blue eyes burned into his, luring him to crave her softness and her gentler view of the world. For two years nothing had touched him. He'd felt like he was dead and that everything he'd once believed in—love, goodness, God, and country, hell, even his university—had been naïve, little-boy illusions.

Then she'd come into his life and had made him want to forget the nightmare. She made him want to believe and hope again, as she did. As Mindy had.

He wanted to sink into Hannah's arms and let her hold him. He wanted to use her so he could forget all the young bodies he'd seen lying shattered in the dirt. But the dream and what he'd done to her had left him feeling too vulnerable and guilt-ridden.

He didn't do vulnerable, because it ripped down the walls that protected him from the pain of his secret memories. He couldn't let her in. It wouldn't help. He had nothing to offer her.

He wanted to make love to her again because sex would take the edge off. But he'd be using her. She didn't deserve that.

"Go back to bed. Get some sleep," he said gently.

"What about you—"

"I'll live. That's the problem." When she lifted her chin to protest, he held a fingertip to her lips. "Shhh."

When she quieted, he got up and dressed in the thin stream of silvery light. Not that he looked at her. He couldn't bear to, partly because of how close he'd nearly come to hurting her, but mostly because her dazzling nakedness and shimmering eyes had his blood buzzing.

He was rock hard. He wanted to sink down beside her and hold her. Just for a few precious minutes. But if he did, he'd weaken and take her.

"I'm going out," he said in a hoarse, clipped whisper.

"Stay."

"This isn't about you. You're not part of my real life, and I'm not part of yours. So leave me be."

"What if I care too much to watch you destroy yourself?"

Why was she so bossy? "You know the rules. I don't want you to care about me—because I damn sure don't care about you."

He strode out of the room and slammed down the stairs.

15

I damn sure don't care about you!

For four, long, agonizing seconds Hannah's heart pounded against her chest as she clutched the sheets around her. Then she tossed them aside.

Rules or no rules, he had no business out there in the dark with a gun and a bottle of booze when he was in such a tormented state.

Would Mindy have let him leave *her* like this? *Hell no!*

But she wasn't Mindy, and he made it plain as day that he didn't care about her the way he'd cared for his wife.

She'd promised not to care. Theirs was to be a short, meaningless affair before they went their separate ways.

But what if she did care? What if staying in bed when he was out there hurting and alone wasn't an option?

Frustrated, she punched her pillow. Stubborn man! Why couldn't he just talk about it?

If only she could forget his vivid curses and anguished cries and his powerful body on top of hers when he'd wrapped his large hands around her throat.

She got up, pulled on a robe, and flew down the stairs. Heedless of the cold and his orders to her, she opened the front door and dashed outside after him.

A chill wind swept across the pasture and brought with it the scent of dry winter grasses, mesquite trees and the salty flavor of the distant bay. Since she wore nothing under the robe, it fluttered, baring her naked legs. Fighting to close her robe, she began to shiver uncontrollably long before she spotted him.

"Liam?"

He was walking slowly, so he hadn't even gotten as far as the barn. When he heard her, he whirled.

"Damn it. I told you to stay in bed. Do you ever, ever, do what you're told?"

She ran up to him. "If you can't talk to me or your friends and family, you could see a therapist."

"Go back to bed!"

"If you want to act crazy and freeze your butt off out here, Liam Stark, well maybe I do too."

When her teeth began to chatter, he smiled. "I appreciate what you're trying to do, Hannah, I really do. But this is something nobody can fix. Not you. Not Gabe. And damn sure, no therapist."

"A lot of macho men like you talk to therapists."

"Whiners. Losers."

"What are you, a man who runs away with a bottle of booze and a gun?"

"You think you know everything because you're a doctor. Well, you don't. People are dead. Men I cared about and was responsible for. Mindy and Charlie. Because of what I did. Because of what I didn't do. How do I fix that? Tell me how!"

"I don't know. I just know you shouldn't be out here alone with a gun when you're this upset." She sank to the ground on her knees in front of him, her posture that of a supplicant.

"Get up," he growled.

"And leave you when you scream in the night? When you're broken-hearted out here with a gun and I'm terrified you'll... you'll..."

"I'll what?" he demanded, staring daggers through her.

"Hurt yourself," she whispered in a low, agonized tone. "How will I live knowing I didn't try to stop you? I-I know you've been hoarding pain meds."

As if stunned by her admission, he sank down beside her.

"Don't be afraid of that." Gathering her close, he brushed her sleep-tangled hair out of her eyes. "I know I can act crazy when I'm asleep, but I'm not ever going to hurt myself. Not when I'm awake."

"How do you know? You saved those pills for a reason."

"And you threw them away, which makes that a dead issue."

"You knew about that?"

"Hell. You saved me the trouble."

"You've got all those guns and you know how to use them. It's so much easier to give in to despair if a person has a gun available."

He thought about his mother, about how abandoned he'd felt when he'd found her and seen the empty pill bottle on the floor. Not that he'd understood at the time what she'd done. He'd just known she was gone and he was alone.

"Suicide always hurts other people. Like I told you before, I don't want to hurt anybody else. The gun is for protection. I don't know who else might be out here. Quit thinking and worrying so much. Go back to bed."

When she refused to budge, his mouth brushed against hers, its heat a subtle warning. "Who's calling who stubborn?" she said.

He sighed. "This isn't working... you and me. I should send you away—early, tomorrow."

"What would that solve?"

"If I go back with you, if I take you now, I'll be using you to forget."

"That's okay," she lied. "I don't care what you do. I just can't leave you out here alone. Not tonight. Not after..."

She bit her lip as she waited for him to decide. Why couldn't she ever matter to the men she loved? Her father? James? *Him?*

Him? He's not one of the men I love. I don't love him. I can't love him! How stupid would that be? I can't! I barely know him...I promised...

Liam pulled her inside and slammed the door. Quickly he laid his gun on the floor and set his bottle on a shelf.

"You'll be sorry that you didn't leave me alone out there," he muttered.

"I'm a big girl. I'll take my chances."

Damn it! Why hadn't he been able to ignore her shattered, pleading eyes and leave her kneeling in the dirt?

His nightmare had wound him up, filled him with self-loathing and remorse and all his familiar bitterness.

He should be in his grave like his buddies. Maybe if he hadn't come home, Mindy and Charlie wouldn't have been on that road. Maybe they'd be alive.

But he hadn't died. His punishment was to live and remember and to know he would go on remembering day after day.

His nightmares seemed to be getting worse since Hannah had moved in with him. Maybe because she forced him to feel and yearn again. It was hellish to crave a second chance at happiness when he knew he was too broken inside to make it work.

He wasn't the first man to come home from combat ruined and embittered, and he damn sure wouldn't be the last. He'd made decisions that had cost lives, committed atrocities that were irrevocable. And for what: a war that maybe shouldn't have been fought. No matter how much he might want to forget or what he thought about the war now, his demons were always there, lurking on the fringes of his mind.

Until she'd come into his life, he'd been able to get up every morning, dress, and work with his men or in the office until he was so exhausted he collapsed. Then she'd arrived with her bossy ways and organizational skills and her desire to tidy up his life and cleanse his soul as if that were as easy as sterilizing a surgical suite. She was sweet and fun to hang out with. In a short time, she'd made him crave normalcy again.

So he was angry again—because he couldn't have what she'd made him want.

Not that she wanted normalcy with him. He was merely a means for her forget James.

"Are you sure you want this?" he breathed against her temple.

"I can't leave you to get through the night alone out there."

He buried his hands in her hair, liking the way its softness flowed over his wrists and arms like living silk.

"All right then." He unlashed the ties of her robe and drew her nearer.

As always, she smelled of floral shampoo and scented soap, and the answering flare of desire and trust in her eyes mesmerized him.

When he pushed her robe over her shoulders, it fell to the floor. He took her mouth, his kiss rough, maybe in a final attempt to scare her into giving up on him and running upstairs.

But she wrapped her arms around his neck and kissed him back with a sweet, welcoming response that heightened his need to possess her. In an instant, the shocking thrill of her mouth moving over his flesh lit every nerve in his body.

Desperation drove him to snug her closer. He wanted to forget, to sink into her body and taste her sweetness, to know the bliss of her comforting arms and touch. When she leaned into him and stroked his earlobe and began talking dirty to him with that soft, melodious, grammatically-proper *Yankee* voice of hers, he hitched in a breath.

When she dictated explicit instructions, listing all the naughty things she wanted him to do to her, his pulse rocketed. "Put your hands inside me and then your tongue."

His hard body flattened her against the door. They weren't going to make it upstairs to his bed. He was too desperate and too out of control. He had to have her. Here. Now.

Usually he undressed and seduced. Tonight he ripped his belt loose and undid his jeans and let them slide to his knees.

Trembling, her eyes went dark and hot when he pushed his fingers inside her slick wet heat. Surrendering when he began to stroke, her knees went limp and her head fell back against the door. His fingers explored deeper, fondling with an erotic precision that made her drip. He didn't stop until he had her quivering and clinging, until her breaths came in shallow, desperate gasps.

"Hannah. Oh, Hannah… I should have sent you back to New York where you belong. I don't know why you stay."

"Don't you? If I hadn't met you, I might have gone the rest of my life and never felt like this."

He laughed, stunned at how good she felt. For a second, joy—the joy of being with her—broke through a crack in the wall of darkness around his heart, and he felt young again and almost carefree.

He knelt between her legs, and with a single thrust of his tongue entered her, causing her to clutch him closer and cry his name.

One taste of her put him in a state of acute arousal. Because he had to have her, he stood up immediately.

"Don't stop," she pleaded in a low, thready tone. "Don't stop."

"Sorry. Can't wait." Cupping her buttocks, his arms crushed her closer as he pushed inside her.

She was slick and warm and shockingly desirable. He lunged once and then again, filling her completely. Inside her he felt huge and hard, like a bull. Wave after wave of pleasure washed him.

"I'm not wearing a condom," he whispered, almost hoping she'd order him to stop.

She clasped him tighter. "It's not that time of the month."

He began to move and, catching his rhythm, she moaned. Whatever explosive emotion devoured him, it had her in its thrall as well. Clasping his neck, she exploded at the exact moment he pulled out.

When it was over, he sank with her to the floor, his arms still tightly wound around her waist.

He was thinking she was the best damn thing that had happened to him in two years until he remembered how close he'd come to seriously injuring her.

A sob in his throat caught him unawares. When she heard it, she stroked his face, gasping when she discovered that his cheek was wet. Then in the next instant, her warm lips kissed his hot tears.

He felt like a layer of ice inside him was melting.

Damn it to hell, was he crying?

In a rage he let out a raw, wild curse. Wiping his face with his elbow, he pushed her away.

"Sorry," he muttered as another awful sob broke in his throat. "I don't know what's wrong with me."

"It's okay. It's okay," she said gently.

"The hell it is." He didn't do tears or break down. "I hurt you earlier tonight. I scared you. And now I used you."

"I was scared earlier. Not for me...for you. I wanted this. I wanted you. Not just for the sex. I wanted to be with you. It always feels so right, so perfect, when we're together."

The awe in her low tone shook him. She was right. It was wonderful being with her. He liked her being in his house, liked having someone to share his day with as much as he liked making love to her... if that was possible.

He wanted to take her in his arms and kiss her again, wanted to tell her that everything was going to be all right, but a fist gripped his heart and squeezed hard.

He was no one to offer comfort. He had to get a grip. "Well, it's not right...or perfect. It's just sex."

She winced at his sharp tone and bit her lips— lips that looked soft and inviting. Lips that were so close he could feel the warmth of her breath caressing his cheek.

*How long had he known her? A week? How
could he already have feelings for her that were
tearing him apart? She wasn't anything special,
damn it!*

Wild to get away from her before he broke
down completely and confided all the pain and
guilt that was in his heart, he yanked up his jeans
and fastened them.

"Don't go," she pleaded.

"Why the hell won't you give up on me? Put
your robe back on. Quit nagging me. Go to bed."

Despite his fierce need to escape her, when he
turned, he couldn't stop staring at her. Her eyes
were sparkling with unshed tears. He'd hurt her.
More than anything he wanted to take her in his
arms and hold her, but he knew if he did, he might
not be able to let her go.

"I care about you. I want to help you," she
said.

"You can't. Nobody can."

"You know what? You're right. Be a big
stubborn crybaby for all I care. Go ahead, go out
there with that gun and bottle and shoot yourself!
You don't care what I think. But what would
Mindy think if she could see you now? Would *she*
be proud of you or ashamed?"

His eyes narrowed. "Don't you dare throw
Mindy up at me."

The cold air rushing through the doorway had
her teeth chattering. "I'll dare anything I want to,
you big, thick-headed idiot!" she said as she
hugged herself.

In a fury, his eyes swept from her lips to her
breasts, then down her belly to her bare toes. "Put

on your robe," he growled. "It's too damn hard to argue with a naked woman who's freezing to death."

She laughed at him, but it was laughter tinged with tears.

Shoot yourself. Hannah wasn't the first to tell him to do that. Nor the first to throw Mindy up to him either.

But *her* saying it, *her* giving up on him, hurt even more than Gabe's doing it had.

He knew he should apologize.

As she stooped to pick up her robe, his mind spun back to the bright, sunny afternoon of Mindy and Charlie's funerals—funerals he hadn't attended because he'd been too cowardly to watch their coffins being lowered into the ground. Instead he'd stayed home in his unheated house, sulking in his favorite chair.

Sweating and breathing hard, he'd held his pistol that contained a single bullet to his head. He'd just pulled the trigger for the second time after spinning the cylinder and was sitting in the hush of his tomblike house after that final, terrifying click, his heart pounding like cannon fire.

"Don't," an unearthly voice that sounded like Mindy whispered.

When he whirled around and no one was there, he'd felt like a fool.

He raised the gun to his head again. Instead of pulling the trigger, he picked up his favorite photograph of Mindy and was staring at her beautiful face for the last time when Gabe rushed in and shouted to him to put the gun down.

Gabe's face was gray, his black eyes huge.

Relief flooded Liam. He'd never been so glad to see anybody in his life.

"You stupid, selfish, cowardly bastard!" Gabe said quietly. "Do I have to babysit you every damn minute?"

When Liam laid the gun down on the table beside him, Gabe grabbed it and checked the chamber. "The next round was live."

"Too bad you came in."

Gabe removed the bullet and handed it to Liam. "Keep that as a reminder that you're a dumb ass, why don't you?"

Half out of his mind with drink, Liam threw the bullet at a wall. "As if I need a reminder." He paused. "If you hadn't shown up, it would all be over."

"For you, maybe. What about me? I would have blamed myself till I died. You know that, don't you? Everybody who loves you would have blamed himself. Me. Hector. Sam. Luli, Sam and Ben's mother. Homer. Even Mother, hard and cold as she is. And a dozen others. Is that really what you want—to pull us down in your sinkhole of grief and make us feel it was our fault?"

Gabe grabbed Mindy's picture and tossed it toward the couch. "What would she think? She didn't have a cowardly bone in her body."

Gabe went over to the wall and picked up the bullet. Then he reloaded the gun, and spun the chamber.

"If you really want to saddle the rest of us with your suicide, then go ahead. Blow your head off." He slapped the pistol into Liam's open palm so hard his fingers stung like fire. "Go on. Make me watch. Make me live with the fact that I handed you the gun you used to blow your brains out." He paused. "Make me live with the image of you dying in front of me."

Gabe's bruised black eyes had been as wild and terrible as they'd been the night Aunt Miranda had told him that Uncle Vince had drowned and Jack had been swept away in the raging creek.

"Damn you, Gabe! Damn you to hell and back." Liam laid the gun down on the floor and kicked it away.

Hannah coughed, bringing him back to the present. "Go on then! Leave me. Take your big old gun. Enjoy your pity party outside in the dark."

When she arched her brows, the fist around his heart squeezed harder. Dark emotions bubbled up.

For a full minute longer he stared at Hannah, willing her to back down, but she didn't. She squared her shoulders and crossed her arms over her chest.

He was tempted to move toward her and slide that robe off her again and kiss the blue marks on her silky-smooth throat, but the coward in him made him stay where he was.

Turning his back on her, he strode down the porch stairs. What he did with his life was his own damn business. Not hers. She wasn't his wife. She wasn't even his girlfriend...and she never would be.

He turned around. In a cold voice he said, "I want you gone—first thing tomorrow!"

Inside the cabin, Hannah closed the door and sagged against it. His parting shot had hurt, but what hurt her even more was knowing that he was falling apart inside.

He was reckless and dangerous, not at all like the obsessively raised, overly-educated, pampered, self-controlled men she'd been used to on the Upper East Side.

But Liam compelled her, not they. Why?

As a little girl, she'd loved fireworks and playing with matches. After she'd lit a fire in a trashcan in her room when she'd been five, her mother had sat her down at the kitchen table and had made her strike one match after the other and hold them until they'd burned her fingertips.

Only when all the matches were gone had Audrey brushed Hannah's hair back from her face and dried her tears with one of her exquisitely-embroidered handkerchiefs.

"I know getting those blisters on your fingertips wasn't enjoyable, darling, but you have to learn you'll get burned if you play with fire."

Hannah sighed. Liam was pure dynamite and so much more dangerous than a box of silly matches.

Even though she was weary, she waited for him a while, tidying up downstairs and writing in her journal. Finally, however, she grew so exhausted she went up to bed.

She woke hours later when the mattress dipped as he tried to steal back into bed.

"You okay?" she said.

He tensed. When she didn't chastise him, he gathered her close. "Better. I took a long walk."

"Good."

"I'm sorry," he whispered. He kissed her on the nape and then held her a few minutes longer before rolling over onto his side of the bed where he lay as stiff as a board with his back to her.

She lay silently in the dark wishing she knew what to say. It was stupid to care so much about a man who could so thoroughly block his emotions. It was time she got back to figuring her own life out.

"I'm sorry too. I called you a crybaby," she said.

"And I told you to leave. Don't apologize. You didn't do anything wrong."

"I deliberately tried to make you feel worse."

"Hush. Go to sleep."

Don't talk. Words are dangerous. Words promote intimacy—something you don't want with me.

She wanted to say more. Instead, she placed the tip of her tongue between her teeth and bore down until she tasted blood.

Yes, she'd shut up. Not because he'd ordered her to. But because he was a man and he had his hackles up. Which meant he wouldn't listen to a thing she had to say anyway.

16

The next morning Hannah's chest ached when Liam wasn't sitting on the edge of his bed drinking coffee while he waited for her to wake up. How quickly she'd grown accustomed to that pleasant routine.

Dressing hurriedly, she flew downstairs. When he wasn't in the cabin or the barn, she went to the garage.

His truck was gone, and he hadn't left a note.

"If you're lookin' for Liam, he went to town to see about a belt for the tractor," Louise offered when they bumped into each other as Hannah was leaving the garage.

"Couldn't one of the hands have gone?"

His trusted secretary flushed. "I asked him that, but he brushed me off. Said he was in a hurry."

"Okay. Right. It's a pretty day. If he comes back, tell him I'm riding Pharaoh."

She'd hoped his wild emotions last night when he'd ordered her to leave might bring them closer, so it hurt that he was avoiding her.

Impatient to get this particular chore over so he could forget about it, Liam braked on the shoulder in an angry swirl of dust a few feet short of the bridge.

Slamming out of his truck into sparkling sunshine and morning air so cool it had a bite, he cursed when he realized he'd forgotten his hammer. Hissing in a breath, he opened the door to the cab and grabbed his hammer off the floorboard. Then he hurried to the back of the vehicle where Cortez had loaded five new crosses into the bed.

Hefting them onto his shoulders, he barely glanced at the sluggish, brown creek with its sand bars and flat banks that meandered through brush country covered with cactus, huisache, mesquite and the occasional live oak. Nor did he note the bone-white sand dunes that edged the bay where he and Mindy had once kept a houseboat so they could fish on weekends.

He hated the creek and the dunes and the bay now and avoided them at all costs.

Kneeling beside the five broken crosses, he laid the new ones on the ground.

He dreaded coming here so much he usually took another route. Because always when he came here, he thought too keenly of Mindy and Charlie, and of Uncle Vince whose body had been found in his car at the bottom of the creek as well as his five-year-old cousin, Jack, whose body had never been recovered, despite months of frantic searches by determined professionals and private search parties. He thought of Kate and the accident that had ruined her life and left her friend Lizzy dead.

Hoping to avoid the town gossips who might pass by and note his presence even if they didn't stop, he worked quickly, gathering and stacking the fragments of the old crosses into a pile before hammering the new ones into the hard, packed earth.

Why did he bother with the South Texas ritual of white crosses, when Mindy and the others had been dead so long?

Because they'd lost their lives here and their lives still meant something.

Don't think. Just get this done and get the hell out of here.

When he finished, he picked up the splinters of wood and carried them back to his truck. But instead of climbing into the cab and leaving as he'd intended, he went back to the five, newly-erected crosses and stared at them.

Five people he'd known, four whom he'd loved, had died here. Here they had experienced their last thoughts, drawn their last breaths.

Too often he wondered what Charlie and Mindy had suffered in those last moments.

Homer had sworn they'd died instantly. But did he know? Or was he just saying that to be kind?

Did anything remain of emotions or passions or love? Or were they just gone once the people themselves were gone?

Hannah wanted him to talk; she wanted a real relationship even if it was to be of short duration.

What was the use of letting himself confide in her and risk caring again, if everything and everyone always went away?

He couldn't do a relationship again. That's why he'd told her to leave last night.

Night had fallen when he finally strode inside the house. Dinner was waiting for him on the stove, and the cabin smelled wonderful. Just as is it used to when he'd come home to Mindy after a long day at work.

The table was set. When he saw Hannah sitting at the opposite end journaling, his heart lifted until he saw how drawn she looked. Then guilt washed him because he was responsible.

"Hannah…Honey…" His low drawl was deep and hoarse with remorse. "You didn't have to cook. I'm used to eating out of cans."

"I know. Out-of-date cans. But I'm not. Princess-and-the-pea syndrome, remember? You doing okay?"

He nodded.

"I cooked fried chicken…without burning the cabin down."

Dots of flour dusted her hair and the tip of her nose.

"Fried chicken… My favorite."

She smiled. "That's why I cooked it."

"Why don't I put on some music and take a quick shower?" He needed a moment before he could face her and all the expectations he sensed she had.

How he hated knowing that ultimately he would disappoint her.

During dinner she didn't probe. Their conversation was light, like that of strangers on a cruise ship.

"That was the best fried chicken I've ever eaten," he said as he took her hand and led her to the stairs after dinner.

At his praise, her voice filled with pride. "I sure wrecked the kitchen though."

"It was clean by the time I got home," he murmured. "Thanks again."

She smiled. As soon as they reached his bedroom, she nipped his nose playfully with her teeth. Then he nipped hers back. For a moment, they clung to one another, but it wasn't long before a new kind of tension thickened the air between them. Dropping their clothes where they stood, they hurled themselves into bed. If they couldn't talk or share, what was left but to forget their quarrel and indulge in wild makeup sex?

When they'd thoroughly exhausted themselves and still couldn't talk, they fell asleep in a messy coil of arms and legs. For a while, he rested peacefully. But when he began to thrash in her arms, she remembered his hands on her throat and slid away from him. His screams weren't as bad as the night before, but taking no chances, she fled to a far corner of the room before she called him by his last name. When she finally managed to wake him, he was coldly rational and in rigid control.

Talk to me. Please talk to me.

Staring at her across the dark with fiercely glittering eyes, he got up and dressed. Then without a word he stalked past her downstairs.

When the front door slammed, unlike the night before, she forced herself to stay where she was.

Shortly after dawn, he crept into the bed beside her and was instantly asleep. She got up and made coffee. Returning to sit beside him, she sipped coffee and watched him sleep while she waited for him to wake up.

Doubtless there were many things she could be doing, but she was so glad he was home safe, there was nothing she'd rather do than hover. Watching the steady rise and fall of his broad chest, she studied the arrogant arch of his dark brows and the sculpted cheekbones. His sleep-tousled hair was as black as ink against his pillow. It made her happy that at least in sleep he looked peaceful.

"Good morning," she said when his thick lashes finally fluttered, his dark eyes flashing in awareness when he saw her sitting in a square of dazzling sunlight. "There's coffee downstairs. I'll get you a cup."

When she came back, he took the mug and sipped with relish. For a long moment he refused to meet her gaze or say a single word; he just stared into the cup and the curl of steam that rose in the air.

Again she couldn't stop looking at him— maybe because she was still so thankful he'd returned to her and was safe. Or maybe because he was so outrageously male and virile he made her toes curl.

Feeling shy, she took a breath and started to rise, but his hand closed gently over hers.

Setting his cup aside, he pulled her close. "Thank you for the coffee. And for being here. For not leaving." Burying his face in the hollow of her throat, he inhaled her scent.

She ran her fingers through his hair and then over the hard contours of his sleek muscles. He must have liked her touching him because he nuzzled her while she stroked him.

If only he could talk about what was wrong. But if he couldn't, she had to accept that. It wasn't like he'd misled her. He'd been upfront and brutally honest about who he was and what he wanted from her. And what he didn't want.

He wanted sex. For a month. Then he wanted her gone.

Foolishly she'd thought a month of revenge sex was all she wanted as well. But after a few nights, their sex was no longer about revenge for her. Her humiliation over James or Nell had lessened. It was Liam who compelled her now.

Because of Liam, she'd moved on. Unfortunately, he was unable to do the same.

"I don't know what happened to you," she said hesitantly. "I just know you're a good man, and that's enough for me. You don't have to tell me anything."

When she felt his muscles bunch beneath her stroking hands, she thought he would reject her again. Instead, he swallowed a long breath and then another and continued to trace her smooth skin with his work-roughened fingertips. Because her body was intimately accustomed to the needs of his, his fingertip kneading her nipple in his special way put an answering tingling knot in her tummy.

"Hannah... Oh, Hannah...honey. It wasn't supposed to be like this."

Hoping for more, she caught her breath as wordlessly he pulled her to him. Taking her mouth, he kissed her lips as gently as he had in the bar, only this time with a heartfelt reverence that made her heart stop.

"If I could be different, I would be," he muttered. "You've made me want..." When he stopped abruptly, a hard lump filled her throat. "But this is all I'm capable of."

She shut her eyes and sighed. "I know *you* believe that."

"You'll be happier if you believe it too. There's something missing in me now. A great big hole." He swallowed again. "It's not your fault."

She thought about her mother and father living in their palatial apartment on Park Avenue where they never spoke or touched each other or connected in any way either physically or emotionally unless they were forced to. They were so divided, they couldn't love their daughters as a normal couple would. Daddy loved Nell, and Mother loved her.

Hannah had wanted to help them too. Unlike Liam, they refused to admit anything was wrong.

"I know more about damaged hearts than you can imagine. There are things I haven't told you, too," she said.

"Maybe I sense that. Maybe that's why I need you so much," he said. "Or maybe I just need this."

"Sex?"

"Hell, yes—sex! You make me feel so hungry for it. Like I'm starved. I don't know why."

Maybe because being alone is so awful. Maybe because in spite of what you think, you're still a decent human being who wants love and acceptance and connection and all the normal things decent human beings want.

"I should send you away," he said.

"Probably. But not this morning. Not when you've started something—something I very much want you to finish."

He laughed. The rich rumble of sound seemed as beautiful as music to her, maybe because it was so rare.

When his black eyes filled with desperate heat, she opened her mouth and kissed him, inviting him to kiss her back. Which he did—long and deeply.

Then, unhurriedly, he trailed his lips down the length of her throat, tracing soft kisses across her belly, her navel, and in between her thighs. When she felt the tip of his tongue against her sex, her breath caught.

His touch was minimal at first, but the persistent light flicking against wet, sensitive flesh soon set her whole body alight.

Don't play with fire.

Hard to follow such wise maternal advice when her amazing warrior lover was doing incredibly erotic things to her.

Powerful sensations and emotions washed her as she parted her thighs. Clasping his dark head with her hands, she dug her fingers into his luxuriant black hair to pull him closer.

Then his tongue circled her secret spot, sending a thrilling frisson of sensation zinging through her, leaving her quivery, open, needy…and frantically on edge.

She felt that everything he did, every kiss, every sweet breath against her skin, every swirl of his tongue upon sensitive tissues was meant to please her and apologize for the night before. Long before he brought her to the sweetest climax she'd ever known, his tenderness had her begging as she clung and clawed the sheets.

Hannah held her breath when he repositioned himself and covered her with his muscular body. As if reading her vulnerability, he cupped her face and kissed her brow. Then he pressed his forehead against hers.

"You are so sexy. So lovely. I'm going to miss you so much."

Unable to speak, she swallowed against the tight lump in her throat.

When he finally lifted his head, he stared deeply into her eyes. Only then did he enter her and begin to move.

Maybe he couldn't confide to her in words as she wished, but she felt he was speaking to her.

You are mine. Mine. All mine. You are special. I care about you more than I can say. Or admit. I don't want to let you go.

Even before they fell into their natural rhythm, which soon built into a flaming conflagration, she had surrendered all of herself to him.

He drove deeper, never rushing her as he carried her to new, exquisite heights. When he finally groaned her name against her throat, she shuddered against him.

After the storm, he held her, his rough fingertips tracing the length of her spinal column vertebra by vertebra, and she knew a peace in his tender touching that had been lacking before. But when a tear traced down her cheek, she turned away so he wouldn't see.

How could she, who'd promised not to fall in love with him, feel in imminent danger of losing her heart to him?

She would have to let him go. Let *this* go.

"Not yet," she whispered.

Not yet.

They made love again. When it was over, he pulled her close and shut his eyes.

She wasn't about to let him totally off the hook. If they couldn't talk about the things that mattered most, maybe they could at least discuss how they were going to celebrate the holiday together.

"Liam, it's nearly Christmas, and we haven't put up a tree."

"What?" he murmured drowsily.

"We're spending Christmas together, so don't we need a tree?"

He sighed. "Honey, I don't do trees. Not since…"

Not since he'd lost his real family.

"Okay. So how do you suggest we celebrate Christmas?"

"Can't we ignore it?"

"I don't think that's healthy for either one of us. Christmas is my birthday, so we have to do something," she said.

"Can we just try to get some sleep?"

"Yes," she murmured, remembering he'd barely slept, "but I won't forget about the tree."

He shifted beside her. "I'm sure you won't. But for now, be good a girl and don't say anything else about Christmas or a tree. At least not until 10 a.m. or so."

"10 a.m. sharp," she teased.

17

Hannah wanted to decorate for Christmas, but she didn't feel she could tackle that without discussing it with Liam. Since he hadn't liked the idea of a tree or of celebrating Christmas and hadn't brought it up, she'd let an entire day and night go by without mentioning it again.

Since she couldn't do anything about the tree without talking to him, and she didn't know how to approach him, she felt at loose ends as she sipped her coffee and stared out the kitchen window at the barn where Liam was hard at work in his office.

In Manhattan she'd never had an idle moment. Not even as a small child. From birth, her perfectionistic, domineering mother had micro-managed every hour of her day and taught her to do the same. Never had there been time to lie back on a blanket in Central Park and feel the breeze in her hair and watch the wind in the trees and the clouds drift by. Or stare out a window.

Hannah thumbed her nails on the countertop. The cabin was immaculate. Every drawer, every cabinet, was in perfect order. She'd even gotten

Liam to help, so she'd been able to box up quite a few items he didn't need. To her surprise, he'd even allowed her to put a few of his precious cowboy hats in a pile to donate to charity.

Her cheeks heated as she remembered the incredible sex they'd shared last night after they'd finished organizing his closet. Even now she couldn't imagine how she'd done what she'd done, she who'd always been so shy when it came to sex. Maybe it had been the extra glass of wine, or some deep desire to do something so outrageous he'd forget his demons.

When he'd led her up the stairs, she'd said, "Let's do something different."

"Bored with me already?" His intense gaze had made her feel naked.

"Hardly. I want to play striptease."

"I thought you were a doctor, a serious intellectual woman, who speaks three languages."

"Four, which means I studied way too much in my misguided youth, so I missed a lot."

"How do you play? What are the rules?"

"We make them up as we go."

He smiled. "My kind of game."

"We could watch each other strip. Or we could strip each other. First you take something off and then I will. Only we don't touch each other."

"That doesn't sound like any fun."

"Trust me," she whispered.

She put on some sexy garments she'd imagined would be fun to take off. Then she downloaded a classic stripper song and played it on her phone. As the music pounded in his tiny bedroom, she began to undulate to the music. When she'd started to blush with embarrassment, he tried to pull her into his arms and snug her close, his hands drifting over her body, she'd almost let herself forget her purpose. Then resisting temptation, she'd pushed free.

"No touching, remember." When he frowned, she loosened the pearl-studded fasteners on her jacket.

His quick grin had inspired her to yank the jacket apart so fast pearl fasteners flew everywhere.

"Take something else off," he'd said. "I'm naked and you're not even down to your pasties and panties."

"That's because you were a bad sport and tore your clothes off with absolutely no finesse."

She loosened a garter and then rolled down a stocking, twirling it around her head before she threw it at him. "I dressed up for the part."

"You put on too many damn clothes." He stalked across the room and seized her by the waist.

"Uh. Uh. No touching, cowboy."

"We're playing by my rules now." His fierce words were muttered against the curve of her neck as he drew her into his arms.

They'd made wild, out-of-control love. Then he'd slept the whole night without crying out once or having a nightmare.

When she'd awakened, he'd been staring down at her while he drank his coffee. Flushing with shy delight, she'd crawled into his arms and snuggled close. As he held her, she'd dreaded the future when they would have to part.

Blinking hard against tears, Hannah had pushed him away, sat up and had run her hands through her hair, ruffling it.

"You've got chores, so I guess I should get up and make us some breakfast," she said briskly.

"I've eaten. You could sleep in," he responded.

"No! But you'd better get to work."

"Slave driver."

Dressing hurriedly after he left, she'd stomped down the stairs and into the kitchen. And now that she was down here, she didn't have a clue what to do.

In no mood to journal or think about her life in New York or to plan for the future she'd begun to dread, she decided to go out to the barn to help Liam. But just as she was grabbing her jacket and heading for the door, she heard heavy boots on the porch stairs outside.

Anticipating Liam, her heart sped up. Not that he usually returned to the cabin this early.

When a knock sounded briskly, she threw the door open and stood ready to be folded into his arms.

Only instead of Liam a tall, dark, man in jeans and a long-sleeved white shirt, who looked a lot like Liam stood in the doorway. Despite the chill, he'd rolled the cuffs of his shirt up, revealing muscular suntanned arms.

"Hi," he said, leaning against the doorjamb in a way that exuded command. "You don't know me, but I feel like I know you, since my cousin Mary Sue is always singing your praises."

"Nice to know I have at least one fan," she said, backing hurriedly away.

Although he dressed more elegantly than Liam, despite his charcoal gray suit, he was tall and dark and every bit as ruggedly handsome.

"I don't believe I've had the pleasure," she said, guessing who he was even before he introduced himself.

"Gabe Stark." Arching a dark, arrogant eyebrow, he thrust out his hand. "Liam's favorite cousin."

"Is that so?" Smiling, she shook his hand. "Hannah Lewis. Glad to meet you."

"Dr. Lewis, right?" he said.

"When I'm in Manhattan. Here, it's Hannah."

She stepped aside when he pushed the door wider.

"Coffee?" she asked.

"Only if it's already made. Don't want to trouble you, ma'am."

"It is. Liam drinks a lot of coffee."

"Right."

When she asked him what he took in his coffee, he said he took it black, and to her surprise, he insisted on pouring the cup himself.

"You've been here ten days and it's amazing the difference you've made in my cousin," he said.

"Maybe I washed a dish or two for him and got him to move his motorcycle and bailing wire to the barn."

"I'm not talking about the sanitary condition of his cabin—which is pretty damn amazing, too. I'm talking about Liam. For two years he's been a dead man walking. Drinkin' out here alone. Not talkin' to folks he's known his whole life. Walkin' the roads at night with a shotgun slung over one shoulder and a bottle of booze in his free hand. Working cattle drunk a lot of days. Now he's sober and calling folks up again. He's waving to people from his truck and stopping to chat. Louise and Cortez says he's a new man."

"Maybe on the surface," she said, speaking more candidly than she probably should have. But then Liam had told her Gabe had tried harder to break through his walls than anybody else. "He still has nightmares, and when he does, he still takes those walks with the gun and the bottle."

"He's better. He may take the bottle on those walks, but he's not drinking."

"I have no right to ask this, and he wouldn't want me to. But what was his wife like?"

He studied her for a long moment. "They grew up together. I don't remember a time when he didn't love her, so it was tough on both of them when he kept signing up for more tours of duty. None of us understood why he did it."

Gabe sipped his coffee. "Mindy tried to talk him into not going back for that last tour. By then he was bound and determined to finish the job, as he put it, for his buddies' sake. Then something real bad happened to his platoon on their last mission. As platoon commander, he was in charge when he and his guys left the Forward Operation Base and went out in the countryside to engage the enemy. Only the enemy knew they were coming, so only two of his guys got back to the base alive. Liam. And his good buddy, Charlie. And Charlie lost a leg."

"Charlie? That's his son's name."

"Liam named his kid after him."

"He's never mentioned him."

"Never goes to see him either," Gabe said in a heavy tone. "Charlie writes him all the time, too, begging him to come."

"I...I guess it's still too painful."

"Whatever happened messed up his mind so badly he got an early discharge—an honorable one—and a couple of medals, including the Purple Heart, but he didn't finish that tour of duty. He can't forgive himself for what happened over there or for Mindy and Charlie either."

"I know, but their deaths just happened; they weren't his fault."

"They are in his mind. The day of Mindy's funeral, I found him up at the big house playing Russian roulette. If I hadn't walked in right when I did, he wouldn't be here."

"Russian roulette?" Flinching inwardly, she shut her eyes.

"Hell, what's the use of going over all of it again? He didn't, so I'd better do what I came to do. Where's Liam?"

"Out in his office."

Gabe stood up. "Thanks for the coffee."

After he left, she couldn't get the image out of her head of a desperate Liam holding a gun to his head.

Hannah thought the gray sky with its foaming clouds that hovered over the flat brush country was spectacular as Liam drove them toward Lonesome. Not that they'd discussed the sky, or much of anything, for that matter.

Driving was so different here than it was in New York. Other than a few eighteen-wheelers and the Border Patrol, there was almost no traffic; and except for the occasional ranch house and its outlying buildings, not much development.

Liam had been quiet for a spell, and much as she hated breaking the peaceful mood and the easiness she felt between them, she couldn't think of a better time to remind him that she was serious about wanting a Christmas tree.

"Remember what we were talking about the other night before we went to bed?"

"We talked about a lot of things."

"I told you I thought we should put up a tree."

"I gave mine away."

"I bet there's a lot where we could buy a real one in town."

He pressed his lips together and kept his eyes on the road. "I plan to make several stops. The truck's gonna be overloaded as it is. There's no room for a damn tree." He stepped on the gas and the truck flew crazily.

"Do you have any ornaments? Or do I need to buy some?"

His jaw hardened. His hand tightened on the steering wheel. "Supposin' I did? What good would they be if we don't get a tree?"

"Great. You do have ornaments," she said, delighted. "Where are they?"

"We're not putting up a tree."

"Are the ornaments in your garage?"

"Stay away from my garage! Away from my house!"

"Okay. Then I'll buy some new ones."

"What the hell do we need with a tree?" he growled, lifting the toe of his boot from the accelerator when signs posting lower speed limits began to appear on the outskirts of Lonesome.

"What the heck's wrong with trying to put a little bit of fun into life?" she replied.

"I should have known this wouldn't work."

"*This*?"

"*Us*?"

"Maybe it would—if you weren't so all-fired determined live in the past."

"Finally! We're in town." He slammed into the first parking space he saw with a vengeance. "I've got some shopping to do. I'll meet you back at the truck in forty-five minutes."

"I hope you're in a more cheerful mood by then," she said.

"Don't count on it."

When he scowled, she laughed.

"Don't you dare buy a tree!" he hollered after her.

18

As Liam marched up the porch stairs, he dreaded facing her. He'd spent the entire day after their shopping trip in town and their silent ride home feeling guilty as hell for denying her the tree. At the same time, he'd been angry at himself for caring so much about disappointing her.

Women. They got under a man's skin like nothing else could.

He pushed open the door and then his boot caught on something heavy. He went flying onto the middle of the floor where he landed flat on his butt.

"I'm so sorry," she wailed from the couch. "You were right about the tree. Bad idea."

When he picked himself up and switched on the lamp, he saw the mesquite tree that someone—hopefully not her—had dragged into the middle of his living room. His gaze shot to the couch where she lay on one side. Her face was white and bruised, her hair disheveled, her eyes puffy.

"Don't tell me you chopped down a mesquite and lugged it back here all by yourself?"

"With your axe. It was supposed to be our Christmas tree. I wore gloves. Everything was going just fine until I fell into some prickly pear cactus dragging it back to the cabin. I wanted to have the tree up before you got here, but I've got cactus stickers everywhere—in my bottom, in my arms and legs, and I can't get them out."

Was that sparkly drop on her cheek a tear?

"Why didn't you call me?" He went over to the couch and was careful not to touch her as he sat down beside her.

"Because I was trying to get them out myself. But every time I pulled one out, I got more in my fingers.

"Glochids," he said. "The needles have tiny little hair-like needles on them. They adhere to anything that touches them."

"I was taking a break, trying to figure out what to do next." She kept her eyes down. All he could see was the lush fan of her damp lashes and the tear on her cheek.

"You were being stubborn," he said gently, drying her cheek with a fingertip.

"That too."

"It's going to be okay. You're in good hands. I've spent a lifetime yanking thorns out of dogs and calves and pigs..."

"Pigs?"

"Cheer up. You'll be my first woman. Now you just stay put while I get my tools."

"Tools?" she squeaked. "What are we talking about here?"

"Duct tape, tweezers and a pair of pliers."

"Pliers?" she groaned.

"I know what I'm doin', honey."

He returned with a roll of duct tape and the other items he'd mentioned. He cut her jeans and panties off and laid her across his lap. Then he pulled the larger needles out of her naked bottom with tweezers or pliers and dropped each needle into a small glass plate he'd brought in from the kitchen. Next he began repeatedly stretching duct tape over the affected areas of her skin and couch and clothes and quickly ripped it off. Within thirty minutes he'd removed all the glochids and needles.

"Why are you so slow?"

"You didn't want the needles breaking off inside you, did you?"

"I think you're enjoying this."

"You were the one who said I needed to put more fun into my life."

"If I could kick you I would—but since I still have needles in my butt, I need you too much."

"So, you'd better behave."

He stretched another strip of duct tape across her bottom and yanked it off.

"Ouch!"

When he finished, she scooted off his lap and rushed upstairs to dress.

"I'll get the Christmas stand and ornaments for you now," he called up to her sheepishly.

"But you said..."

"I was a prick. It's Christmas. I'll get the stand and ornaments and put the tree up for you. I'm starving. Do you feel up to scrambling us some eggs and making some toast for supper?"

"Sure," she said as she descended the stairs. "But you don't ever go up to that house."

"Hey, it's just the garage."

"But Gabe...he told me what you nearly did there...the day of Mindy's funeral."

He flushed. "Damn him for that. He had no right to tell you."

"I'm sure he was only trying to help. Look, if you tell me where they are, I'll get them. Please let me."

"I'm not going inside the house, and I'm not going to shoot myself, okay?"

Scowling, he opened the door. "I'll be back for those eggs."

But long after the eggs and toast were cold, he hadn't returned. Finally, she grew too worried to wait any longer. Tearing out of the cabin and down the porch steps, she ran all the way to the big house.

He wasn't in the garage like he'd said he'd be.

Her heart pounding, she let herself into the darkened rooms of the lower story. She flipped on a light switch and made her way to the staircase.

"Liam?" she called as she climbed the stairs. "Liam?"

When he didn't answer, her heart began to thud as she rushed from room to room, her panic growing. Finally, she saw a bar of gold light beneath a door at the end of the hall.

"Liam?"

"In here," he answered.

"When you didn't come back, I..."

"You were afraid you'd find me holding a gun to my head?"

"No!"

His face gray, he sat in a rocking chair in Charlie's room clutching a black and white bear against his chest.

"This is Zebo. Charlie didn't go anywhere without him."

"All right."

"We lost him in Landa Park once and had to go back and search every trash container. When we couldn't find him, we had to buy a new Zebo. So, technically, this is Zebo 2."

"Okay."

"I walked the rooms, opened closets and drawers, touched everything, *her* things, Charlie's things, even my things. I've never been able to do that before."

"And? How're you doing?"

"We were so happy. And then suddenly, it was gone. Just like that...all gone..."

"I know." Strangely that's how she'd felt in New York...like her life there was simply over. Gone.

"What do you call the American Dream when it becomes a nightmare?"

"It's not *all* gone. You're alive. You had a wonderful marriage. That means something. Maybe it's not about how long you have with someone..."

"Is that the kind of feel-good bullshit you share with your patients because you think it makes them feel better?"

"I think I told you that in my practice all I do is ask them questions about their habits, drug allergies, medications, and medical history. Then I put them to sleep and never see them again."

"So you don't know what the hell you're talking about."

"I know it's hard...losing people you love, spending Christmas with a stranger when you'd so much rather be with the people you care about."

"You're hardly a stranger."

"You know what I mean. You had real life with them. And I'm not someone you even want to talk to, much less be serious about."

It crushed her a little when he wasn't polite enough to argue.

"Still, you saved my life," she said. "Or at least you saved me from a terrible fate. So, I want to be your friend. Friends help each other. I want to help you. Is that so terrible?"

"You can't help me. You're nothing like me or the people around here. The only people who could help me are dead."

His words and tone cut her, but she didn't flinch. Despite his rejection and her feelings of helplessness, she forced herself to try once more.

"You're right about us being different—at least on the surface. I grew up in a palatial apartment and was taught from birth that people in my world were better than everyone else on our glorified island as well as everyone else on the entire planet. My father was old money; my mother was the perfect socialite who made sure she and all of us were friends with the "right" people."

"I don't want to hear this."

"Then cover your ears because even though you won't talk to me, I'm going to talk to you. In my mother's house everything is perfect...on the surface."

"The pillows match?"

"Oh, yes. My parents are the perfect couple, and everywhere they go they are feted and admired. They are excellent conversationalists and can intelligently debate the world's affairs for hours. But when they talk to each other it is always about what they wish to accomplish materially. They totally support one another's goals and tolerate one another's faults. Daddy gives Mother everything she wants. They are married in every sense of the word but one—they do not share a bed or interfere in each other's personal lives—ever. They are in pain, so much pain, but they are cold to each other. I have no idea why they married each other or stay married. Sometimes I think they may hate each other. Or at least, Mother hates Daddy."

Despite what he'd said about not wanting to listen, he was staring at her with rapt attention.

"Growing up in that home, I felt much was expected of me, but I felt almost no love. And I craved love, so I couldn't let them down. I had to be perfect...like Mother... to please her...but I could never be perfect enough. And if I wasn't, it reflected on her...diminished her."

Liam nodded slightly, as if he understood what she was trying to say.

"My father has a Wedgewood copy of the Portland Vase, the original being one of the most cherished treasures of the British Museum. I'll never forget the first time he told me about the vase. The original is an extraordinary example of

Roman cameo-glass created around 25 AD. It was
perfect and rare until William Lloyd, a madman,
smashed it to bits in 1845. The vase has been
restored several times, but there are missing
pieces, so it is no longer perfect."

"Why are you talking about a damned vase?"

"Because it means something to me."

"What?"

"I don't know. Maybe just that in my family
we're not good at gluing things back together
either. We want perfection. I think it's odd that
my father keeps this replica of a shattered vase
that has been glued back together. Sometimes I
can't look at it without crying. Then there's my
sister..."

"The one who's dead to you?"

"Twins are supposed to understand each other,
to have secret bonds, but it's like she and I are
creatures from different planets. We don't
understand each other at all, and we've always
been such rivals. No matter how poorly she did on
some project, Daddy would champion her while I
had to be perfect. She always loved our chauffeur
and used to hang out with him in the garage as
much as possible which hurt Daddy. Pete taught
her about cars, and she ended up repairing
automobiles for a living. Automobiles! People
like us don't run body shops. I'm a doctor like
Daddy. But despite her odd or maybe rebellious
choice of careers, she's the one he brags on."

"And you resent her?"

"I should be wise and mature, I know. I guess
what I'm trying to say is that I imagine a lot of
people look at me, where I was brought up, what

I've made of myself, and they think I'm living the American Dream, too. But it hasn't ever felt like the American Dream. Not for one second. Even my picture-perfect, high-society wedding turned out to be a bust. So, I think you're lucky if you ever felt like you lived the dream. I think you're even luckier if you ever felt like somebody really loved you, and you loved them back."

Liam sat silently. His non-response to her statement made her feel vulnerable and exposed.

"Okay—I'll go now," she said. "Eat my cold egg. And in the morning, I'll see about packing and getting myself back to New York City where I probably belong. You don't have to do a tree or have Christmas. You've been awfully kind to put up with me this long. Awfully kind."

"Awfully kind? Hell!" His eyes were as black as night as he sprang from the rocking chair. "I don't want you to go, and I'm gonna put up that tree for you—even if it is the ugliest tree I ever saw. And then you're gonna decorate it. And you're gonna stay here as long as we originally agreed, if that's what you want."

He slid his hand behind her neck and drew her toward him. "At least I hope you'll agree to stay because it's damn sure what I want."

When his breath brushed her cheek, she felt a fluttery sensation sizzle inside her. "And maybe tomorrow I'll tell you about Mindy. Because you are my friend."

She took his hand, pressed his fingers.

"But not tonight," he continued. "Tonight's going to be about you and me."

His mouth was so close to hers she inhaled sharply.

"Who knows, darlin', maybe we'll make love under the Christmas tree—even if it is the ugliest tree in all of Texas," he said.

He ran his hand down the length of her hair, traced the shape of her ears with a fingertip.

"Kiss me," she whispered.

She felt him go still, felt the tension between them build and thicken.

Afraid to look at him, Hannah kept her eyes down.

"Not here. Not in this house," he muttered fiercely. "Later."

"Promise?" she said softly.

He nodded.

True to his promise, he didn't draw her into his arms until after they'd returned to the cabin, eaten and she'd hung the final ornament on their tree.

Only then did he come to her, turn her toward him, and fuse his mouth to hers. Pulling her down, he flattened her against the floor near the tree. As always, for the brief time that he made love to her, she felt that he belonged to her completely. The tenderness in his smile and eyes afterward when he led her upstairs was too perfect for words.

It was only later when he screamed and she woke him up that loneliness and desolation washed her again. He was as lost and tormented as ever and as determined to leave her and wrestle his demons out in the dark alone.

Would she ever matter to him? Would he always be in love with Mindy?

19

Hannah wiggled her nose. She smelled coffee. Rich, dark–roasted coffee—the special brand she couldn't live without and had ordered the online when she'd decided to stay with him.

When she opened her eyes, Liam smiled at her and handed her a cup.

"So this is what rich people drink. Nectar for the gods," he said, sipping from his own cup.

"You like it, too."

"It's good, but I can't see myself getting hooked on coffee the local grocery doesn't stock."

"Just you wait and see."

"I said I like it, didn't I?"

"You always choose it over the other stuff you have when you make the coffee. You just don't want to admit it's special."

"When you've spent as much time in combat as I have, you figure out real quick that a low-maintenance lifestyle is less stressful and more efficient."

"Right."

"The more things you gotta drag along, the harder it is."

"We've had this conversation before. I'm the heroine in the *Princess and the Pea.*"

"I've got enough baggage as it is without addin' on your fancy, over-priced coffee." But he kissed her on her nose to soften his words before heading back downstairs.

After she dressed and went to the kitchen to pour herself a second cup of coffee, he came up and put his arms around her.

"I'm sorry I left you last night."

"It's okay."

"I wanted to stay."

"Then why didn't you?"

"Because I'd rather walk than lie in that bed staring up at the ceiling. This morning, just for you, I'm gonna try very hard to talk about Mindy. I don't know if I can, but I'm gonna try because that's what you want, and like you keep sayin', you're my friend."

"That means a lot, Liam."

"But first there's somewhere I have to take you."

"Where?"

"Why don't you just get in the truck with me?"

When he turned south a mile from the house onto a caliche road that passed by a pretty, man-made pond and wound through one stand of wind-tangled oak after the other—oak motts, he called them—she was fairly sure she knew where he was going because she'd often ridden this way on Pharaoh to visit the pond.

He stopped when he came to a chain-link fence. Above the gate a simple, hand-painted sign read, White Tail Ranch Cemetery.

He got out of the truck and came around to her side. Putting his arms around her waist, he helped her down. Then he took her hand in his and led her to the southwest corner of the graveyard where the stones were more modern and legible. When she read the names carved into granite beneath a large live oak tree, she marveled that he'd brought her with him to Mindy and Charlie's graves.

He let go of Hannah's hand and sank to his knees. "I've never been to their graves before. Oh, I tried to make myself come. Lots of times. But I just couldn't. Not without you. I hope Mindy doesn't mind too much."

"I don't think she will."

"If I was crazy from what happened to my men in the war, I went ten times crazier when I lost her and little Charlie. It nearly broke me. I went through two years of hell...until you walked into that bar and tempted me into kissing you. Then you headed off toward Dead Man's Curve in the same kind of weather Mindy had been driving in when she lost control of her car. When I saw those truckers follow you, I had to make sure you were okay. You mattered to me even then."

"I did?"

"Savin' you was a gift. It made me feel...if not whole...better...like I could still get something right."

"I'm glad. Because none of what happened to you before was your fault."

"If I hadn't been so anxious to see Mindy, she wouldn't have driven in that weather."

"She made the decision to drive that night in those conditions."

"You tellin' me I should blame her?" His eyes flashed.

"No. She was worried about you and wanted to be with you. She knew the weather was bad, but she took the risk. People drive in bad weather every day and make it."

"You've got a point—logically—I guess."

"Of course, I do." He pulled her close and held her for a long time. Then he got up. Hand in hand, they walked back to his truck. Without speaking, he drove her to the cabin.

"See you tonight," he said in a low, easy tone as he kissed her brow at the foot of the steps. "I hope that's enough talkin' for a while 'cause it sure wrung me out." He turned but then whirled around and shot her a long, lingering glance before he headed toward the barn.

As she started up the stairs, she was thinking over what he'd said when her phone buzzed in her hip pocket. Pulling it out, her hand tensed when she read Uncle Tommy's number.

She didn't want to think about James, her family or the future. But if she were going to move forward on the annulment, she had to talk to Uncle Tommy.

"Hello," she said.

"Hannah! Oh my God! It's you! I can't believe you answered!"

"N-Nell?" Hannah bit her lip in shock.

"Don't hang up—please!"

Hannah's heart knocked against her rib cage. "I blocked you because I have nothing to say to you."

"That's why I called on Uncle Tommy's phone. Hannah, please…please just listen to me."

Nell sounded strange, almost desperate.

"Why should I?" Hannah said.

"Because you didn't see what you thought you saw."

Hannah sucked in a breath. "Really?"

"I spilled champagne on him. I was wiping it off."

Even as Hannah's heart raced, she tried to tell herself she felt totally calm, indifferent even. "Well, your lipstick was smeared all over your face. And his. And I don't know where else."

"Not where you think. We kissed. He didn't want to. It was my idea. I kissed him."

"He looked like he was enjoying the hell out of himself to me."

"He's always wanted you. I swear. I-I didn't want to ruin your life. I really didn't. I-I thought I loved him, and I didn't think you did. So, I…made this stupid play for him…b-because I thought maybe I could make him see that he felt something for me. I-I told him I wanted to kiss him goodbye. But it was a mistake. He didn't want me; he wanted you. I made a horrible mistake. I'm very, very sorry."

"I don't care," Hannah said.

"Hannah…please…"

Hannah didn't know if she could ever forgive her twin, and she was surprised that she could even listen to her absurd excuses and apology.

Not that she wanted James or maybe even her old life back. And no way could she ever trust Nell alone with Liam. Not for two seconds.

"Okay." Hannah forced herself to breathe in and out very slowly. "You've said what you wanted to say, and I've listened. I'm not saying I believe you, and I definitely don't like the part you played in ending my relationship with James so publicly and at such cost to our parents, especially Mother."

"But?"

"I don't forgive you. I can't. But…maybe you did me a favor, the way you often do when you pull one of your stupid pranks. You forced me to question why I was so focused on my career instead of on James. You made me realize marrying James was a mistake, and now that I've met someone else…"

"Someone else?"

Hannah hadn't intended to say that. Why was she confiding in Nell, of all people?

"In Texas," she said. "A cowboy."

"Does he like art…or opera…or fundraisers?"

"Look, I don't really want to talk about him. It couldn't possibly go anywhere. But I need some time here, so don't you dare tell Mother about him or where I am."

"She's very angry with me for what I did. She wouldn't speak to me or allow me in the house after it happened. But then she became so upset that you never called her or answered when she called that she finally broke down and asked me to call you and try to make things right."

"I can't talk to her right now. She has all these huge expectations. She'll be so disappointed in me if... What am I doing? I can't believe I'm even talking to you."

"I'm sorry."

"Sorry doesn't cut it this time. I have to figure out some stuff on my own. Furthermore, if you ever even think of going after Liam or any other man I might become interested in, ever, I don't know what I'll do to you. I mean it, Nell. Do we understand each other?"

"I promise," Nell whispered. "I really am very sorry."

"I'm afraid I'm not going to get over this for a while...if ever."

"Please..."

"And don't call me again. I don't need your apologies or explanations. I don't want to have anything to do with you."

After she hung up, Hannah felt freer, as if some dark cloud had lifted off her. When she walked outside a few minutes later, Pharaoh came up to her and started sniffing her pockets, and she pulled out a carrot.

"Is this what you're looking for?"

That afternoon Hannah started a pot roast in a slow cooker and then left again with Pharaoh to go on a long walk to clear her head.

She thought about her mother and the life in New York her mother was so determined she lead.

Why does she want me to be like her... when she's miserable?

When Hannah returned, she found a tiny Christmas present with her name on it under their tree. Pleased that he'd taken the time to select something for her, she smiled.

Picking it up, she shook it. Mystified, she was still smiling as she replaced it underneath the tree.

"Is that pot roast that smells so great?" Liam said when he came back to the cabin that evening.

Over dinner they talked about their day. She told him that she'd spoken to Nell.

"I'm glad she called," Hannah said. "I can't forgive her, but we needed to talk. I felt relieved after she hung up."

"So, is she still dead to you?"

"Okay. Okay. You were right. I'm not indifferent, so maybe she isn't dead. But I haven't forgiven her. I don't know if I ever well."

"You should probably call your mother," he said.

"Can we talk about something other than my family?"

"Ladies first."

Hannah told him about the birds she'd seen on her walk—a green jay, a green heron, which wasn't green, coveys of quail, an owl, wild turkeys, three northern pintails, and two Mexican ducks. And of course she bragged on the pot roast she'd cooked.

"In New York, I never have time to cook. I buy carry-out."

"I bet it's expensive—like the coffee you're so set on hookin' me on."

"You can eat cheap in Manhattan if you want to."

"But you don't, I bet."

"I've been known to eat the occasional hot dog from a street vendor."

"Really? When was the last time you did that?"

When she confessed she couldn't remember, he laughed.

"That's just one example."

"How come you people enjoy throwing your hard-earned money away so much?"

How could she explain the highly-tuned status games women like Audrey Lewis played on the Upper East Side? And not only the women. The men were just as bad.

Everything was about having more. A woman thought nothing of spending $15,000 on a designer purse from Paris because so many in her tribe spent more and would despise her if she didn't. A mother had to send her children to a *certain* school, the right school. She had to serve *certain* foods and eat at the right restaurants where she had to make sure she sat at the right table. There were dozens and dozens of unspoken rules every woman who was anybody knew, dozens of games to be played...and, more importantly, won. The most important was to look stunning *all the time*.

"We don't think we're throwing our money away. In our world, such 'investments' are necessary." She wasn't about to confess how much it cost just to keep her hair the color and shape it was.

"Hmmm," he said, studying her. "To change the subject, how would you like to go to a Christmas dance?"

"A dance? For real?"

"You could wear one of those sexy getups from your revenge wardrobe. Maybe those sexy red boots of yours," he said hopefully.

"So you're telling me how to dress."

"Just makin' a suggestion."

"You don't ever want me telling you how to dress."

"I'll make an exception for this occasion."

"What exactly is this occasion?"

"My Aunt Miranda..."

"The aunt who raised you?"

"Yes. She's throws a dance every year out in her barn at Christmas. She's sulked these past two years because I didn't show up. So I thought this year maybe I'd surprise her."

"I've never been to a barn party."

"Oh, her barn isn't like any other barn around here. She calls it her party barn. It's got concrete floors and heating and air-conditioning. And she keeps it clean as a whistle and throws all her big shindigs in it because she doesn't like entertaining at El Castillo."

"El Castillo?"

"The big house."

"When?"

"Tomorrow night."

"That's not much notice."

"All we have to do is dress and drive over."

"Men," she whispered. "I have to figure out what to wear and then put an appropriate outfit together..."

"Nobody'll care what you're wearing, honey. They're all too curious about you and me."

When Hannah finally descended the stairs the night of the party wearing a red dress that clung to her curves, Liam drew a long breath and shot to his feet.

"You're beautiful."

Blushing, she twirled to show off her legs.

"What the hell did you to do to your hair?"

She'd washed it and had blown it dry, so that it fell in a straight golden curtain to her shoulders. It was the sophisticated style she favored in Manhattan rather than the ponytail she'd worn while living with him.

"You look great," he said. "Why am I surprised? This is the real you, right?"

He wore a white, long-sleeved shirt, pressed jeans, and boots.

She went to him and traced the edges of his white collar with a fingertip. "You don't look half bad yourself."

He kissed her softly, carefully, so he wouldn't mess up her lipstick. Still, even that light brush of his mouth against hers got her heart pounding.

"Now don't you go flirtin' with the other men," he whispered, letting her go. "We'd better save the kisses and hugs for later if we're going to make it to Aunt Miranda's party."

When he kept smiling after he released her, she took his hand and squeezed it. He seemed happy, she thought, happier than she'd ever seen him.

How wonderful it was being with him when he was like this. If only…

She was a doctor. Her career had forced her to face harsh realities rather than to let herself believe in wishful fancies.

Only a fool would let herself fall for a man
whose life was so different from hers, a man
who'd warned her he could never be hers.

20

Miranda's barn was brilliantly lit and sumptuously decorated. A marvelous aroma drifted from the platters piled high with barbequed ribs and chicken legs and other finger foods. A band played while prominent Texas politicians made conversation with movie stars, who had prestigious cattle spreads in Texas.

A full-sized oilrig ablaze with white Christmas lights had been erected in between the Castillo and Miranda's party barn as a tribute to North Star Oil and Gas, the company which Miranda owned and operated, even though members of her board, tired of her high-handed, managerial style, and Gabe, whom she'd ousted, were vying to dethrone her.

When Hannah and Liam stepped into the barn, heads turned and conversations stopped. Feeling conspicuous and out of her element in the awkward silence, Hannah's grip tightened on Liam's arm. Suddenly a tall, silver-haired woman on the other side of the barn held up her hand in an imperious gesture, and the avidly-curious throng parted as she and a man at least a decade younger than she headed toward Liam.

"It's about time you got out," the woman said by way of greeting. "He's been positively maudlin, hasn't he, Wes, if one can be positively maudlin?" The older woman's companion's quick laugh grated on Hannah's nerves. "I suppose *she's* the reason." After staring pointedly at Hannah, the woman turned to Liam. "And you were going to love Mindy forever."

Hannah felt Liam tense as the woman laughed and thrust out a wrinkled, clawlike hand.

"Miranda Stark," she said, introducing herself.

Hannah forced herself to smile and take her hand as Liam introduced her to his formidable aunt and the man at her side, Uncle Wes—the man she'd married almost immediately after her first husband, Vince, had died and her son, Jack, had vanished. Due to the vast fortune Miranda had inherited, there'd been talk of foul play. Hannah remembered this from that first time when she'd googled Liam and his relatives and had read some of the old news stories and police reports about his Uncle Vince's accident and his cousin's disappearance.

Miranda lowered her hand and gazed down the length of her nose at Hannah. If the older woman was pleased with what she saw, she did not show it. On the contrary, she pressed her mouth into a rigid line and frowned. Not that this bothered Hannah, who was used to games of this sort in New York. Wes, however, regarded her with such an excessive amount of male interest, she blushed.

When Liam's aunt took his arm and led him into her barn, Hannah was left to trail dutifully behind with Wes.

Friends and family surrounded Liam. Clearly uneasy in the throng, he came to her and took her hand and led her away from Wes. When asked, Liam refused to discuss how the two of them had met or to describe in detail how he'd bested the truckers and saved her, so Wes and a few of his pals cornered her at the first opportunity and bombarded her with the same questions.

"You'll have to ask Liam if you want the details. I was so scared it's all sort of a blur," Hannah said. "I'm just so glad he showed up."

"I own The Dove. Liam's like a brother to me, so they'd better not show their faces in my place again," Hector Montoya said darkly. "Can I get you a drink?"

"Water."

"This is a party."

"Make it sparkling water. With a lime."

Wes, whose cheeks were red, frowned.

Hannah hadn't had an alcoholic beverage since she'd been in Texas because she hadn't wanted to encourage Liam to drink, but after Liam ordered a club soda and lime for himself and brought her a glass of wine, she weakened and took it. Whether it was because of the wine or because she was at a dance with Liam, who was smiling and tapping the toe of his boot to the music as if he were enjoying himself, she began to relax. She'd felt so humiliated at her wedding reception, she'd wondered if she could ever face going to a party again, but it felt good to be out with Liam and to be around people again.

When the band began to play the next song, Liam led her onto the dance floor and swirled her around. His handsome face grew flushed, and his eyes shone with pleasure every time he glanced down at her. James had never once looked at her the way Liam did. She should have known months before the wedding to break it off. Instead, she'd ignored whatever doubts she'd felt and had gone ahead with "the plan."

Other men asked her to dance. When she accepted, Liam danced with different partners too. But mostly he danced with her, especially the slow dances. During the waltzes and slow numbers, he pulled her to him, his arm firm around her waist as he skillfully guided her around the dance floor.

She liked feeling the heat of his body against her own, the thud of his heart, and the warmth of his skin. Tracing the length of his neck with her fingertips, she liked it when he snugged her closer and ran his hands down the length of her spine. What she didn't like was the way everybody, especially his uncle Wes, watched them. Were they all remembering Mindy and making comparisons?

At one point, she and Liam were alone on the dance floor, and everybody stood on the sidelines as Liam spun her around. When the music finished, he executed an impressive dip that left her breathless and had their audience clapping.

"Remember how he used to always do that with Mindy," Wes said loud enough for everyone to hear.

Liam flushed. Letting her go, he took her hand and pulled her from the dance floor.

"Where' Gabe?" she asked when she found herself alone with Liam.

"I told you. He thinks he should run the family company. So, Miranda kicked him off the board. He has his own company, of course, but they aren't on speaking terms."

"But she's his mother."

"So? Gabe speaks his mind. If you cross her or my uncle, she can be incredibly difficult. Take it from somebody who's crossed her. Gabe's every bit as smart as she is and maybe a whole lot smarter. He's definitely richer. And that galls her. She liked bullying him. He's a major stockholder and has a lot of friends on the board who want him reinstated."

After the dance was over, Liam drove her home. As always, she was amazed at how empty the country roads in South Texas were compared to the roads in New York. Except for a few lone pairs of headlights near Dead Man's Curve, they saw no other vehicles.

When they reached the cabin, he helped her out of the truck and pulled her into his arms. "I felt happy tonight when we were dancing."

"I'm glad you had fun," she said. So did I."

"No. I said I felt happy," he repeated.

She absorbed his meaning. "Okay."

"I didn't think I could ever feel like this again. It's scary...me believing I might be able to be happy again."

"Is that really so bad?"

"I don't know. Maybe. 'Cause I know how easy it is to lose everything."

"Wouldn't it be scarier to think you'd spend the rest of your life miserable?"

"I've been thinking about that a lot." He leaned inside the truck and turned on the radio, quickly flipping the dial until he found a station that played country music.

"We're in luck. That's a waltz." Tightening his arm around her, he began to waltz with her across the driveway "I've missed dancin'."

Bright stars, a sliver of moon and inky velvet sky whirled above her. Not that she noticed. She was staring into his eyes and savoring the heat of his body pressed into hers. As quickly as he'd started dancing, he stopped and kissed her hard. Slowly her arms wound around his neck. He didn't stop kissing her until they were both breathless.

"I didn't like them watching you and wondering about us. It isn't anybody's business what I feel for you."

What do you feel, she wanted to ask, but bit her tongue. The warmth in his eyes and smile had to be enough for now.

"I was thinkin'," he began almost shyly.

Her breath caught. "You were, huh?" She ran a finger down the length of his crooked nose. Then she traced his high, sculpted cheekbones. He was so magnificently handsome. She felt happier, more natural, as if she were her real self with him, than she'd ever felt in New York.

"Do you think maybe…after you go…I could come to New York and see you sometime? When it's convenient, I mean. This is a yes/no question, so you can say no, and I'll accept it. I know we had a pact to end this thing. And I'll stick to it, if that's still what you want."

"What if it isn't?"

Suddenly tension she hadn't known she felt drained out of her.

"What are you saying?" she whispered in a low, breathless tone.

"You're still gettin' that annulment right?"

"Most definitely," she stated.

"Then it means I care about you, and I don't want to let you go. At least, not yet. We're friends right?"

Her heart raced. A huge lump formed in her throat.

Calm down. It's not like he's asked you to stay or committed himself in any way.

It's not like I could, even if he asked, so there, Liam Stark!

You could stay.

How? My work, my whole life is in New York.

You weren't so sure about that when you ran away. You're a doctor. You could work anywhere. You could get a Texas license. Practice here. You could.

"Shut up," she murmured angrily to those warring voices in her head, not realizing she'd spoken aloud.

"What?"

"Not you, silly!"

"Then who?"

"Never mind. Your lips felt good a while ago. Just hold me and kiss me some more."

"Now you're trying to distract me 'cause you're hoping I'll forget you talk to folks who aren't really here," he teased.

"Don't be silly."

"You've done it before."

"Have not!"

"Then it's okay if I come see you."

She wrapped him in her arms. "Yes! I'd love to show you New York."

His dark eyes tender, he lowered his head and kissed her. She closed her eyes. With his hands in her hair and his mouth on hers, she felt that maybe someday he might truly love her as she'd longed to be loved her whole life.

21

"Honey! Wake up! Now!"

At the hard note in Liam's voice, she sprang to a sitting position.

Towering above her, his mud-streaked face was grim. His jeans and boots were even filthier. As was the floor. He was so upset he'd probably trailed mud all over the house.

"What is it?" She pushed her hair out of her eyes. "What's wrong?"

"It's that damn fool horse you like so much. Somebody left a gate open, or he figured out how to open it. He's in the pond. On the island. Only it's not an island any more. The damn thing is sinking under his weight. He's in so deep, he can't get out."

"Quick sand?"

"Sort of. He's in up to his back, and I need some help getting' him out. Cortez is fifty miles down south on the Hondo Division with all my best hands."

Flying out of bed, she pulled on one of the old sweaters she'd bought in the second-hand store in Lonesome.

"At least I finally know you like Pharaoh," she said.

"The hell I do. He's more trouble than he's worth. I'm gonna sell him for glue for sure after this stunt."

"No—you'll sell him to me before you do that." She sat back down on the bed and yanked on a pair of jeans.

"You live in New York City."

"So? I'll rent a stable. I'm rich, remember?" Without bothering to use a brush, she pulled her hair back in a ponytail. "I'll ride him whenever I can."

"Right, you have so much free time, you being a big, fancy doctor and all. He'll love being locked up in a gloomy cage in a city."

"I'll explain to him that it beats being turned into glue."

"Hey, I was just kidding."

"Good, or I'd rethink our relationship. And I'd remind you about Mindy watching you from Heaven. I bet you never kidded *her* about turning him into glue?"

His face paled, and the haunted look she hated was back, clouding his eyes.

"Sorry," she whispered, instantly remorseful.

"Hey, lighten up. Guess I had it coming. And you can mention Mindy…any time you want." He shrugged and headed down the stairs.

Together they grabbed boards and scraps of wood from a pile in the barn and loaded them into the bed of his truck. Then they drove out to the lake. When they reached the tiny pond, Hannah's heart quickened when she saw the water was indeed over Pharaoh's back.

Pharaoh's ears were back and his dark eyes were wide. When he saw her, he shook his head, snorting and neighing wildly.

A knot of terror twisted in her stomach. "My poor, big darling," she cried in a calm tone. "We're going to get you out!"

Then she hurled herself out of the truck and ran to him.

"Stop!" Liam yelled after her. When she ignored him, he gave chase and caught her when she was knee deep in the cold, gooey mud.

"What are you doing?" he yelled.

"Let me go!"

"We've got to build a bridge or a causeway to him first, or you'll sink too."

"Oh." She felt stupid for not having asked him earlier what all the boards were for. Not that she admitted it as she trudged grudgingly after him back to shore.

With him directing, they worked quickly, laying boards in the mud. They had to stand on them so they'd sink a little, so the mud would hold them, and they wouldn't float.

Since they had to get in the water, the work was so wet, muddy, and cold, she was soon shaking all over. Not that she complained. Ignoring her chattering teeth, she worked steadily, wordlessly by his side.

It took nearly an hour for them to construct their causeway and reach Pharaoh. Then she stroked the animal and fed him a carrot and an apple to distract him while Liam secured a thick rope around him. After that Liam quickly tied the other end to the hitch on his truck.

"Are you sure this is the thing to do? Aren't you afraid you'll hurt him? Cripple him maybe?" she asked.

"Considerin' what'll happen to him for sure if I don't, I'm willin' to take the chance. You suggestin' we leave him here and let him drown?"

"I was wondering if you've talked to a vet."

"Why would I do that? He's not sick."

"I guess that would be like asking directions, and men like you never ask for directions."

"I've been dealing with horses my whole life."

"We doctors consult each other when we have a problem."

"I ask for advice too—when I *need* it."

Being a man, he wasn't going to listen to her. But that wasn't why she shut up. She was suddenly remembering the way he did everything with sureness and an unspoken expertise. She was thinking that maybe, just maybe, he knew a thing or two about getting his horse out of a jam. He'd saved *her* life, hadn't he?

"Okay," she whispered grudgingly.

His smile was a bit too smug for her liking.

Without another word, he got in the truck and started the powerful engine. He inched forward until the slack went out of the rope. Then he stopped.

"Keep an eye on Pharaoh. Tell me if he gets into trouble. And step away from the truck. If the rope breaks, I don't want it flyin' back in your face."

"Okay."

Pressing her lips together, she backed away from the trailer hitch, watching the horse as the pressure from the truck moving forward forced Pharaoh to take a single step onto the homemade causeway, and then another and then another. After the first three or four steps, the job became easier as the horse got out of the deeper mud and moved onto the boards and into shallower water.

When Pharaoh clambered to shore, he shook his head, spraying water in all directions. Then he neighed wildly.

"Stop," she yelled. Liam got out and went with her to check the horse.

After he'd run his hands over every part of the animal and found him sound, he said, "I'll walk him back. You drive the truck. He needs to be groomed and fed and to have some quiet time in a stall. Damn fool horse. He probably just did this so he'd be the center of attention."

"Pharaoh, don't you listen to him. It wasn't your fault."

"Who walked himself out onto that island and got stuck, I'd like to know?"

"Don't listen to him," she said as she handed Pharaoh another apple, which the gelding chomped gratefully. "I'm sure if he could talk, he'd explain everything."

"I can't believe you're rewarding him. What about me? He caused me to lose half a day of work, and he gets an apple. What do I get?"

"You were wonderful, so you get a kiss." She turned from Pharaoh and put her arms around him.

"I'm kinda dirty."

"So am I," she whispered. "I feel like a mud wrestler."

"Now you're turning me on."

"If you get lucky, you'll have Pharaoh to thank."

He laughed as she kissed him on his muddy mouth.

"Maybe I'll keep him after all," he murmured. "But you're shivering and your teeth are chattering, so get in the truck and turn on the heater. Drive yourself to the cabin and take a long, hot shower."

"What about you? Your teeth are chattering too."

"I'll be fine. I'll walk him to the barn and clean him up first."

She drove straight to the barn without bothering to shower or change. Instead, she worked on getting everything ready before Liam returned. Then together they hosed Pharaoh off with warm sudsy water. After they toweled him dry, they brushed him until his coat gleamed and the mischievous gleam returned to his eyes.

They weren't quite finished when they heard a horn honk outside.

She wrapped her arms around Liam. "We did it! We saved him!"

"Thank you. I couldn't have done it without you." He took her hand and folded it against his cheek.

"Now you're gonna do a little jail time for that trick, old fella," Liam said, letting go of her hand so he could lead the gelding to a stall at the back of the barn.

Normally Liam allowed the horse the freedom of his loafing shed and a four-acre pasture. If Pharaoh chose to seek shelter, it was available. If he chose to run around in a storm, that was his choice too. But Liam had said Pharaoh needed to rest for a while and to stay out of mischief.

As Liam was pouring a bucket of feed for Pharaoh, Hannah heard the horn outside again. Who could it be? Nobody had ever driven up to the ranch and honked like that before. Had somebody gotten lost and wandered here by mistake?

When Liam returned, he took her in his arms, and she forgot about the horn. "You're gorgeous. Even more gorgeous than you were all dressed up last night."

"You're crazy."

"Those wet clothes stick to your body and outline your shape, you know."

Feeling happily exhausted after all their hard work and pleased he could find her sexy even now, she smiled up at him.

Gently he traced the lines of her muddy face with his fingers. "You were wonderful out there. It was nice...you working beside me. Used to..." His voice trailed off, and the shadows came back into his eyes.

Was he thinking of Mindy? At the thought, Hannah's throat tightened. Mindy had worked with him too, of course, countless times.

Suddenly his gaze warmed, and Hannah knew that he was thinking about her again. As he continued to look at her, her own mood brightened. Without speaking, he kissed her long and so deeply Hannah felt like her soul was rising up to meet his.

He'd said he wanted to keep seeing her. Maybe in time he would forget the past or at least put it behind him.

I love him, she thought, lacing her fingers through his.

I love him with my entire body and soul and want to be with him forever.

She pressed her body closer to his, finding peace and reassurance and excitement too.

"Maybe we should go to the house and take that long, hot shower together," he murmured a little while later. "We could curl up under some blankets till we get toasty warm."

"And then what?"

"You tell me," he whispered, his breath falling lightly on her skin.

The impossible had happened. She loved him. And she had the hope that he was beginning to love her.

As he stared into her eyes, she felt that he was her whole world, that nothing else mattered except him.

Her heart thudded a little harder. She was clinging to him and nodding happily, when somebody stepped on the horn outside the barn again and didn't let up.

"What the hell?" Liam growled.

Letting her go, he headed purposefully toward the barn doors.

When he pushed the doors open, and she saw the stretch limo, her hand flew to her mouth.

"No!" she whispered, running after him. "No. Shut the door! Don't go out there! Please!"

"Why the hell not?"

"Please… please…"

But it was too late. Liam was already outside, striding toward the limo to investigate.

She ran after him and took his hand and tugged at it to pull him back. He put his arm around her possessively. "What is it, honey? What are you so scared of?"

She clutched his hand fiercely as she stared into his eyes. "They've come for me. It's my family…my mother for sure…and no telling who else."

"James?" Turmoil that held grief and pain and profound loss and maybe jealousy too flashed in the depths of his dark eyes as he studied her. Then his features hardened and just like that he shut her out. "You think your husband's come for you?"

"He's not my husband."

"In the eyes of the law, he damn sure is." Liam's voice was low and completely devoid of emotion. "Of course, he's come. I told you he wouldn't let you go."

"Let me talk to them," she pleaded.

He arched a brow. "Okay. If that's how you want to play it, I'll respect your wishes and remove myself from the picture." His voice was hard and rough.

"You're being obtuse."

"Am I?" He gazed down at her. "You're married to another man, and he's come for you!"

"I'm getting an annulment."

One of the rear doors of the limo opened and James, who wore a three-piece gray suit, unfolded himself from the sleek automobile. Tall and dark, he cut a dashing figure.

"Hannah," he called, his voice overly authoritative and not the least bit friendly as he eyed Liam.

When she wrapped her arms around Liam, a muscle in Liam's jaw jerked. "He's your husband. It's time you dealt with him. With your marriage. With your *real* life."

"Liam, no..." When she touched his arm, he flinched. "Please don't shut me out."

"Honey, we always knew it had to end. It's just ending sooner than we expected."

She could feel her blood pulsing desperately through her ears. "But last night you said you wanted to see me in New York."

"Last night was a dream." His eyes were deep and dark and so beautiful they filled her with profound misery. "Maybe everything here between us has been a dream. Honey, we both know how easy it is to shatter dreams. Maybe this is for the best."

"No! Don't shut me out," Hannah cried as a wild spasm of grief ripped through her.

"Go home to your people where you belong. You're a doctor. You're important, too important to waste yourself here on me. You've got nothing here. The sooner you realize that, the better."

"Liam, please..." She tried to speak, but somehow could find no words.

"Go home," he repeated coldly. "Like I said, we both knew we were on borrowed time."

He pulled her close, touched his forehead to hers. She felt the violent rhythm of his heart pounding against her breasts. For a few brief seconds, he held her as if she were very precious to him. "You belong in New York," he whispered into her hair. "Deep down you know that. We've got to end this—now."

Did she belong in New York? The mere thought of returning depressed her.

She made a childish face at him. "How can you be so sure I belong there when I'm not sure about anything?"

There was no emotion in his voice now. "You were hurt. Go home. Be happy."

Letting her go, he spun savagely on a mud-caked boot heel and strode back to the barn without once looking back at her...while she couldn't take her eyes from his long, jean-clad legs until he slammed the barn doors. Then she stood there aching all over with emotional torment, her pain so intense, it was almost physical.

When James walked up to her and laid a hand on her shoulder, she whirled around. That he should see her weak and on the verge of tears, infuriated her.

"Why are you even here?" she demanded as a hateful tear streaked down her muddy cheek. "Why, when I told you not to come? When I told you I wanted an annulment?"

"Because I—because *we*—want you to come home."

"Define *we*?"

"Your mother, your colleagues at the hospital...everybody."

"My mother's the main one behind you coming here, isn't she?"

He didn't deny it.

"Damn you! I can't deal with you...not after what you did at our reception! With my sister, of all people. I'm not ready."

"I don't blame you for feeling the way you do. I don't like myself for doing what I did. Nell doesn't like herself either."

"Why didn't you both just stay in Manhattan?"

When his mouth tightened, she knew for sure he hadn't wanted to come. When he refused to argue or defend himself, her anger at him lessened a bit. She didn't really care about him anymore. Liam's rejection was what was killing her.

"I was happy before you drove up," she said. "So happy." She bit her lip. "H-happier than I've ever been in my whole life."

"That's good."

"No thanks to you! Or Nell! When you showed up—you destroyed everything."

His shoulders sagged. When his blue eyes filled with compassion, she remembered that whatever he was or wasn't, he'd been her trusted friend once. Even Nell had defended him and blamed herself. Still, Hannah had seen what she'd seen. He hadn't looked unhappy with Nell at *their* reception. Quite the opposite.

"Okay," he said, "I admit I wouldn't have come on my own because I respect your feelings. But your mother was worried you're not thinking straight. She thought since I was responsible, I

should come. I felt like she was right, that I
should do something to fix this mess."

"Maybe I'm thinking for myself for the first
time ever. Thinking about what *I* want for a
change. *"*

"Good," he whispered. "I'm glad. I hated
knowing I'd hurt you. I don't like thinking I hurt
you again by showing up here."

He looked so contrite, Hannah had to fight
feeling sympathetic toward him.

"I'll do whatever you want," he said.

When Nell came running up, looking lovely
and every bit as chastened as he did, with her dark
hair framing her pale face, Hannah turned on her.
"How dare you tell everybody where I was!"

"I didn't tell them. I swear. Mother hired
someone. And I'm sorry about what I did. I
wasn't thinking about hurting you at the wedding
reception. Really, I wasn't."

"Stop apologizing! I don't care about the
reception anymore, okay?"

Hannah didn't want to deal with Nell's
apologies or their lifelong rivalry either. Not now,
when her heart was breaking. "And Mother and
Daddy? Are they here too?"

"We're all here," Nell said. "We came
together. In the family jet."

Of course.

"I really am so sorry for what I did," Nell
repeated in a rush. Her brown eyes held so much
pain Hannah softened a little. "It wasn't Colt's
fault. I mean James's fault. James didn't do
anything. I swear it. He was just there. I threw
myself at him."

"He didn't look like he was objecting."

James flushed as he turned to Nell. "I was as much to blame as you."

"We already discussed this on the phone," Hannah said. "Do we have to go over it again?"

"It's just that I'm so ashamed," Nell said. "I love you so much and ever since you disappeared, I've been worried sick about you!"

"Don't say that!"

"But I do love you."

Even though something in her sister's voice touched her, at the same time, Hannah felt twisted. Her sister had betrayed her on a profound level, and she didn't feel capable of closeness with her.

"That's a little hard to believe. Did you want attention? You always want the limelight. Or did you just want to hurt me?" Suddenly Hannah really wanted to know. "Sisters, twins especially, should have each other's backs. What's wrong with us? Why do we always compete?"

"It wasn't about you this time. I did it because I love…" Nell's frantic gaze darted beseechingly to James whose face was cold and set. "I-I just did it. That's all. And it was awful of me. Selfish. And I feel awful about it. I'm truly sorry, Hannah."

"Well, I felt awful too…until I came here and met Liam, who was going through far worse than you or I could ever imagine. He and I, we're friends, and I was hoping I could stay with him a while longer…and that maybe he would…" Remembering his tender expression last night

when he'd asked her if he could visit her in New
York, her desperate gaze drifted to the barn.

Liam was lost to her.

"But all of you are here now," Hannah said.
"And he wants me to go. Whatever we had for a
few short days is over."

"So, you'll come home now?" James asked, a
faint note of impatience with the situation edging
his voice now.

"Why not?" Hannah whispered even though
she didn't want to.

"Do you need to get your things?" Nell asked.

Feeling the weight of her former life falling
upon her shoulders like an unwelcome harness,
Hannah stared at her twin in confusion. If she
couldn't have Liam, what did she have in that
cabin that mattered? Her revenge wardrobe?
Shirts, a pair of boots, several pairs of jeans from
a resale shop, none of which she would ever wear
in Manhattan?

"I suppose I need my purse and phone," she
said in a low, mechanical voice. "They're in that
cabin over there."

"You've been living *there*?" Nell whispered,
her mouth falling slack. "We went to that big
house and knocked, but nobody was home, so we
drove to the barn."

"Maybe I should take a quick shower and
change," Hannah said, remembering what a mess
she was. "It'll just take a moment."

When she went into the cabin, James and Nell
waited for her on the porch. Inside, the first thing
Hannah saw was the Christmas tree. She turned
on the lights, causing the tree to sparkle. When the

ribbons on their gifts glittered, she knelt and
picked up his gift to her. Like a child she shook it
again and listened, wondering what was inside.
On a label, Liam had written, "Happy Birthday!
Merry Christmas!"

Closing her eyes, she pressed the gift to her
heart. Then very carefully she set it down by the
one she'd bought him.

She'd never know what he'd chosen for her. If
their relationship was over, she didn't want some
keepsake to remind her of all she'd lost.

Slowly she arose. Turning out the Christmas
lights, she marched up the stairs to shower.

When she came out of the cabin dressed in an
old shirt and a pair of jeans, her face free of
makeup, her wet hair slicked back in a ponytail,
she carried her purse, a hastily packed suitcase,
and grocery bags that she'd stuffed with all her
things.

Cupping her elbow, James led her to the limo.
When Hannah climbed inside, Audrey, who was
swathed in black fur, looked both joyous and
distressed as she gazed at her.

"Darling, it's so good to see you. You'll be
glad to know I've sent Claude to your townhouse
nearly every day to water your flowers and to
dust. And James has moved his things out."

James sighed. Claude was her mother's maid.
Her mother had bought the townhouse, which was
an elegant residence in Sutton Place, a cozy,
affluent enclave, for her as a wedding gift with
money from one of the family trusts. James,
who'd spent most nights there, had moved a few
of his things in already and had planned to move

in formally after they returned from their
honeymoon. It was good to know she wouldn't
have to deal with him.

Hannah brushed a tear from her cheek and
nodded weakly. "Thank you."

"There...there," her mother soothed, patting
her own golden hair. "No need for tears. You'll be
fine once we get you home where you belong and
into some decent clothes."

Her father shot her a cool, indifferent smile.

Letting out another sob, Hannah turned her
back on her sister, James and her parents and
stared at the barn, hoping...hoping.

What did she hope for?

That a tall handsome man caked with mud
would come out and call to her? That she'd order
the driver to stop and open her door and fly into
his arms? That he'd sink to his knees and beg her
to stay? That she'd say yes, yes, and she'd stay for
the rest of her life?

These people and New York were her reality.

The barn doors remained firmly shut, so she
didn't order the driver to stop. Instead she
watched the barn and his cabin grow smaller as
the limo sped quickly down the narrow ranch road
toward the highway. Still, long after the shack and
the barn had disappeared, she continued to stare
out the back window.

Only when they hit the highway did Hannah
turn around. Facing her family and James, she felt
as if they were from an alien universe and
invisible walls shielded her. Thankfully, her low,
mumbled responses soon placed such a pall on
everyone, even her mother, who knew exactly

what Nell had done and was obviously furious with her, stopped grilling Hannah.

Beside her, Nell was as white as a sheet and as rigid as a post. Heart-broken as Hannah was, she registered that her twin truly regretted what she had done. James, who sat opposite them, stared straight ahead and said nothing as well.

Since her mother wanted nothing to do with Nell, Hannah wondered why she had thought it necessary to bring Nell and James along and make this journey so much worse than it had to be. Her mother was controlling. Maybe she considered it part of their punishment.

The tension in the limo soon became unbearable. Her father had nodded at her once but had said nothing to her. As always her parents neither looked nor spoke to one another.

Pressing her lips together, Hannah stared out the window. Not that the flat ranch land was much to look at.

Somehow she had to get through this. She had to get the annulment, go back to work, and move on with her life.

But how could she, when everything she cared about was rapidly receding in the rear window?

22

Manhattan during the Christmas season was no place for grief. The streets that were decorated gaily for the holidays were too noisy with cars and pedestrians rushing to get to work or to get home or to buy what they needed or to get through one more day.

Hannah, who had lived in the city her whole life, craved silence and felt as lost in the bustling metropolis as a newly arrived immigrant. She wanted to burrow in a hole and lick her wounds, but her mother wouldn't leave her alone.

Audrey had to know exactly what Hannah had seen that had made her run away. When Hannah refused to discuss it, her mother told her what she'd surmised.

"I saw James and Nell together right after you left, and I knew by the guilty way they looked at each other that you'd caught them doing something horrible. You would never have run away otherwise. And I think they've been seeing each other."

"That's fine. I don't care about them any more."

"Of course you do! I asked Nell to explain herself, and she did. Her version of the truth was so awful, I banished her from the house. Of course your father defended her like he always does."

"Why does he do that, Mother?"

Her mother ignored her question. "I didn't care what he said. I simply couldn't have her back in our home. But then when a couple of weeks went by and I couldn't find you, I grew so desperate I finally enlisted James and Nell to help me. Not that dealing with them was easy for me. Let me tell you, the trip to Texas with them was excruciating, but it was worth it—to find you."

"Can we not talk about Nell and James?"

Her mother nodded. "The sooner you put all that behind you and move forward, the better."

"Other than not wanting James back in my life. I don't know what I want. Things have changed, Mother. I've changed."

"How?"

"I'm not sure. I can't blame Nell and James completely for what happened. I don't think I was in love with James, but I was so out of touch with who I was, I didn't even know it. Maybe James and I looked like the perfect couple to you and your set, but we weren't. I think he was a safe, acceptable choice. And maybe that was what I was for him. But we didn't love each other deeply. I'm afraid if I resume my old life, I'll make the same mistakes all over again and lose touch with who I really am. There are certain expectations here...that don't exist in other places."

"We are civilized."

"Or maybe our choices are more materialistic."

"Which is sensible."

"I'm not *me* here. There's too much noise. Too many social demands. I think I may need to move out of Manhattan and live at a slower pace."

"You can't mean you'd throw everything you've worked so hard for away. People would give anything to have your position here."

"But I wasn't happy here, Mother."

"You could have fooled me, before the reception. Why didn't you come to me? Why did you run?"

"Maybe I needed to get away from this city…and you and figure this out on my own."

"Something like this happened to me when I was your age, but I wasn't so foolish that I let it change the course of my life."

"Maybe you should have."

"What?"

What happened to you, Mother? I've always wanted to know."

Anger and hurt flashed in her mother's eyes. Then her slender face grew smooth. "It was a long time ago."

"Tell me."

"It doesn't matter any more."

The raw note in her mother's voice made Hannah doubt her mother. She thought of her mother's tense, perfect house; of her marriage that wasn't a marriage.

"You're wrong! Why do you and Daddy live on opposite ends of your co-op? Why don't you ever talk to each other or sleep with each other?"

Her mother's mouth thinned. "There are all sorts of marriages, darling. Ours is very successful...in its own way."

"On the surface..."

"That's harsh."

"He freezes me out the way he freezes you out. I'm his daughter and I don't know why. I'm sorry, but your choices aren't working for me any longer," Hannah said. "I don't think they ever did. It was just that I loved you and wanted you to be happy, so I tried to please you."

"Darling..."

"I have to figure this out on my own. You can't help me."

"But..." Her mother's eyes sparkled with unshed tears. "I love you. I love you more than anything. I can't lose you."

"But don't you see, you need more in your life than me! You're not supposed to live vicariously through me."

"You're all I have."

"It doesn't have to be that way—for either of us, Mother."

Audrey, who couldn't accept the uncertainty of her daughter's future, phoned her incessantly, demanding that she act like her old self. She wanted her to see her old friends, go to their Christmas parties, and assume her former responsibilities. Hannah hated their ongoing battles, but her mother wouldn't listen or let up. She had Hannah's friends call her, too.

It was all important to her mother that Hannah decorate for the holidays, so her mother had come over with Claude to install a wreath of feathery white lights on her front door. Her mother had had a tree delivered as well, a well-shaped spruce complete with a stand.

It was so like her mother to concentrate on superficial appearances even when the foundation of Hannah's life was crumbling.

Listlessly Hannah watched her mother direct Claude to string the lights and hang the ornaments. When the two of them finished, Hannah, feeling vaguely nauseated, turned her back on her mother and the exquisite tree that symbolized the lavish, showy life she no longer found attractive and rushed to the bathroom where she threw up.

Feeling weak and drained, she returned to the living room. At the sight of Claude and her mother rearranging a pile of wedding gifts, a wellspring of sorrow so deep she couldn't fathom it squeezed her heart.

Hannah remembered shaking the one gift Liam had bought for her.

"Happy birthday! Merry Christmas!" he'd written.

Unbidden came the memory of Liam's tenderness as he'd held her that last time after they'd made love. Lying in his arms, she'd stared up at the lights of *their* Christmas tree afterward, thinking the misshapen mesquite the most beautiful tree she'd ever seen.

"What?" her mother said from behind her in exasperation when she saw how near Hannah was to tears. "What are you thinking about? Not *him* I hope!"

"Would that be so awful? He's a very nice person."

"He's highly unsuitable."

"He has two college degrees."

"From a school nobody who's anybody ever heard of."

"He owns a huge ranch."

"In the middle of nowhere. And he looked like a barbarian."

"Because he isn't into impressing people."

Her mother's expression tightened. To her mother, New York was the *known* universe. "It will help if you stay busy. You should return each and every wedding gift as soon as possible, darling."

A tear splashed down Hannah's cheek. "You're right. I-I'll do it."

"When?"

Suddenly Hannah's slender body felt heavy and lethargic in her high-backed chair, so she sat up straighter.

"Immediately. I promise." Then her tummy flipped, and she felt like she might throw up again. "Mother—just go. I don't feel well. I've got a virus and I need to be alone. I'll do it. Things are going to work out. I'll be my old self in no time. I promise."

Her mother's brows drew together.

Thankfully the nausea passed as soon as her mother left.

Her mother invited her to dinner or to lunch or nagged her into coming over to help Daddy make his mulled wine on a daily basis. When Hannah visited her parents, who as always carried on separate conversations with her, she felt increasingly alienated, especially from her father, who seemed unusually withdrawn.

I don't want to end up like them. I don't belong here. This isn't how I want to live.

Her father's lack of concern and her mother's constant attentions were too much for Hannah, who missed Liam more every day rather than less. When friends invited her out, she refused or put them off. But she couldn't ignore her mother.

"Mother, you don't have to call me all the time or come by," Hannah said one morning when her mother showed up when Hannah was feeling sick to her stomach again. "I'm fine."

"Fine? Then why do you stay locked up in your townhouse like a recluse? You're as pale as death. In your whole life you've never lounged around like this. I'm beginning to think we should get you to a doctor."

"I'm a doctor. I'm fine."

"All I'm saying is that if you insist on not seeing people, you should at least get something done at home before you go back to work, darling."

Hannah was no longer sure she wanted to go back to her former job or stay in New York.

"Why won't you let me send Claude over to help you pack up all those wedding gifts and address them for mailing?"

"All right," Hannah finally relented. "Send Claude. That's very, very kind of you."

"You will write notes to all our friends who sent them, yourself, won't you, dear?"

"Mother, please… Stop!"

"If it would help, I could come over and draft the notes for you, and you could copy them in your own handwriting."

"No. I'm a grown woman."

Her mother sighed. "He's not right for you. You need to forget him. You know that, don't you?"

I'm trying, Mother.

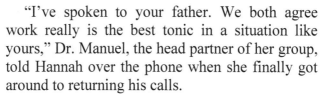

"I've spoken to your father. We both agree work really is the best tonic in a situation like yours," Dr. Manuel, the head partner of her group, told Hannah over the phone when she finally got around to returning his calls.

He'd spoken with her father? As if she were a child? That hurt because her father hadn't come to see her once to express his concern to her personally. She'd become a doctor to please him, but nothing she'd ever done had really mattered.

Pushing the little button in and then out on the end of her ballpoint pen, Hannah stared listlessly at the gardens and East River.

"We're under-staffed," her boss pressed. "We need you."

Hannah sighed, hating herself for feeling guilty. "I haven't been feeling well lately." That at least was the truth. Her tummy refused to settle down. "If you don't mind, I'll return on the day we originally agreed upon. I'm afraid I need some time…to sort things out."

"Like I said, work would get your mind off yourself."

She shook her head. "I'm sure you mean well."

His tone sharpened. "So, you're not coming in?"

"No. But thank you for your concern, Dr. Manuel."

Like all doctors, her boss was used to getting his way. Thus, he'd sounded extremely dissatisfied when he'd hung up. Usually his displeasure would have been enough to send her flying back to the hospital to please him...and her father. As always, Dr. Manuel was so sure he was right. But what did he know about what she wanted?

As she walked around the townhouse, she noted all the boxes that still needed to be unpacked. Wedding gifts were piled high in the dining room. Even the page she'd copied from her calendar and stuck on her fridge with her wedding date circled in red was still taped there.

She had so many things to do and no desire to do any of them. Sitting down at her piano, she placed her hands on the keys and then quickly withdrew them.

How long was it going to take for her to get over Liam? She had a feeling that it wouldn't be a matter of days or weeks, but months, or years even, before she felt halfway alive again.

Indeed, *when*—no, *if* she got over him, would she ever meet anyone from her own world who excited her on a primal, honest level half so much?

Or was he so special she would spend the rest of her life as she'd spent most of her life before she'd met him—doing what other people expected her to do?

When she stood up, a wave of fresh nausea hit her, only this time she felt dizzy too. If she didn't start feeling better soon, she was going to have to quit telling herself that her sickness was psychological and go to a doctor.

Heaving in a breath, she sank into a nearby chair and pulled a faux fur blanket over herself. When the nausea passed, once again she told herself it had to be psychological.

She was off work, wasn't she? That meant she could do exactly what she wanted for the rest of the day—which was exactly nothing.

Pulling her phone out of her pocket, she turned it off. If Claude or her mother rang her bell, she wouldn't answer.

Today, miserable as it was, would be hers alone. Tomorrow—maybe tomorrow—she'd be able to face dealing with the wedding gifts, her mother, and thoughts about her future.

Shutting her eyes, she wondered where Liam was and what he was doing.

What if she never saw him again?

23

"$245.00 please," the pretty cashier said, batting her lashes at him.

Liam was about to hand her his credit card when a blast of artic air swept inside the feed store along with a pair of voices that of late were way too familiar.

He whirled around so fast, he dropped his wallet on the counter. When Gabe and Homer stormed up to him, he said, "Hell."

When they smiled, Liam's jaw hardened.

"Can't a man come into Lonesome and buy feed and treats for the most cantankerous horse in the county without bein' pestered by the likes of you two?"

Gabe's face was flushed from the cold and he was rubbing his hands to bring warmth into them. "Have you called her yet?"

"She's married," Liam said, gritting his teeth.

"She ran away from the bastard, didn't she? Would have gotten herself killed if you hadn't scared those truckers off, am I right?" Homer said. "You admitted she didn't want to leave."

The cashier handed Liam his receipt and credit card.

"What's your point?" Liam demanded as he slipped his credit card back into his wallet.

Homer heaved a feed sack onto his wide shoulder and carried it out to Liam's truck as Liam carried the other one.

"Homer's getting as tired as I am of watching you sulk," Gabe said.

"So, don't. Leave me the hell alone." Liam opened the door of his pickup and climbed inside.

"You used to have goals and you used to face life head-on," Homer said.

Until I screwed everything up.

"Aren't you supposed to be chasing bad guys or something?" Liam asked.

Homer smiled. "I can catch 'em later. Hassling you into not being a total idiot seems way more important. By the way, I spoke to the Mexican authorities the other day about those truckers. The couple they hit down there with their vehicle died. Looks like those fellows are going to spend a stretch in a Mexican prison."

Liam sucked in a breath. "Good."

"You want her," Gabe said. "She's the best thing that's happened to you since…"

"I gotta go," Liam said.

"Right," Gabe said. "Bury that hard head of yours in the sand."

"You two through?"

"Not quite." Gabe held up an envelope. "This arrived at El Castillo a couple of days ago. Hank gave it to me and asked me to pass it on to you."

Hank, who was Miranda's ranch foreman, had been the closest thing to a father figure Gabe and he had known.

"Been carrying it around in my pocket for a spell...been meaning to drop it by your place."

When Liam saw Charlie Hazlet's Wimberley address on the long envelope, guilt flashed through him. Frowning, he snatched the letter from Gabe and pitched it onto the floorboard.

"You should go see him. I don't know how many letters and cards this makes," Gabe said.

"Hell. You people never give up, do you? This is none of your damn business. You know that, don't you?"

Pregnant? Pregnant! Never in her wildest dreams had she imagined...

How could she be a doctor and not have guessed immediately?

She was only a few weeks along. Normally morning sickness didn't occur so early. Liam had protected her. Why would she have thought she was pregnant?

Pregnant? It was funny. No, it was miraculous how one's life could change in a heartbeat. Hers had changed when Liam had kissed her in that bar. Only she hadn't wanted to see it.

But she saw it now. She was pregnant with his child. Her life here had felt all wrong when she'd fled New York, but she'd felt clueless about what she could do about it.

She was going to have Liam's baby. Suddenly Hannah knew exactly what she had to do, and because she did, she felt an immediate surging of her spirits.

Was it only yesterday that she'd assured her mother she would definitely stay in New York and go back to work as planned—even if her heart was breaking?

And then today because of a pregnancy test she'd bought in the drugstore two blocks from her townhouse, everything was different.

She was pregnant. No, they were pregnant.

She could not raise *her* baby, no *their* baby in Manhattan. She could not teach their baby to be like her parents—pillars of their community even though their whole life was a lie.

Her mother had lived through Hannah for years. Maybe it was time Hannah lived her own life and set her mother free to face the truths in hers. She couldn't make her mother happy by doing what her mother wanted, and she certainly couldn't make herself happy that way.

Hannah's phone was ringing in her bedroom, but she ignored it. With the familiar hot bile threatening to rise in her throat, Hannah threw the pee stick in the trash, washed her hands for a very long time, dried them, and then walked out of her bathroom.

No wonder her stomach virus hadn't let up. No wonder odors bothered her and she'd begun to crave sardines, pickles, anchovies and salted eel. Eel? She, who loved sushi, had never been a big fan of eel.

Her phone stopped ringing, and then began again. It was probably her mother, who wanted her daughter's life to be as it had always been.

But it wasn't. Nell and James had blasted her out of her old life, and now she was pregnant with a child she had no intention of raising as she'd been raised, in a world of lies and secrets and false values. She didn't want to micro-manage her child as she'd been micro-managed.

Mother and all her assumptions about what Hannah's perfect future should be could wait…indefinitely.

Telling Liam she was pregnant couldn't, but she wasn't going to text him or call him.

No. Hannah had some packing to do and a plane ticket to San Antonio to buy.

This was one bit of news she intended to deliver in person.

Tires squealing, gravel flying, Liam took the turn off Ranch Road 12 in his truck at sixty miles an hour, which was way too fast on that narrow, hilly road for his heavy vehicle.

Two miles later, he took a sharp right and turned onto a narrow strip of asphalt that cut through Charlie's ten-acre spread and wound up to his sprawling, limestone ranch house.

Liam hadn't warned Charlie or his wife that he was coming. Too afraid he'd chicken out if Charlie had sounded the least bit down, Liam had hopped in his truck, slammed his foot on his accelerator and headed north as soon as he'd read Charlie's letter.

Much to Liam's surprise, Charlie, who looked as fit as ever, was up on a ladder stringing Christmas lights under the eaves of his house.

When Liam braked and got out of the truck, Susan, who was holding the ladder, turned.

"Oh, my goodness. Charlie, look who's here!" she cried, flushing with joy. With a sunny smile and without the slightest hesitation, she ran into Liam's arms.

He hugged her hard, maybe because she wasn't giving him a choice.

For months Liam had tortured himself, wondering if she'd hate him because Charlie had lost a leg.

"It's so good to see you," she said, burying her face in his wide chest. "You have no idea how much your coming means to him," she whispered. "And to me."

Liam fought to control his surprise and pleasure at her warmth. "It's good to be here," he said in a low, husky voice. "It's good to see him out of that damn wheel chair."

"Hell, it took you long enough," Charlie said as he slowly descended the ladder. But once Charlie got down, he was smiling as he strode toward Liam.

He walked without a limp, Liam noted, realizing he must have a prosthetic leg.

"How've you been? I wrote. I called. I e-mailed. What does it take to get through to you down there?"

Liam flushed with guilt. He hadn't read more than one or two of his letters or answered many of his emails. And he'd had to get very drunk to send the two or three emails he'd managed to send.

"I'm fine. Sorry I've been such a poor correspondent."

"I thought maybe you'd written me off," Charlie said.

Liam shut his eyes and took a breath. For a second or two he was back in Afghanistan, surrounded by the enemy, fighting for his life as his men fell around him. A wave of horror had him shuddering.

No. He'd written himself off because he'd led his men into a trap. He should have seen the attack coming, should have saved them. It hadn't mattered how many of the enemy he'd killed because nothing he'd been able to do could bring his men back.

There was so much he wanted to say he was sorry about, so much he wanted to tell Charlie he regretted, but his throat felt choked and he couldn't get out a single word.

"Hey," Charlie said. "I knew you'd come...when you could."

"Damn it, I should have been here for you."

"You're here now," Charlie said quietly. "Like I said, I always knew you'd come."

"You had more faith in me than I did. I had no intention of ever comin'."

"But here you are. You're a good man. The best. Hell, when we lost everybody, and I was down, you stood up to those bastards and fought like a single man platoon and accomplished our mission. Then you saved my life. I was lucky to serve under you. The guys would have been proud."

Liam, who felt no pride in what he'd done or the medals he'd received, hung his head.

"How about some coffee?" Charlie offered. "You still like coffee, right?"

Liam laughed. "Some things don't change. Coffee sounds great."

A small, dark-haired little girl who couldn't be two yet, stumbled out of the door as they were heading inside.

"Daddy!" she shrieked, her face lighting up when she saw Charlie.

"Right here, baby," Charlie said, backing up. "Come to Daddy."

When she toddled up to him without falling, he clapped.

"I want to fwy, Daddy."

When Charlie picked her up, she held her hands out like wings and pretended to fly as he swung her back and forth above his head and then slowly lowered her back to the ground.

"Again," she ordered. "Do it again!"

"Milly, this is my friend, Uncle Liam," Charlie said.

"Uncle Liam?" she said, staring up at him. "He's even bigger than you."

Liam sank to his knees. "It's nice to meet you, Milly. Your daddy sent me your picture."

"He did?"

"It's in my pocket."

Blushing and chewing her bottom lip so she wouldn't smile, she stared at the ground shyly.

"Can I see?"

When he pulled out her picture, her grin lit up her face.

"I was a baby!"

He laughed at her outrage. "And you're all grown up now."

She laughed.

"I'm coaching again," Charlie said as the three of them went inside. "Football. At the high school. And ranching on the side. Life is good."

Charlie was obviously trying to concentrate on the future instead of the past.

"Man, am I glad you came. Have a chair. I've been worried sick about you, bro. It had to be tough...losing Mindy and your little Charlie right after losing..." He looked away.

The two of them sat down at the kitchen table.

"It was hell," Liam whispered, his voice rough with restrained misery. He swallowed, fighting to maintain control. As always, he felt explosive, enraged, helpless and terrified because he knew there was no way he could ever get past the losses and the horrible mistakes he'd made.

As he remembered his men lying dead and Charlie down and wounded as he'd fired madly, pain washed him, black and dark, like flood waters against a dam. When he began to cry, he couldn't stop. Soon great hacking, broken sobs shook his entire body.

"Why is he cwying, Daddy?"

"Why don't you go outside and play, baby girl?"

Saying nothing as Liam shuddered convulsively and the scalding tears fell, Charlie simply sat beside him quietly and waited.

When Liam was finally done, he wasn't thinking about Mindy or Charlie or Charlie's beautiful little girl, Milly. Instead, he saw

Hannah's mud-streaked face, her blue eyes teary and empty after he'd firmly set her aside, telling her she belonged in New York with James.

Liam had sent her away, sent the woman he loved away, and he was in hell because he had. What he wanted right now was to open up to her just like he'd opened up to Charlie and tell her how hard he'd tried to save his men, to tell her how hard he'd fought to kill every last murdering bastard who'd shot his brothers to pieces right in front of him. To tell her he would have gladly died instead of Mindy and Charlie and his men.

But he hadn't died. He was alive, and finally glad to be alive, so he wanted Hannah to circle him with her arms and kiss his damp eyelids and tell him she believed in him as Charlie still did, despite everything. Why hadn't he given her a chance?

"Hell, I'm every bit as stubborn and headstrong as Gabe always says I am."

"What?"

"Nothin'," Liam said, hunching lower.

Liam hadn't given her and their love a chance because he hadn't thought he deserved a second chance. Then Charlie had sent him a picture of Milly, who'd been grinning in the picture, and for no reason at all, he'd felt a faint glimmer of hope.

"If you hadn't sent that picture of Milly, I wouldn't have come here," Liam admitted aloud.

"Man—am I glad you did," Charlie said. "Can you stay for supper?"

"Sure. I'd like that. I've missed you, bro. I've missed you so much, missed everybody."

"Me too. But, hey, we've still got each other. We came home. Because of *you*, I came home. Because of you, I have Milly."

Liam shut his eyes. Again he saw the tear streaking Hannah's muddy face and her trembling lips after he'd told her to go back to New York.

He thought of his lonely cabin and how lost he felt every time he came home to its hellish emptiness.

He'd sent her away when she'd begged him not to. She'd called him, but he hadn't answered her calls. Or texts.

It was time, way past time he called her...just to make sure she was okay up there with her husband and family and her *real* life.

Friends called each other, didn't they? They checked up on each other, didn't they?

He wouldn't tell her he loved her or that he needed her. He wasn't that selfish. But he would damn sure make sure she was okay.

24

Liam punched the Lewises' doorbell, stepped back and then glanced up at their discreetly-positioned security cameras.

From the doormen dressed in regal gold and black livery to the marble lobby and the brass and oak elevator that had whisked Liam up to the Lewises' penthouse, everything about the their building on East 79th was designed to impress and intimidate.

It had been hell getting this far, but when one of Hannah's neighbors at her building had told him she'd left town, he'd tracked down her parents, thinking they would know where she was. First, he'd had to convince the doorman to let him up. The doorman had called her parents. Only after they vetted him had he finally been allowed access to their private elevator.

From behind the immense door he heard slow, methodical footsteps approaching. The knob turned, and a rail-thin, elderly man in black tails, who looked like he belonged to another century, opened the door and bowed low. "Whom shall I say is calling, sir?"

As the man's cold gray eyes inspected him, Liam was glad he'd worn a suit.

"Liam Stark. I'm looking for Hannah Lewis."

"I'm afraid the lady hasn't lived here for some time, sir."

"She isn't at her address on Sutton Place."

The man, who was as pale as a vampire, hesitated.

"I'd like to speak to Mrs. Lewis then."

The man opened the door wider and stepped aside. "If you'd be so kind as to step inside, I will inquire if she is available."

Liam nodded.

The butler showed him to a palatial sitting room with tall, gilt-edged windows that was furnished with stiff, carved chairs upholstered in red silk. When he sat down on a spindly antique that looked like it belonged in a museum and groaned under his weight, the butler stiffened.

The house with its gilded ceilings made him long for the smell of grass, the expanse of a big blue sky and the warmth of a more democratic locale where everybody called everybody by their name or nickname, whether they were rich or poor.

With an effort, Liam forced himself to stay in his seat until he heard the tap tap of a woman's heels hurrying toward him on marble floors. Arising, he greeted the tall, fashionably thin woman with glossy, pursed lips, who swept into the room. Dressed in black with diamonds at her throat and wrists, her golden hair swept back from her regal face, Audrey Lewis exuded an air of impatience, hauteur and entitlement.

She held out her hand, which felt as icy when he took it as her voice as she introduced herself.

She withdrew her fingertips instantly, as if touching him had been an unpleasant necessity. Still, she managed a smile, even if it was cool and failed to light her eyes which he noted were the same jewel shade of blue as her daughter's.

"I'm Liam Stark."

"I know who you are, Mr. Stark, and I'm in your debt."

He lifted his brows.

"Hannah told me you saved her life."

"Well, now, Ma'am," he began in protest. "Anybody would have…"

"I want to thank you for what you did. Hannah is very precious to me."

"I'm sure she is, ma'am."

"Please sit down.'"

She seemed surprised when he waited until she sat. Then she winced when the antique groaned under his weight when he did sit.

"Sorry, ma'am."

"What can I do for you?"

"I'm looking for Hannah."

"All right…but why are you here? Why didn't you call her or text her? Or e-mail her? She doesn't live here. Why drop in on me at this hour?"

"I've tried to contact her. When I couldn't reach her, I went to her residence, but she's gone."

"Maybe that should tell you something."

"I want to make sure she's okay."

"I'm sure if she wanted to talk to you, she would have answered. Or called you herself."

He didn't tell her that Hannah had called and texted a week or so before, but he'd deleted her messages without listening to them or reading them.

"I have to make sure she's okay," he repeated stubbornly.

"Okay? She's the last thing from okay. After Hannah obtains her annulment, she's leaving New York. She quit her job at the hospital. She doesn't want to live in this city any more. This whole thing has turned into an incomprehensible nightmare."

She really was getting an annulment. She really was going to be free.

"Do you have any idea how hard she's worked to achieve all the goals she's achieved? No—*you* wouldn't. She had friends here, the right kind of people. People in high places, people who are willing to help her in every way they can. She had so much to be proud of. None of us can understand why she's throwing it all away."

He stared at her, trying to make sense of what she was saying.

"You're all wrong for her." She gave him a long, meaningful look. "Surely, even *you* can see that. Not that you wouldn't be perfect for a lot of women."

"Just not your daughter," he murmured.

"She's used to the finer things in life."

"I can see that."

"You can't give her what she's accustomed to."

There was a dull ache in his chest. "No, ma'am, I can't."

What had he given her in the brief weeks they'd been together? Grief, darkness, nightmares. Chores, long walks, and a troublesome horse to deal with. A lousy cabin to live in. On top of that, he'd been moody as hell.

Other memories hit him. He remembered holding her down in his bed the first night she'd come upstairs when he'd awakened feeling furious and violent.

But from the first moment he'd seen her in the bar, he'd wanted her—no, craved her.

He remembered their first kiss and the sex that had always been more than mere sex. He remembered the exquisite sensation of feeling huge inside her and the tenderness he'd felt afterward. He remembered her warmth and her sweetness when she'd lain nestled against his body in the dark with her arms around him. How quickly he'd grown to care for her.

Maybe he'd saved her life, but she'd saved his soul. And now that she had, he didn't know how he'd face the rest of his life without her.

Audrey's lips curved. "I'm so glad we understand each other."

"Where the hell is she?" Liam demanded. "I have to see for myself that she's okay."

"She left a week ago. If I knew where she was, you'd be the last person I'd ever tell." Her voice was cold. "The very last. She's gone. She didn't tell any of us, not her sister or her father, where she was going." Her blue eyes glittered with hurt and outrage. "This is your fault! If you care about her, stay away from her! You're the last person she needs to see. You'll destroy her."

Was it only a week ago that Hannah had left?

Liam felt heavy and lethargic. The knowledge that Hannah had left New York and hadn't once tried to contact him ate at him as he sat in the bar of his Manhattan hotel, nursing a club soda with a dash of lime.

He needed a real drink, but he could feel himself slipping into the familiar darkness of bitter hopelessness, so he didn't trust himself.

Like a blind man he would have to seek all the familiar paths that would enable him to get through day after bleak day alone, without her. Chores, work…liquor. No. Not liquor. This time, he was going to do it without the liquor.

She'd begged him to talk to her, to open up, to share. To give of himself. Just a little. Instead, he'd repeatedly rejected her.

He loved her. He wanted her forever. He didn't care that she was from a different world, that her family would never accept him as a suitable husband for her.

Why hadn't he faced the truth of his feelings and simply told her how much she mattered to him?

Why had he been so afraid to put himself out there and fight for her?

Because to love was to risk losing everything again.

So, instead, he'd been a coward and had told her it was over and sent her away.

So, now it *was* over, and he had to live with the knowledge that he'd lost everything that mattered to him again—lost the one woman he loved, and that this time it really was his fault.

25

It was nearly ten p.m. when Liam braked in front of his cabin. He should have been here hours ago, but grounded flights and innumerable delays due to bad weather had had him impatiently pacing in several crowded airports. He'd almost regretted not commandeering one of the family planes to fly him back and forth. But being a rancher, he was not prone to extravagance.

The cabin was dark except for a faint glow coming from the left window as he grabbed his suitcase out of the backseat.

Funny, he didn't remember leaving any lights on. When he went to unlock the front door, he tensed when he found that it was already unlocked.

Warily he pushed it open and slid his suitcase inside. Then he went back to his truck and got his bird-hunting gun. After stealing back onto the porch, he stood to one side in the dark, waiting, listening.

"Don't shoot," said a soft, musical voice from his living room that made his heart catch.

"Hannah?"

When she stepped out onto the porch looking flushed and lovely in the moonlight, he felt dizzy with happiness.

"Don't be mad," she whispered. "I had to come."

He laid the gun down carefully.

"I'm not mad."

"I knew if I called or took your calls, you'd tell me not to. And I had to come. There was something I had to share with you...even though I know you don't want me."

He took a long breath. If only she'd have him, he intended to spend the rest of his life telling her how wrong she was about that.

"I went to New York to make sure you were okay," he admitted. "I spent all of today on planes and in airports."

"You went to New York?"

"To find you. But you weren't there."

"I quit my job."

"I saw your mother. She told me you were going to do that."

"I can't imagine you and her together. Not even for one second. She blames you for everything."

He smiled. "When you didn't answer your phone or e-mails, I didn't know who else to contact. But, you're right. She's very upset."

"Don't you want to know why I left New York?"

"More than anything."

"For starters, I felt like I could breathe in Texas, maybe for the first time in my life. Everybody speaks to everybody here. I felt free in this environment. Then there's another tiny little reason... I'm pregnant."

"What?" His deep voice cracked.

"With *your* child. With *our* child. As soon as I knew, I realized that I didn't want to raise our child the way I was raised, and that, in fact, I wanted to raise our baby near its father. It's okay if you don't want me, but if you're at all interested in our baby and being part of his life, I want to relocate to Corpus Christi or Kingsville... or, if that's too close, San Antonio."

"But I do want you," he whispered, hardly daring to take the next breath because he was so afraid she'd reject him.

"You do?"

"I love you. I went to New York to tell you that I love you and want you and that I can't live without you. And I'll love our baby too. I'll love you both with all my heart. Just like I loved little Charlie."

Slowly Liam wrapped her in his arms. "I've missed you so much."

"I missed you too. I was so miserable in Manhattan. Nothing was right about my life in New York without you," she said. "My parents have problems, but they have to solve them on their own, especially Mother. I'm through trying to prove myself to them."

He leaned his forehead against hers and stroked her hair gently. "I need you. I need the baby. I love you. The baby and you being here makes this the best Christmas ever. I'm just afraid I don't deserve you."

"Don't say that! Don't ever say that again."

"What about your career and your fancy life? Are you sure you won't miss your setup in New York?"

"I'll have to get a Texas license, but after that, I'm sure I'll do just fine here. Doctors can work anywhere. I'll figure it out. Not that I could live in this cabin forever... me being the princess-and-the-pea type and all."

"I'll build you a proper house...one you can fill with antiques and matching pillows. Or maybe we can just update the family place...now that the ghosts are receding."

She smiled. "I know now that I don't want my mother's life. That that is the last thing I want."

He traced a finger along her jawline. Then slowly he lowered his mouth to hers. Cupping her chin gently, he kissed her long and tenderly.

"I love you. I want you to stay...forever. I love you so much that tomorrow I'll go into town and buy you a fancy new Christmas tree."

"Oh, no you won't. Like I told you, the one thing I've learned is I don't want fancy. I love this one and I've got the marks on my bottom to prove it."

He smiled.

"I've been sitting here remembering how it sparkled as I lay beneath you while you made love to me," she said.

"You grew up in a palace."

"But I feel like I was under a dark spell until you set me free."

"I feel exactly the same way."

Laughing, unbelievably happy, Liam pulled her to him. "Will you marry me?"

"What do you think?" she whispered against his lips.

"I think you're crazy if you say yes."

"Is that a nice thing to say about your future bride?"

When his arms tightened around her, he kissed her again, with purpose this go-round, because he didn't intend to stop for a very long time.

"All my life I worked so hard for any scrap of affection or approval. I love the way you kiss me and the way you look at me," she whispered. "You make me feel so loved. And so cherished. I've wanted to feel like this my whole life. Always."

"And you always will. I promise."

Kneeling in front of the five crosses at Dead Man's Curve as Hannah stood beside him, Liam laid a Christmas wreath of red roses on the ground and whispered goodbye to his darling Mindy and little Charlie. Because he wasn't one hundred percent sure about Jack, he whispered a prayer that wherever he was, he was all right.

"If you're out there somewhere...alive, I hope we see each other again in this life."

When Liam finally stood up, he shook the dust off his hands before turning to Hannah. Funny, how the pain of the past had dissipated...not in one abrupt moment...but slowly as he'd built happier memories.

Taking her in his arms, he kissed her gently. He'd lost so much here, his uncle and his cousin, Jack; Mindy and his little Charlie, and, of course,

Kate, who refused to come home and Lizzy, her best friend, who'd died.

But he'd found Hannah here, too. They were going to marry and have a child. They were going to make a new life together and be happy.

He lifted his mouth from hers and stared past her to the sluggish brown creek with its sand bars and high reeds without really seeing any of it, without remembering the tragedies that had taken place here. Because of Hannah, his grief was fading.

Not that he would ever forget those he'd loved and lost, but now he was focused on his love for Hannah and their baby and the bright future they would share.

"You're everything to me now," he whispered into her hair. "You know that, don't you?"

She clung, pressing her face into his collar. "You're everything to me, too."

He would never take her for granted because he knew that no matter how much time he thought they had to love one another, it would never be enough. He kissed her again and then again, never wanting to let her go.

"We have to get back to the cabin. It's Christmas, remember?" she whispered. "We left that turkey cooking. And...and I can't wait to open my Christmas present and see what you got me."

"Materialist."

He laughed. It felt good to laugh. It felt so damn good to hold her in his arms and laugh like a man who didn't have a care in the world.

"Happy birthday," he murmured, feeling his love for her well up inside him.

"Thank you. I always wanted somebody to look at me the way you do."

"Forever," he whispered. "For as long as we both shall live."

THE END

If you enjoyed this book, it would be so lovely if you left a review on Amazon, Barnes & Noble, or on your favorite retailer's site.

Nell's story is next.
Enjoy the following excerpt from
HIS FOR ONE NIGHT ONLY
The second book in Ann Major's LONE STAR DYNASTY Series!
Coming soon...

1

"You can't go in there, mister!"

The hell he couldn't.

James Colton hadn't followed the wrecker hauling his Jag whose front-end damage Nell was responsible for through Manhattan's dense, afternoon traffic on icy streets clogged with holiday shoppers all the way to her lousy body shop in Queens to be told no by some vacant-eyed teenager with too many tats and a ring in his nose.

It was bad enough that Nell Lewis had started tongues wagging when she'd popped out of a big cake in a silver bikini and had come onto him at his bachelor's party, a male-only-affair.

Hell—when she'd danced and sat on his lap, the guys had gone wild. He had too; not that he'd let on.

But the real grief she'd caused him, her twin sister and *his* bride, had occurred at their wedding reception.

Nell had destroyed his marriage, his career and his car, and she had to pay.

He wasn't leaving until he settled the score.

James pushed past the boy in black and rushed headlong into her shop, only to be stopped by a blast of rock music so fierce he clamped his hands over his ears. For a second or two he failed to see the shapely, feminine leg encased in skin-tight denim peeping out from underneath the crumpled hood of some unlucky sod's smashed Mercedes.

"Nell!" he yelled.

Oblivious to him, the toe of her paint-spattered jogging shoe continued to gyrate in time to the music.

Not for the first time he wondered what an Upper East Side princess, who'd been raised with a silver spoon in her mouth, was doing running a body shop.

With one swift movement he yanked the electric cord of her boom box out of the wall outlet.

"Craig?" she called in that velvety voice that could send a frisson of heat through him when he least expected it.

No, it's me—Colt," he muttered, cursing silently when he used her special nickname for him. He was James to Hannah, James to Tom

Lewis, his boss, James to everyone who counted in the rest of the world, damn it.

He knelt over her and hollered louder. "*Nell!*"

A piece of metal clattered onto concrete beneath the Mercedes.

"Ouch!" she cried when she banged her head as she scooted out from under the car too fast. Then she was beneath him, helpless, trapped under his larger male body just like he'd wanted as she rubbed her injured brow. He got hard instantly, which infuriated him.

Nonplussed, he found himself staring down into chocolate-dark eyes that widened in shock and pain even as her olive-tone skinned paled. Once again, her dark eyes lured him.

How was that possible? She was Hannah's fraternal twin; younger by a mere three minutes. Nell was his best movie buddy when Hannah had been too busy for him, which had been all the time lately, since Hannah was a workaholic doctor.

Nell looked so small and feminine and adorable, so utterly defenseless with her bruised brow, he almost softened.

For years everybody had warned him Nell was an outrageous flirt and had a wild reputation. Not that she'd ever come across like that to him— except maybe on that first day when he'd met her. Sure, he'd known she'd never been the student Hannah was and that Nell lacked her twin's ambition. Just as he'd known Nell had such a passion for cars the twins' father had gone against their mother and financed a body shop for her in the hopes Nell would settle down at something, no matter how unsuitable it was for a young woman of her upper East Side background to run such a place. But to everyone's surprise, she had.

Not once before the reception had Nell ever flirted or dressed sexily around him. She'd gone without lipstick and had worn baggy sweats and had acted sweet and innocent, so why should he have been wary of her?

Idiot! Too late he'd learned she was about as innocent as a Death Stalker scorpion, a vile tempered creature that had bitten him on his tour of duty in the Middle East.

Well, now that he had her underneath him and in his power, he should have felt some relief. But over the past few days, his anger had morphed into a tangle of conflicting, unsavory emotions, one of which was lust. Ever since the reception he'd thought of nothing but her, dreamed of nothing except the taste of her forbidden mouth.

His pulse beat harder. How could he find her so beautiful when her creamy cheek was streaked with black grease and her nose with a dab of white paint? How could he want her when she'd cost him his bride and his career?

One kiss—that's all they'd shared.

Even knowing that she'd played him to one-up the brilliant, high-achieving sister she was so jealous of, he wanted to kiss her again. Just looking at the curve of her sweet mouth had his lower body heating and hardening despite the frigid temperature in her shop.

Damn it, she owed him way more than a kiss for destroying his relationship with Hannah and taking a wrecking ball to his career.

"Colt? What are you doing here—slumming?" Nell demanded in that sultry tone that got to him.

His mouth curled. "I brought my Jag in. Believe it or not, your services come highly recommended." He let his gaze slide from her mouth down her curves.

"Talk to my service-writer," she hissed on a blush.

Good, his insult had stung. "I came to see you. This is your mess. You have to clean it up."

"No. You made it clear you think I'm a tramp and despise me."

He didn't deny what she said.

"Go back to your fancy office on Park Avenue and hang out with all those rich hypocrites you admire so much."

Why had he ever confided in her about his ambitions? Because Hannah had usually been too busy to listen. Because he'd considered Nell a friend.

When Hannah had warned him Nell was troubled and had always resented her and didn't get on with their mother either, he'd taken more of an interest in her than he probably should have...maybe because he could relate to troubled. But she'd always behaved like a normal kid sister around him...until the night before his wedding.

"Thanks to you, there is no fancy office. Your uncle sacked me this morning."

"Your work was probably sub-standard. Uncle Tommy would employ the devil himself if he produced."

"He fired me because you popped out of that cake at my bachelor's party in a silver bikini and ended up on my lap! And because of what you did at the reception."

"Because of what they *thought* I did," she amended.

"You embarrassed the family, so they closed ranks to protect their precious name."

"I tried to warn you what they were like. We didn't do anything. W-well hardly anything. Okay, you let me kiss you goodbye behind closed doors, and I spilled a little champagne on you. And wiped it off. Big deal."

"Tell that to the jury," he growled.

"Why are you here? Shouldn't you be trying to make up to your precious Hannah—*your* wife?"

"She wants an annulment, and your uncle Tom's agreed to handle it. Because of you, I'm out."

"Do you want her back?"

He wished he could taunt her and say, damn it, yes, he did, but when Hannah had called him and told him it was over, he'd felt relieved, if the truth be told.

Nell had gotten inside him when she'd kissed him. He still didn't understand how that was that possible. For years all she'd been was his movie buddy who had a penchant for stealing his popcorn.

No more. He'd kissed her and held her. Now it was as if he lived and breathed her. He thought of all the times they'd fought over his popcorn after she'd sworn she didn't want any because it would make her fat, only to steal it once they were in the dark movie theater; thought of all their heartfelt conversations that had happened after those movies when Hannah had worked late.

Nell had listened when he'd told her why he'd been so thrilled someone like Hannah, who was old money, whose much-respected family was practically Upper East Side royalty, would have him. Nell had listened when he'd told her about his low beginnings and how he'd wanted to be looked up to, instead of despised.

He'd thought he knew exactly what he'd wanted until Nell had kissed him. Now it was the sweet taste of Nell's mouth that he hungered for, the silky texture and delicate curves of Nell's body that he desired.

What kind of lowlife betrayed a wife like Hannah an hour after he'd exchanged his marriage vows?

Yes, Nell had come onto him wearing a red, low-cut gown in a private room at her father's club, but he should have thrown her out as soon as she'd started asking him why he'd chosen Hannah.

"You don't belong with my sister. You'll never fit into her world. Don't you see? She only approves of the guy you're pretending to be. You're like me," Nell had said. "I've never fit into their weird Upper East Side world, and neither will you."

"That's a lie." He'd wanted to prove her wrong so badly.

"You can't live down your low beginnings…any more than I can," she whispered, lifting her champagne flute to lips that were as vivid as her gown. "Believe me, I've tried—even harder than you—and a whole lot longer."

"What low beginnings? You were born filthy rich on the Upper East Side...to a family that's considered royalty."

"That's all you know. I bet you've never told Hannah or Daddy that your daddy was a glorified garbage man at Fresh Kills Landfill."

He'd sucked in a breath. "I'm proud of my father."

"But you didn't tell them about him." She sipped her champagne with a smile. "You told me."

"I was going to tell them. I will tell them."

Still smiling, she stepped closer and lifted her palm against his cheek, each gentle fingertip burning his skin as Hannah's never did.

"I don't think so, and I don't blame you. No way would my mother or my perfect sister or any of the women from their elite, moneyed ranks ever accept you if they knew who you really are. You told me...because you knew I wouldn't care."

"Everybody knows you're damaged and that your taste in men is questionable."

"Is that what Hannah told you?" A muscle had tightened near her mouth, but her fingers stroked his neck before moving down his torso, their light heat causing every muscle in his body tense. "Well, I like you, Colt, *because* you're not perfect—*because* you're all too human."

His world had shifted.

Never again would he see her as Hannah's safe, *misunderstood,* younger twin who'd preferred hanging out in the garage tinkering on cars with the chauffeur to her family.

He should have made her go, but her feather-light touch and the memory of her on his lap at his bachelor's party had him wanting to taste those red lips and touch her everywhere.

So, he'd kissed her—and wrecked his life.

You might also enjoy Ann's *Texas:*
Children of Destiny Series

*Passion's Child (*Book 1*)*

In Name Only
Nicholas and Amy were madly in love until
Nick broke Amy's heart and she ran away. When
a life threatening illness threatens Triple, the child
she loves as her very own, Nick suddenly returns
determined to claim what's his.

But can Amy forgive him for his part in the
cruel circumstances that forced her to deceive him
in the most terrible way?

Destiny's Child (Book 2)

In love with her worst enemy
Ever since Megan MacKay's father lost the
MacKay ranch to neighboring rancher Jeb
Jackson and vanished, after asking Jackson to
look after her, Megan MacKay resented Jeb
almost as much as she desired him. When she was
sixteen, he rejected her, and she vowed to hate
him forever.

Now she's all grown up and such a handful, his
feisty pilot is the last woman Jeb wants to desire.
Then a passionate kiss makes Jeb realize that he
wants to possess her a whole lot more than he
wants her land. But can he win the one woman
who's so stubbornly set against him?

Night Child (Book 3)

World-famous ballerina Dawn Hayden had no memory of being torn from Kirk MacKay's arms and abducted as a child. She didn't know the cause of the darkness at the center of her being which made her reject love and feel driven to dance every waking moment.

Then suddenly she found herself in danger again, and a mysterious stranger, who seemed dazzlingly familiar on a soul deep level, set her free and captured her heart.

Kirk MacKay felt responsible for young Julia Jackson's abduction. Haunted by her loss, Kirk rushed across the world to save still another kidnap victim, the lovely ballerina, who was the same age Julia would have been and who was wearing a necklace exactly like Julia's.

Ann Major Classics

Texas: Children of Destiny Series

Book 1 – Passion's Child
Book 2- Destiny's Child (Coming soon)
Book 3- Night Child (Coming soon)

Men of the West Series

Book 1 - *Wild Lady*
Book 2 - *The Fairy Tale Girl*
Book 3 – *Meant To Be*

Stand alone novellas

Santa's Special Miracle
The Baby Machine

Short Story

In Love With The Enemy (free)
One Night? Or Forever? (free)
I Will Find You (coming soon)

New Releases by Major Press LLC

Lone Star Dynasty Series

Book 1- Love With An Imperfect Cowboy

All books can be found at Ann's Website
http://www.annmajor.com/

ANN MAJOR
E-BOOK LIST (Harlequin)

The Golden Spurs Series
The Girl with The Golden Spurs (Bk 1)
The Girl with the Golden Gun (Bk 2)
The Throw-Away Bride (Bk3)
The Bride Hunter (Bk 4)

The Fantasy Series
Midnight Fantasy (Bk 1)
Cowboy Fantasy (Bk 2)

Stand-alone Novels
Secret Lives of Doctors' Wives
Wild Enough for Willa
Marry a Man Who will Dance
The Hot Ladies Murder Club
Her Pregnancy Secret
The Amalfi Bride
A Cowboy & a Gentleman
A Scandal So Sweet
His for the Taking
Terms of Engagement
Marriage at the Cowboy's Command
Ultimatum: Marriage
To Tame Her Tycoon Lover
Mistress for a Month
Shameless
Love Me True
Nobody's Child
The Accidental Bodyguard
A Cowboy Christmas

http://www.annmajor.com/booklist.cfm

ABOUT THE AUTHOR

ANN MAJOR is a *USA Today* bestselling author, who lives in Texas with her husband of many years. Newly-retired, he harbors ambitions of encroaching on *her* territory, so she faces new challenges on the domestic front. She has three grown children and several grandchildren. A former English teacher, she has a master's degree from Texas A&M at Kingsville, Texas. She is a co-founder of Romance Writers of America and a frequent speaker at writers' groups.

Besides her writing, Ann loves to hike in the mountains, sail, kayak, travel, and play the piano. Most of all she enjoys her friends and family... and, last but not least, her *muy macho* cat, Jack.

Connect with Ann

Made in the USA
Lexington, KY
21 April 2016